Queen tide

a Novel by
DONNA FISHER

Publisher: SHESAW PRESS

Typesetting and Cover design by Circecorp Design.

Queentide /Donna Fisher - 1st ed. © 2021
ISBN: 978-0-6451421-0-5

I acknowledge this novel was written on the unceded land of the Gayemagal people.

I pay my respects to Elders past, present and emerging, and I extend that respect to all Aboriginal and Torres Strait Islander peoples.

I honour and thank them for the stories they have told and the stories they are yet to tell. And I recognise the need to listen when they are shared.

'Woman is not born; she is made.'

ANDREA DWORKIN

Chapter 1

Bodie Hughes had seen it all. Not because she'd reached a significant age. Time on earth didn't equate to understanding it. There were plenty of folks with walking frames, but not a single clue. No. She had seen it all because she had looked behind the curtain. The one most people pretend isn't there.

Sometime around 1965, Bodie decided there was more to life than pot roasts and white weddings and hitched a ride to San Francisco, which seemed back then to be the opposite of Idaho. She was escaping. Looking for freedom from her mother's expectations and a life so small it would've crushed her in a matter of years. She stopped being Doris from Idaho and became Bodie from San Francisco, who smoked hash, hung out with musicians and could drink any man under the table. But all that freedom left a tooth-stripping saccharine taste in her mouth, warning her it was entirely artificial.

The miniskirts and drugs were a distraction from the pretty beaded curtain that hid the truth from hip women like Bodie. The terrifying truth. They were not liberated. Just like the Dorises from Idaho, someone was still chaining them to the kitchen sink. They were just too high on the hype to see the shackles.

When a colleague had to leave the office after getting married, Bodie took a peek behind that curtain. Then a friend died from a backyard abortion, and the curtain opened just a little more. Another got committed by a cheating husband because it was cheaper than divorcing her. It was then that Bodie tugged at the curtain until the damn thing fell. Until she was staring the dragon in the eye.

For sixty years since, she'd fought it with protests and doctorates and women's collectives. She'd even chased it halfway across the world. But she had failed to defeat it on this new battlefield. In fact, since the last pandemic, its fiery breath seemed to have got hotter. It had come up with unpredictable ways to hurt women. To keep them scared and in their place.

But Bodie had a new tactic, one the dragon wouldn't see coming. And that's where Janet De Marco came in. Janet wasn't as old as Bodie, but she knew the dragon just as well. As a female lawyer, even just to become a female lawyer, she'd had plenty of battles with it. Janet had even got some spears through its thickened hide. The occasional scorching she'd got in return had made her more determined to keep on fighting.

But she knew, just like Bodie, that they were losing. Women were losing in Australia. All over the world. Even though women like Janet De Marco were fighting for them. Swinging at the Australian Government when it kept its 'temporary' powers. Hammering the judges when droves of abusive men walked free because of the 'unique mental pressure' of the bushfires and multiple lockdowns. Janet didn't like to lose. And recently, she'd been losing a lot. She was tired. They were all so damn tired. But Bodie was sure her idea would be like a hit of caffeine and sugar. Straight into the veins.

Bodie waited for Janet to finish reading, looking over the lawyer's perfect bouffant with the glossy silver streaks. She ran a hand through her own messy spikes and wondered how two women who looked so different could think the same.

'Jesus, Bodie.' Janet De Marco moved her glasses to the end of her nose, removing the barrier between her eyes and Bodie's. 'Legally, yes, nothing can prevent you from doing this. Of course, we both know you didn't need a lawyer to tell you that. But, practically, do you think this is possible?'

'Yes.' Bodie reminded herself to sound confident. Less tired. 'I do.'

Janet raised her eyebrows. 'You really think you can get the numbers?'

'If I can expand the support base, get the other groups on board. If I can make them see we all win if Queentide wins, I mean, if the Women's Party wins,' Bodie scrunched her eyes and fists. It was hard not using the name of the movement she'd spent years establishing. 'Then yes, I...' Bodie corrected herself again. This was not about her, she reminded herself, 'We. We can do this.'

Janet smiled. She knew Bodie struggled to find the right words to ask for help. It was a foreign language she hadn't bothered to learn. She was feeding her the lines. 'So, what do you want from me?'

Bodie breathed in, 'Legal advice. Free. There are many people who will want us to fail.'

Janet nodded. A little too enthusiastically.

'And they will have more resources than you. I get it.' She waved her hand, the sunlight catching on the gold and gems on her fingers. 'This firm is at your disposal. But you will need more than a room full of lawyers. You are going to need people that understand election processes. Not just the policy stuff. The backroom stuff. The *backstabbing* stuff. You know? You will need PR and marketing. A shitload.' Janet paused, narrowing her eyes. 'And I can't imagine the media are going to lend you a megaphone. You are going to need someone loud enough without one. You'll need to create your own media. I'll put some feelers out. Leave the hiring to me.'

Bodie finally let go of the breath she'd been holding. 'Thank you, Janet.'

The offer of help felt like drinking a shot of bourbon. Endorphins flooded her veins. The unfamiliar sensation, the relief, of someone taking some of her load had altered her balance. It made her feel not quite complete. Not in control. Drunk. Scared. Trying to regain her composure, Bodie focused on Janet's face. The worry she found there instantly restoring the weight on her shoulder.

'You know what you are getting into here, Bodie? What *we* are getting into, right? You know the discipline that is going to be needed to pull this off?' It was a loaded question – a direct hit to Bodie's heart.

'If you are worrying about Insley, don't.' Bodie intended her voice to be a full stop on the conversation of her granddaughter. But Janet wasn't one to be punctuated by someone else. Even Bodie Hughes. She aimed again.

'I'm always worried about Insley. Where is she now?'

'Doing what Insley does, saving the world one woman at a time.' Bodie's smile failed to land, crashing into a frown. 'Single-handed.'

'She can't be making trouble once you start this Bodie. If you've any chance of succeeding, Queentide needs to come across as utterly respectable. Not a word anyone would use to describe Insley, not even you. You might hide Queentide on the ballot paper, calling it the Women's Party, using some semi-defunct political party as a Trojan horse, but everyone will know you are the one on the inside, steering it through the gates of Canberra. We can't have your family turn up in court for killing someone.'

That blow struck hard. Reaching too many nerves. Bruising a memory too close to the surface. Insley, still so small she needed a cushion to see the judge, calmly, too calmly, explaining what she had seen her father do. Bodie, still jetlagged, biting her lip, so she didn't cry. Trying to be brave for her granddaughter, as she heard how Celeste, her daughter, had died. She decided that day to move to Sydney to take care of Insley. As well as you can take care of a wildflower.

'We'll have a meeting in a few days. I may need you to help convince the others of the change of direction. In the meantime, let me buy you lunch. It's the least I can do.' Bodie talked before Janet realised the damage she'd caused and scrambled to apologise. Or worse. Ask Bodie how long it had been now. Twenty years, almost? Bodie didn't have an answer. When you lost a daughter, you didn't count it in years or even days. You counted it in unmade memories. For Bodie, that was incalculable.

Oblivious or relieved, Janet shook her head. 'Sorry, I've got a client now. A paying one. Hopefully.' The obese emerald prevented her from fully crossing her fingers, and Bodie stopped feeling bad about the pro bono work. 'But I'll be at the meeting. Helen is going to hate this.' Bodie let out a heavy sigh. Helen's research had inspired Bodie to start Queentide, but her rigid opposition to politicising the movement was limiting it. Helen believed in playing fair, even in an unfair world. Bodie had too, but now time was running out.

'You are going to need my help, or at least my moral support.' Janet looked down at her rose-gold watch. A Rolex. 'Jesus, is that the time? My client is probably already in reception. She sounded positively terrified about coming in. Poor girl. I'll walk you out.'

Janet was already on her feet. Bodie took the hint and started stuffing the files and laptop back into her cavernous patchwork knapsack.

'Is she in some kind of trouble, this new client?' Bodie couldn't stop herself from asking, even though she knew she couldn't, shouldn't, help. Not now.

'All the people I meet are in some kind of trouble.' Her eyebrows raised, and her glazed lips curled into a cynical smile.

'She's left her husband. I know little more than that.' Janet scanned the office for anything out of place and found an offending crooked file. 'Oh, except that he, the ex-husband, is Ben Henderson. You know that young politician? Minister for Bullshit.'

Bodie knew him well enough to grimace when she heard the name. The author of the Discrimination Bill, a policy that made it legal for women to be sacked for 'morally offending' Christian bosses, or any bosses, in fact.

Bodie remembered there was always a woman with him at press conferences. The wife. A polished prop for the cameras, proof the Bill wasn't all that bad – how could it be if a woman was standing right next to him? The accessory didn't talk. Or smile. Bodie remembered seeing her nearly cry once. She didn't even know her name. How could she not know her name? How had Bodie Hughes let a woman become scenery?

She had to rectify this. 'What's her name?'

'Er ... Lilith?' Janet picked up a legal pad. 'Lilith Green. She's already gone back to her maiden name. How d'you like that?'

Bodie liked it a great deal. She'd left a name behind in Idaho. It was too heavy with guilt to bring with her. She wondered what was weighing down Lilith's old name.

The phone on Janet's desk buzzed, slightly startling them both.

'And she's here.' Janet looked around, exasperated to see things out of place, even though, to Bodie, it seemed just fine. Except Bodie's mug, off the coaster, on Janet's glass desk. Bodie picked it up, then saw the circle it had left behind, so put it down again. But Janet had already witnessed the crime and tutted at Bodie. 'Come on, old woman,' Janet said as she shooed Bodie out of the office. 'Let me make some money so I can work for you for free.'

Bodie and Janet were still laughing as they emerged into the clinically clean reception. Bodie saw an out-of-place bundle of creases perched on the white leather sofa. The face and body as crumpled as the clothes, as though this woman had collapsed in on herself and didn't have the strength, or inclination, to straighten herself back out. Their boisterous entrance had startled her. She jumped, her teacup sloshing its contents on the saucer.

'Oh, I'm so sorry, my dear. We are so loud. Can I help you?' Bodie made her way towards the bundle, but Janet cut her off.

Gliding across the room, her two arms open, purposefully blocking Bodie. The bundle lifted her chin, quickly glancing at the door as if she were working out how long it would take to reach it. Then she locked two hesitant eyes on Bodie, giving her an intense but wary once-over. Bodie smiled in as friendly a manner as she could muster, then turned to busy herself with Ed, the amiable receptionist. Bodie had lived around nature long enough to know you don't corner a wounded animal. It might die of shock. Or attack you. She couldn't tell which way this one would go. She asked Ed about his weekend, giving one ear to his most recent dating antics and the other to Lilith Green.

'Lilith. Lovely to put a face to a voice.' Janet listened to the apologies. For spilt tea on the sofa. For her clumsiness. For bothering Janet. 'Oh please, don't worry about that. Ed will take that for you.' She gathered up Lilith Green and, with an arm around the younger woman's shoulder, swept her clean past Bodie. 'Come on through.'

Bodie lingered and watched Janet settle her into a conference room, a place without Bodie's coffee stains on the desk. Janet gave a quick dismissing wave and closed the heavy glass door behind them.

Bodie forced herself to leave. If she was going to pull this off – if *they* were going to pull this off – she was going to have to let others swing the sword. She just wasn't strong enough to do it on her own anymore. Besides, she found out long ago, the hard way, that she couldn't save them all. It was time to stop. There was a new plan.

Wearily leaving the office, Bodie considered the train. She realised she had no energy for dragon fighting that afternoon. The young women would have to deflect the words and hands themselves. Bodie couldn't always be there. She wouldn't always be there.

With a heart as heavy as her feet, Bodie took a taxi to the community. It was the place she shared with the women she had saved, back when she thought that would be enough. Enough reparations. Enough to halt the accumulation of unmade memories of her daughter.

But living with these women, these pseudo-daughters, was like swimming in an ocean of missed moments – an ocean whose currents got stronger every day. Exhausted in the backseat, she prayed that what she had planned would be enough to slow its movements.

To finally lay her daughter's memory, and her own mind and body, to rest.

Chapter 2

'So, Lilith. What are we doing here?'

It wasn't unkind, but it was sudden, catching Lilith by surprise. Like a band-aid being ripped off by a well-intentioned parent. Lilith remembered how much per hour Janet De Marco cost and decided brevity felt good.

Lilith's face felt raw from the scratch of the lawyer's sharp eyes. She wondered what other women said to Janet the first time they came into her office.

She tried a few explanations on to see if they fit. *I'm scared of my ex-husband. His friend fired me when I fled my marriage. There are just no jobs. I'm using the last of my money to see you. I'm worried about my children. I have no one else to listen to me, just you, a stranger. Someone I'm paying.* They all fit perfectly but were uncomfortably heavy. So she picked the lightest one to wear.

'I suppose I just want this over with.' The lawyer looked at her, a smile tickling the corner of her shiny oxblood lips. 'Oh, the custody thing, I mean. Not this meeting.' Both women knew Lilith meant the meeting.

Lilith's heart was thumping so hard. She was sure Janet De Marco could hear it. The lawyer sat still. Silent. Like a fox hunting a rabbit. Waiting for the prey to come to her. The room was cavernous and empty. Nowhere to hide. Lilith's skin prickled, those sharp eyes scraping over her again.

Lilith spoke, hoping to stop the lawyer's painful gaze and to stop the sound of blood flooding her brain. 'I need help. Your help.' She tried to grab hold of the escaping words, but they were too panicked, struggling hard to be free. 'He's threatened to take the kids from me. He's contending the next election. You know that, I guess.' The words echoed off the bare walls and timber-slab table, confirming their existence. This was really happening. Lilith Green was really in a solicitor's office, trying to divorce her husband. 'He's said if I don't keep quiet, he will prove I'm an unfit parent.'

Janet seemed unmoved by the words that had left Lilith trembling. She just scribbled on a pad and asked, 'Keep quiet about what?'

'About our separation. Ben doesn't want any controversy during the election.' Lilith twisted the strap of her battered handbag around her fingers. The tips went white, but she didn't release the pressure.

'People get divorced all the time. He's not seeking election in some conservative little village. He's the member for Warringah, isn't he? Northern Beaches? Half the population there are on second marriages. I can't see divorce being an issue.' Janet paused and put down her pen. She detected a new scent. She lowered her voice and her head, concentrating that gaze on Lilith again. 'How bad was it? Police ever called?'

'He never hit me.' The words jumped out eagerly, almost before Janet finished speaking. Waiting for the familiar cue. Lilith turned her head to avoid Janet's eyes, but not before she saw them flash with recognition. Or resignation.

'Sure. Okay, so let's say there was no violence. People don't leave happy marriages. He cheated on you?'

'Well, yes, but that's not why I left. I mean, he didn't leave me for someone else. There were just ... others.' Lilith lashed herself for betraying Ben, for proving his point. He couldn't trust her. Too late. The lawyer had turned a key and cracked the door open. Enough to see the skeletons, smell the blood. Lilith didn't want to stay locked in there with them any longer. 'I was suffocating. He was suffocating me. He controlled everything. Money, the kids. Where I went, what I thought ... it got terrible after the 2020 lockdowns, so much time together – you know how it was ...' Tears disobediently sprang up, Lilith wiped them away before they could reach the creases carved around her eyes.

The lawyer handed Lilith a tissue without even looking up. This was routine for Janet De Marco. Somehow that made Lilith feel better. This was just something to deal with, like removing a tick burrowing into your skin. The tears had dried before the tissue even reached her face.

'So he's a bastard, and he doesn't want anyone to know. Would that be about right?' Janet said.

Lilith nodded. If she didn't speak, she could pretend, at least to herself, that she wasn't betraying Ben. Lilith had done it for twenty years. She could do it for another hour.

'And he is blackmailing you, with this idea of you being an unfit mother,' Janet continued.

'I wouldn't say blackmail ...' Lilith offered.

'You don't have to. I'm saying it.' Janet's voice was as sharp as her eyes. 'And what grounds does he have for suggesting you are unfit?'

'Well, I don't have a job now. I'd hung on to it through the recession, but then I left Ben. My boss was Ben's friend. He told me he couldn't keep me on after all. Now I'm running out of money. Fast. There are no jobs, at least not for someone like me. Ben's still in the house. I had to leave. I've got somewhere, but it's small. It's not good enough for the girls, and I'm struggling even to pay rent there. He knows it will be hard for me to get another job – I don't have a profession, I suppose. I'm only a secretary, you see. He knows I'm on antidepressants. He knows I find it difficult to cope ... with life. But they *are* helping me. He says I drink too much. He's right, I suppose, but I never do it in front of the kids. I ...'

Decades of Ben's words squalled around Lilith's head like confused birds. She was useless. Hopeless with money. Disorganised. Annoying. Weak. Too shrill. Too quiet. Too emotional. Untrustworthy. She couldn't tell now if these were her own words or memories of one-way wars with Ben. Unsure, she stopped speaking.

'That's not grounds. That is Ben's opinion of you,' Janet said decisively. 'And that is only worth what you allow it to be.' She tapped the side of her head with a long nail, matched to the colour of her lips. 'If you don't evict him from your head, he will trash it. He will make you unfit.' She went back to her pad. 'And him, how is he with the girls?'

'He is a good dad,' Lilith said.

'That is not possible,' Janet batted back.

'No, he is.' Lilith tried again. 'He loves them.'

'He loved you too, Lilith,' Janet responded. 'Some people react to love in dangerous ways. Like they have an allergy to it.'

Lilith contracted every muscle in her face. Determined not to give anything away to this fortune-teller in front of her. But Lilith knew it was no use. Janet had seen the clues before, on hundreds of other faces.

'He's a good dad. I mean, he wants to see the girls. More than I expected.'

'How often does he see them?'

'He has them about half of the time.' Lilith tried to read the curling words on the pad to see if she was getting the answers right. 'Maybe more. There's nothing formal. He tells me when he wants them or when his mother will collect them.' Lilith paused. 'I suppose that's why I'm here. I don't think that's good for the girls ... not having a routine.'

Janet looked up from her pad. 'It's not great for you either. It must be unsettling.'

'I'm only worried about the girls.' Lilith tried to keep Janet on an easier path. She followed.

'Okay. Let's talk about the girls. They're twins. Five, yes? Great age.' The lawyer didn't wait for the nod. She was used to being right. 'So they are young, there are no plans in place and a threat of violence.' The lawyer raised a hand to stop words coming out of Lilith's open mouth. It worked. 'They're young enough for us to get this fast-tracked. If we get a decent judge, the interim hearing might be set for six months.' Janet saw Lilith's concerned face. 'It's the best we'll get. Family Court is jammed. These changes they brought in have slowed everything right down.'

A rabbit ran through her veins. Lilith couldn't hide the alarm in her voice. 'I have to take him to court?'

Janet raised her eyebrows in response. Lilith felt stupid. What had she expected to happen?

'No,' she blurted. Lilith imagined Ben in a courtroom. The cameras waiting outside. How angry he would be with her. How much more difficult her life would become. 'I can't do that. It will ruin his career. Isn't there another way? I just want some-one to talk to him, to make him stop threatening to take the girls away.'

Janet stretched her short arms across the timber slab and placed both hands over Lilith's outstretched palms. 'This will not be easy, Lilith. Since the last royal commission, the courts assume you are lying. There were so many domestic violence orders sought after the pandemic, the commission decided it had to be because women were making it up to get custody. Taking advantage of the situation. It was a more comfortable assumption than facing up to all the domestic violence going on and then having to do something about it. They didn't want to acknowledge the new epidemic the old one had created.

'So, if we start this and lose, they will say you've lied and committed parental alienation. Ben will get full custody. So we must get evidence. Hospital reports, statements from friends, that sort of thing. We have to prove that you and the children are being subjected to domestic abuse.'

The words crashed into the room. Lilith didn't want to see them. Raw, like grazed skin. Gory and pulsating. If he was an abuser, then that made her a victim. It meant she was putting her children in danger. An unfit parent, after all. Adrenalin soared through her limbs. Her pulse speeding up as the rabbit thumped on her chest, making it hard to breathe.

'I think I need some time. I don't think I can decide today.'

'Sure.' Janet quietened but continued to speak. 'You're paying me, so at least let me give you some advice. The court process is hard, but staying silent is even harder. For you and your girls.'

Lilith stood up, defying the shake in her limbs. Janet was wrong. Katy and Hannah were fine. Ben was a good dad. He had to be. She had left her marriage only two months before and was already struggling to pay rent and keep her sanity. Lilith wouldn't be able to care for the girls on her own. She couldn't prove to anyone that Ben was abusive. The scars and bruises he left were on the inside. It would be his word against hers, and he was so much louder.

It was time to leave. There was nothing for her here. Lilith would have to look for sanctuary elsewhere.

Lilith extended a hand down to Janet, still sitting as upright as a queen on a throne. She took it, looking surprised. Lilith felt a little pleased that she had ended the meeting and not the lawyer.

'Thanks. I'm sorry I wasted your time. But I'm just going to see how things go. I'm sure that once the stress of the election is over, Ben will settle down.'

Janet slowly stood, making a little sigh as she did. Lilith

thought she heard bones creaking. She had appeared young when they first met. She looked at Janet's hands placed on the table. Past the jewels and gold, Lilith could see the sunspots, the crepey skin resting on the aged oak.

'The election is almost a year away, Lilith. I hope for your sake, and your girls, that he manages stress well.'

As the lawyer turned towards the bookcase behind her, Lilith clenched her teeth and flinched at the memories of Ben's deadlines. She remembered the rainbows the broken glass would scatter across the room as it exploded near Lilith's head and settled at her feet. Janet turned around, a small book in her hand, which she passed to Lilith.

'This is a gift. For you.'

Lilith turned the compact book over in her hands. Her mouth relaxed as her fingers stroked the buttery, midnight leather and found an embossed insignia. A crown made of waves. Unread books and their promise of temporary escape had always made her smile.

'Thank you. It's a lovely cover. What sort of story is it?' Lilith said, playing her usual role of peacekeeper.

'Actually, you get to decide that. I've found it means different things to different people. But there are some universal truths. I think it will give you some guidance.'

Lilith shuddered. Religion hadn't helped her mother. Constant praying hadn't stopped the cancer. She politely slipped it in her worn handbag, trying to hide the heart stickers the girls had used to decorate it. She said goodbye before Janet could exhume the faith Lilith had buried with her mother.

Outside the room, Lilith sidestepped the office cat sitting at the door. She squeezed her way out of the small opening to deter the cat from making an escape. But it remained on the rug, yawning. Lilith closed the door, surprised that it didn't want to run away.

Chapter 3

Lilith hadn't ventured into Sydney since the redundancy. Macquarie Street rippled with people looking down at their phones and not where they were heading, assuming others would avoid them. They did. After the virus had left, the social distancing remained. People became even more insular, even less trusting after a year of conditioning. Lilith's phone remained in her bag. Since her mother died, no one called. Except Ben. He rang. Too many times.

She decided to walk through the park to escape the people and see if the leaves were changing colour. Lilith wanted a sign that summer, with its heat and fires, was ending. It had gone on for too long.

There was a building site near the crossing. Workers sat with feet dangling from the scaffolding as they watched office workers flow across the path. As Lilith neared, she heard their voices. Jeering and rowdy, trying to out-shout and out-crude each other. Jostling for alpha position. They had plenty to work with, a street full of women on lunch breaks looking for a sanctuary from their workday.

Lilith noticed one of these women juggling a container of food, a phone and a handbag. Her shoulders down as though she carried a heavy sort of sad that Lilith recognised. Lilith wondered what had happened to this still-young woman. Had she lost something? Found out something? Was her life not turning out to be the romantic comedy she thought it would be?

The woman pressed the button at the crossing, and Lilith saw the phone cradled in her neck was slipping. She chose to sacrifice her lunch to save it. But it dropped into the puddle of salad that preceded it anyway. A cheer came from the building site as the unforgiving fabric of the woman's skirt stretched as she bent down.

She cleaned her phone with a napkin she'd salvaged from the wreckage. Without her prop, she couldn't pretend to not hear their comments. They passed them back and forth to each other, bouncing compliments and insults like a game of tennis, a woman used as their ball.

Lilith saw she was just a child, really, underneath the carefully applied face. The face she'd learned to do from YouTube. The one that was supposed to make her look 'fierce'. The mask was now slipping with tears she couldn't stop. Lilith knew about masks. She'd worn one herself for a long time, slowly forgetting who she was while she'd hidden behind it. Then one day, it was ripped off. And there she stood. Unmade. An incomplete person.

The child looked about ten years older than her children. Lilith imagined her girls walking down the street in a few years. She shuddered at the idea of them being treated that way. Waves of people continued to roll by, dredging up more and more anger for Lilith. Had people always not cared? She had to do something. She had to help. It was what she'd expect someone to do for her daughters.

'Can't you see she's crying? Isn't it time to stop?' Lilith's voice wasn't loud; in fact, it cracked a little as she spoke, but the lights were red. The traffic had stopped to let pedestrians cross. So it was momentarily quiet. And Lilith's words were dropping into the vacuum. So the builders heard her. They were stunned. Perhaps thinking themselves invisible after years of no one answering back. Perhaps they thought they were in a bubble, and no one heard them.

Lilith turned up her volume, drowning out the memory of others' voices telling her to quieten down, to not make trouble. 'Did you hear me? She's crying?'

The builder with the tattoo sleeve answered, 'Maybe if she smiled, someone would want to fuck the miserable cow.'

The one next to him wouldn't be outdone, 'I'd still do it from behind. Won't be able to see its miserable face from that angle.'

Lilith looked around. The people continued to flow around her, like a stream passing by a rock. There were two police officers, men, close enough to have heard, but they didn't stop. Had the builders done nothing wrong? Could it be that this was now considered okay? The police crossed the road, laughing. Lilith was trapped in the bubble with the builders. People didn't see or hear her either.

'Why do you do this?'

'Cos it's fun, sweetheart.' The tattooed one again. 'Looks like a while since you've had some fun. Come around the back, and I'll sort you out. I don't mind the old frumpy ones. I like an old baggy one sometimes.'

Lilith felt tears welling, but she swallowed them down, the saltiness burning the back of her throat. But not because of the builders. Not because they had hurled something hurtful towards her. She'd been hit with much worse by Ben. What crushed her was seeing the woman she'd defended vanish into the crowd. Leaving Lilith on her own. Maybe she had thought Lilith could handle it because she was older, or perhaps this was just how women survived now. By sacrificing each other.

Lilith spat the bitterness in her throat back at the builders, 'Oh, just fuck off and die, would you?'

The builders look shocked, as though Lilith had pushed one of them off the scaffolding. 'Nice language. No wonder no one wants you. You want to be careful, love. There are laws now against making threats like that. I should report you.'

Lilith wanted to yell and not stop, to drown them in her sadness and anger. But people were staring. She was out of the bubble. Visible again. Audible. A middle-aged woman swearing in the middle of the street. Inside, she screamed. On the outside, she ran. Across the road and down into St James station. Underground. Beneath the city. Hidden. She wondered what would happen if she just stood and yelled into the tunnel. Letting her anger journey deep into the darkness. Would anyone stop her? Would someone join in?

She shook her head, trying to remove the impulse, then scanned the platform, like a reflex, looking for the people to avoid. But there was no danger today. A young couple in school uniforms, kissing and giggling. A middle-aged man with a briefcase. A woman with a pram. An empty carriage slid to a stop in front of her but, out of habit, Lilith didn't get in. Instead, she walked a little further, entering the same carriage as the kissing couple. They didn't even notice her take the seat behind them. They had earphones in, heads resting on each other. Oblivious to Lilith's existence.

Lilith still didn't relax. She couldn't relax on the train. Or the bus. Or the ferry. Lilith couldn't switch off that slight alertness she had carried with her all these years. The fear that kept her safe. She had to look out for the person who might sit too close. She had to fear the man that stared just that little too long. She had to run, fast, from the man that suddenly got off at her station and followed her along the platform. It all made her so very afraid. And just a little bit livid. Silently livid.

The doors to the carriage still weren't shut. Lilith wished they would so she could be on her way home, where it was safe. If she locked and checked the doors and windows and didn't answer the door to strangers.

She wanted to hold her girls, hold on so tight they couldn't grow up and start moving through this awful world, feeling the fear that she did. Lilith didn't want them to feel scared, but they needed to. Her girls needed to know that the world was cruel and dangerous, especially if you were female. She needed to teach them to tread lightly, to watch where they walked. Because if they fell or if someone tripped them, no one would help them. No one could help them. Not even their own mother.

Lilith jumped at the loud beeps, the warning to stand clear. The couple didn't flinch. Too absorbed in their phones and each other to notice, giggling at something on the boy's phone.

Finally, the train doors slid shut, and the carriage shuddered down into the tunnel, the lights failing to come on automatically at first. In the darkness, Lilith pulled her bag strap hard around her fingers and closed her eyes, fighting every urge to accompany the train in its screeches and screams. A chorus of voices from the past patted her on the head. No one likes a loud woman. There's a good girl.

Chapter 4

Lilith was greeted with an army of small shoes standing on parade at the door, waiting for their little generals to march them towards their next adventure. They would wait a while. Ben had taken them to his mother's beach house, and they wouldn't be back until Saturday. She wondered which shoes they had on their feet. The girls wouldn't have chosen them. Ben would have decided. He always did. She wondered what they were doing in the shoes he had chosen. Were they building sandcastles? Eating ice-cream? Missing her?

Lilith still hadn't acclimatised to this new environment. This in-between place where a mother went to bed, not knowing what her children had worn. What they had done. What they had felt. Not being warmed by the fire of their love in their *just-one-more-hug*. Or hearing it in their *love-you-more-than-cupcakes*. The air was thin here. It made Lilith confused. Like walking into a room and forgetting why you went there. Lilith would wander through her empty days, not sure what she was supposed to be doing.

She blinked away the tears, clutching two bottles with one hand. They clinked together like chains on a moored boat as she drifted towards the tiny kitchen. She put one bottle in the freezer, one in the fridge.

She shrugged the battered bag off, letting it land heavily on the bench. The old buckle finally broke, and the contents spilt out like a wave, depositing driftwood on the sand. Lilith looked at the broken bag and the debris, not able to decide what she should do. Nothing, she decided. She wasn't leaving the house for a few days. Ignoring the mess, she retrieved a wineglass from the top shelf, where the girls couldn't see them. Only used when the girls weren't around. Just one glass, she told herself. Just to unwind.

That was a lie. She knew she would drink until she passed out. She found peace in the oblivion. But then she would wake up with more regrets. So she'd drink again.

She went through the mail, waiting for the wine to chill. There wasn't much. She had only lived there for a couple of months. There was a letter from the real estate agent terminating her lease. In her rush to make an escape plan while she was still feeling brave, she had accepted a four-month lease. She believed the agent when he said that it would be extended. How would she find a new place? Lilith had almost burned through the redundancy money. There wouldn't be enough for a bond on a new home. The current bond wouldn't be released until she'd moved out.

The labyrinth Lilith found herself in was continually changing. Just when she thought she saw the way out, the hedgerow walls would grow over the path. Her escape plan was not to fight it but to wait for winter when it would die back, revealing a clear way to escape. There had to be a happy ending. So she crumpled up the letter and retrieved the bottle from the freezer. It was barely cold, but there was enough heat in the late summer air to make the bottle sweat, leaving small pools of water on the counter. Lilith reached into the freezer and loaded her glass with ice cubes, knowing she would have drunk most of it before the ice melted. The familiar weight of the glass in her hand made her feel anchored. She took a sip, the gentle burn in the back of her throat relaxing her like a log fire. She floated down the long corridor to the creaking back deck. The last of the evening light was seeping away, leaving red stains on the sky and bruised blue-grey clouds. Children were squealing louder than the nesting cockatoos and rosellas. It was still sprinkler weather. Lilith wondered if Ben had allowed Hannah and Katy to play in the water. They loved it, but he hated the mess more. She poured the wine to the top of the glass, taking a gulp before the cubes had resettled.

Lilith realised she had left her phone inside. She liked to look at photos of the girls when they were away. When she was drinking. Something that would pull her back from the brink she was pushing herself further towards. She went back to the kitchen and rummaged through the wreckage of her handbag. The phone hadn't spilt out. As she reached into the ruptured bag to find it, her fingers found instead the warmth of leather, the book the lawyer had given her. It was in the phone's way, so she cast it aside, throwing it carelessly on the countertop as she grasped the phone at the bottom of the bag. The book fell onto the faded grey linoleum tiles.

Feeling guilty, Lilith picked it up. She had been taught to treat books with respect. And this one was beautiful. Simple. The leather was rich. The colour of the ocean just before a storm. Dark enough to hide the biggest reefs. Its pages were edged in gold, the same as her mother's old bible, which was buried with her. Her hands folded over it in her casket.

The lawyer hadn't seemed religious. At least not the type to fall for the sort of religion that enticed people with expensive books and television shows. Curious, she opened the first page. *Queentide* was written in bold font. 'To Eve. Being you wasn't the crime.' And bibles didn't have dedications or author photos. She looked at the picture of an older woman. Bodie Hughes. The kind but stoic face floated above a chunky blue sweater, reaching up to her ears. Her white hair was cropped close to the sides of her head but haphazardly styled into a shock of spikes, ever so slightly reaching to the side, like pampas grass that had been cowered by the wind. Her eyes were dark and bright. They made Bodie look switched on. Alert. Ready for whatever life threw at her. Not like Lilith's muddied and mottled mix of greens, like a damp forgotten forest. Her face was familiar, but Lilith couldn't place her.

Her biography mentioned the women's liberation movement, civil rights protests, and teaching posts in Gender Studies across America. Then there was a chasm before she landed halfway across the world, in Sydney, where Bodie Hughes now ran Queentide, a feminist movement that ran women's shelters. Lilith pondered that the movement bore the same name as the book. Bodie had probably been quite busy since the 2020 pandemic. It had become a habit to remove women from their homes if they reported abuse. It was cheaper than jailing the men.

There was a small card stuck between the pages. Probably the lawyer's business card, Lilith thought. She removed it so she could put it with the crumpled letter.

Queentide Support Meetings: Tuesdays @ 6pm

Rm 10, Building 1, Sanctuary Park, Manly

Call Bodie Hughes – 0474 272 019

Sanctuary Park was the new name for the abandoned army barracks, which was slowly being turned into a feminist hipster village. Gun turrets were now used for yoga practice, and artists occupied the storerooms where artillery had been kept for a war that never came. It was just a few minutes from Lilith's little shack, up the hill past the big, glazed houses, the type of home she used to live in.

What sort of book had support meetings? Lilith scanned the

text for clues. There was no table of contents or even a blurb on the back cover making promises to the reader. She read the first line.

What if you aren't broken; what if you are breaking free?

Self-help. Lilith closed the book. She couldn't be fooled. She couldn't help herself. She *was* broken. She cut herself daily on her own sharp edges, could see the cracks where the blows had made her incomplete. She wasn't free, not even a foot out of the door. She was just playing house. Daydreaming.

In moments of startling lucidity, usually at the very edge of a hangover, the first ray of consciousness would find her. Lilith would know she wasn't any freer than when she'd taken the children and driven away three months ago. She remembered her wine, growing warm and stale on the patio table, and returned to it. The phone and book held absentmindedly in her hand.

The volume of children's voices was diminishing. Bedtime was approaching. She wondered if her own children were in bed. If they had already brushed their teeth. To not know the answer felt like a failure of motherhood to Lilith.

She placed the book on the table. Carefully. It really was beautiful. She traded it for the wineglass. Making sure the beads of water didn't come into contact with the leather. The sharp corners of the ice had receded, and waterfalls of droplets were running down the glass. She slid it across her forehead. It was a humid night. She scrolled through photos of the girls – smiling, frowning, pulling silly faces. She stopped when the tears blurred her vision and dropped into her glass, diluting the tepid wine even more.

She downed it in one gulp. Perhaps the contents of the bottle would be colder. She reached for it, but the book was in the way. She picked it up, feeling the leather smooth against her fingertips. She put her glass down so she could hold it with both hands. She flicked through the golden-edged pages. A few sentences caught her eye. She scanned paragraphs to get a sense of the book. Then she went back to the beginning, to the very first line, to make sense of the paragraphs. By the time the sky was too dark to read, she was into Chapter 3. The children had left their yards, replaced by the mosquito whines and cicada clicks.

She fetched the night lantern. The one Katy used to find Lilith when she had one of her bad dreams. She put it on the table and started Chapter 4, quenching a thirst she didn't know she had.

She kept on drinking in the book, stopping only to grab a blanket when the night air got too cool. A family of black flies had entered the open, almost full bottle of wine and drowned. She finished the book just as the sky developed, like an old photo in a dark room. The colours were like a child's painting. Simple. True. The warmth of the clouds comforted her, and the final words of the book sounded like a lullaby.

This is just a phase of the moon. The tide will eventually change.

She fell into an easy sleep, still holding on to the book.

She woke in the heat of the late Saturday morning to the buzz of lawnmowers and neighbours stoking up barbeques. As her brain pulled itself out of the fog, memories danced at the edge of recollection. Like a hangover, not letting her remember why she felt the way she did. But it wasn't the overfamiliar regret of a drunken night she was feeling. It was hope. Something she almost didn't recognise. It had been so long. She breathed in the smell of stale alcohol from the wine bottle on the table, making her feel proud.

As her hands straightened up the house, getting ready for the girls to come home, even though that wouldn't be until Tuesday, Lilith tried to arrange the jumble of thoughts in her mind. Books, at least the ones she chose, had always been an escape for her, allowing her to sail away on their pages for just a little while. But this book was different. It made her stand on the shore and survey her own land. But now she needed to map what she saw and figure out where she wanted it to lead her.

She looked at the card, abandoned on the kitchen bench. The support group. The next meeting was also on Tuesday. She could go, but she'd have to take the girls. But then the thought of gathering up her scattered bones and trying to reassemble them in front of strangers made her veins jump. Bodie Hughes's number was on the card. She could shortcut the mapping, just ask for directions. She punched in the number before she or the rabbit had fully woken up. An even-toned American voice answered, speaking against the beat of a metronome. Asking her to: Leave. A Message. After. The Tone. It made Lilith calm.

Lilith babbled her name and number and hung up. She hated the sound of her own voice – Ben always said it was pitchy. Hard to understand. Worrying that he was right, she rang back five minutes later. But this time the voice was live, with the same rhythmic, hypnotising beat.

'Hello, Lilith, I've been expecting your call. The first one. Not this one.' Her voice was warm, friendly. But definitive.

'I'm sorry, I thought perhaps you wouldn't be able to understand my message, so I called back to leave another one. I didn't mean to bother you.' Lilith felt the need to apologise.

'I understood it, Lilith. It was very clear. And please, no more apologies. So, it seems we have a mutual friend,' Bodie said.

'Oh, do you mean Ms De Marco? Yes, she is my lawyer. Sort of. She gave me your book. It's beautiful,' Lilith replied.

'Yes. I saw you in reception, actually. You looked like you had things on your mind,' Bodie said gently.

Lilith remembered now why the face was familiar. She was the woman whose laugh had startled her. Lilith felt ashamed. She didn't want Bodie Hughes to have seen her that way. She didn't want to be the woman who couldn't hold a teacup. Her veins started twitching.

'I was such a mess …' Lilith said apologetically.

'Please. You were just fine,' Bodie laughed gently. 'Everything looks a mess in Janet's office. The place is so clinical. She told me she had given you one of the nice copies, the leather-bound one. She likes to give the pretty ones to her clients. I think she likes them to have a beautiful thing to hold on to in the dark times, a reminder that the world isn't all bad. When you feel ready, please read it. The words might help you too.'

'I have read it.' Lilith wanted a gold star from the teacher. 'All of it. When I said it was beautiful, I meant the words, not the binding. Although that is beautiful too.'

There was a stillness. Lilith worried that she had said something wrong. That she had reduced Bodie's work to a trinket, a china doll too beautiful to be played with.

'You've read the whole thing?'

'That's right. I read it all. Overnight.'

There was the stillness again. Lilith wondered if there was a fault in the line or if Bodie didn't believe her.

'Well, you must need some rest now. Will we see you Tuesday? The details are on my business card. It should be a good session. We have some … interesting … guests. I think you will benefit from it.'

'Oh, I'm not sure if I will come to the meeting. I really just wanted to call you, and …' She paused. What was it she wanted, exactly?

'You've read the book, Lilith. You can stop there, keep the knowledge on a shelf, let it grow dusty. Reminisce now and then about the night you stayed up to read a book by an old woman who thought she could make the world a better place. And, for a day or so, you believed her. That will be a beautiful memory to hold on to. Or you can do something with it. See what you can turn it into. Something better than beautiful. Something useful.'

'But I have my girls from Tuesday.'

'That really that isn't a problem. We've many women with children of all ages in the community. That's where we meet. It's the first one Queentide opened, actually. They will find themselves in good company. So will you. We will see all of you on Tuesday. There are no signs, but there is a map at the entrance. I am sure you'll find your own way, Lilith. You've come this far with no help. Goodbye, my dear.'

The phone call was over. A decision had been made, but not by Lilith. The rabbit twitched. Lilith put her hand to her chest. *It isn't far, friend. Only up the road.*

Chapter 5

Bodie turned on the stove and put the ancient coffee pot on the ring. She retrieved the honey and lined it up neatly next to the nobbled ceramic cup that one of her former residents had made her. She knew all the other women thought the cup was ugly, but Bodie loved it. Her fingers, all crooked and bumped, seemed to fit into the crevices of the brown, home-pottered cup, like vines around a tree trunk. It gave warmth to her arthritic joints and held an obscene amount of coffee. That ugly mug made Bodie very happy indeed.

As she waited for the pot to brew, she called Janet. It would be at least twenty minutes before the coffee was even remotely drinkable, and Janet would only want to talk for two. It was office hours. She would be busy, but she would still make time for Bodie.

The phone barely rang; Janet picked up on the second ring. 'Bodie. What's she done now? Which judge do I need to call?'

'And good morning to you too, Janet. I'm not calling you about Insley,' Bodie said indignantly.

'Well, that's a relief because I think I've used up every get-out-of-jail-free card for her now.' Janet took an audible sip. It would be a coffee from the overpriced place in the lobby where they scorched the coffee. Fast service, terrible baristas. Bodie looked at her silver pot on the stove – it would be worth the wait.

'So what's up? I can't do lunch today if that's the reason for the call. I've got a defamation case I need to prepare for. Those weasels from MASC are at it again – Male Activists for Social Change, huh! Harassment, more like. MASH, that's what they are.'

'Insley has been doing a bit of digging on their members recently. If you need some help gathering evidence, she could help you for a change.'

'I have a mountain of evidence,' Janet huffed. 'The arseholes blatantly posted lies about her on Facebook, said she'd committed medical malpractice. She lost a load of clients, really clear-cut stuff ...'

'So what's the issue?'

The issue is finding a judge in this town who will rule against the boys' club. Getting a conviction against MASC members is basically impossible these days. Even for a male lawyer. My friend Joe – you know Joe, don't you? Big guy. Came on one of our climate marches? Anyway, he was representing a woman whose house had been vandalised by her ex-husband. A MASC member. Family Court didn't want to know about it. So she brought a civil case. The judge said she had driven him to it by constantly reporting him to the police. He'd been stalking *her* for months. She ended up paying his costs and got told off by the judge for wasting the court's time. Honestly, Bodie, it's worse than forty years ago.' Janet finally breathed.

'We will prevail, Janet. It won't be like this much longer. It will be worth the wait.' Bodie tried to sound confident.

'Yes,' Janet said, sounding hesitant, 'but will you and I be triumphantly walking off the battlefield or playing our angelic horns in celebration from on high?'

'I'm far from dead, Janet De Marco.' Bodie felt indignant. 'And so are you.'

'True,' Janet said, 'but sometimes I just feel so tired of it all.

You know?'

Bodie knew. She changed the subject.

'Well, as we are both so ancient, I'd better get to my point in case one of us kicks the bucket in the next few minutes,' Bodie joked and smiled when she heard Janet guffaw. 'The reason for my call, Lilith Green. The client you gave my book to on Friday?'

'I don't think she's my client,' Janet said. 'She left the office in a way that makes me think she's not coming back.'

'Well, she called me on Saturday morning. She'd read *Queentide*.' Bodie paused. 'In one night. Just after she left your office.'

'And then she called you?' Janet asked incredulously.

'And she's coming to our meeting tomorrow night.'

'This is Lilith Green we are talking about? The ex-wife of Ben Hamilton?'

'The same.' Bodie eased herself into a seat at the dining table. The conversation was lasting longer than she expected.

'She didn't leave me with the impression of someone ready to listen.'

'Maybe she's listening for someone else.' Bodie span the tarot card she'd carried into the kitchen with her as she spoke. It was an old habit, one that helped her think. The card had been given to her by a woman, Harriet, from the place in Nevada. Harriet used to read for the others, but she would refuse to do Bodie's cards. When Bodie had to leave, suddenly, to take care of Insley, Harriet gave her the card, declaring that Bodie would always try to steer destiny. Harriet didn't say if it was a good thing or not. Bodie had always assumed it was, but lately, her confidence was wavering.

'You think she's a plant?' Janet asked her directly.

'It makes me nervous when politicians' wives call me out of the blue.' She straightened out a corner of the card. It was getting a little dogeared. 'I'm going to get Insley to check her out.'

'Jesus, that's all the poor woman needs,' Janet said, 'Insley on her tail.'

'Oh Janet,' Bodie replied quickly, 'Lilith will never even know. Insley can be discreet when she wants to be.' Bodie thought of the secrets Insley carried around. The things even Janet didn't know about, and Bodie only suspected. Insley was in a constant state of discretion; she just used her brashness as a distraction. 'Look how she has been about her relationship with Kathleen. It's still only a few of us who know about that.'

'Okay, sure,' Janet said sharply. 'But if you want my opinion, and I'm guessing you do as you've called me while you are waiting for your morning coffee to brew. And by the way, how you drink that molasses is beyond me,' - Bodie smiled at her friend's knowledge of her routine - 'Lilith Green is genuine.'

'You sound very confident.' Bodie replied.

'I am confident.' Janet's voice was reassuring. 'Putting aside the fact that I can read people very well, just look at the facts. She only called you because I gave her your book. She does not know we are friends. Probably never even heard of Queentide until she read the book and would have no idea I am one of its founders. I doubt feminist activism was a hot topic of conversation with Ben Hamilton.'

Bodie thought this through. It made sense. Ben Hamilton would hate Queentide and what it stood for, but he had never paid them any attention. Why would he? To him, they were just a bunch of angry women to be ignored, like insolent children. To be given the silent treatment. Bodie was banking on people like him underestimating them. Before they knew what hit them, Queentide would be all grown up. Then they could make the rules.

'Okay, I'll buy that.' Bodie hesitated. She was coming to her real reason for calling. 'So why did you give her the book?'

'She didn't randomly pick me off Google. She came to me for

a reason. I'm a damn good lawyer with a reputation for getting results in custody battles, especially where there's domestic violence. At least the best you can expect in the current system.'

'Is that why she left him?'

'You don't need me to answer that, and I can't answer that. Lilith might not be my client, but I still can't divulge what we discussed.' Bodie could picture Janet winking.

'Fair enough. But you gave Lilith the book because you thought it would help?'

'Yes. God knows she needs it, but she didn't want it from me. At least not yet. I thought your hand might look a little more inviting than mine. More like it was about to pull her into a hug than drag her through a messy court case. She needs to be in one piece before she can even attempt to run that gauntlet.'

'And you think I can put her back together again.'

'Well, she's read the book already. There's the first piece.'

'A big piece.' Bodie laughed gently. 'Who does that? Who reads a book like that in one night, then calls the crazy woman that wrote it?'

'Someone ready to change?' Janet offered.

'Someone with balls of fucking steel,' Bodie replied.

'She's got them too. They're just hidden among the broken pieces.'

'And that's why you want me to help her?'

'Yes.' Janet took another sip. 'And it's why I want her to help you.'

'Help me?'

'She's the ex-wife of a high-profile misogynistic politician. A politician we know is as crooked as they come, and who is a front for MASC ...' Janet left the trail open for Bodie to follow. Bodie got there quickly.

'You said she was fragile. I can't put her through something like that, even for Queentide.'

'Eggs are fragile, even on the outside. But they are strong enough to keep a new life safe,' Janet said patiently. 'You just need to give her the right conditions.'

'I don't know Janet. This feels as though I am using Lilith.'

'You will be using each other. Lilith will get stronger, and so will Queentide. It will be worth it, Bodie, for both of you.' Janet sighed. 'For all of us.'

The pot on the stove whistled. They had been talking for an awfully long time.

'I've kept you long enough, Janet. Good luck today. I hope you get those bastards.'

'I'll do my best, Bodie. Enjoy your coffee. I'll see you at the committee meeting this evening. Convincing Helen of your new strategy will be easy compared with this trial.' Janet laughed.

Bodie screwed up her eyes. 'I hope so. I don't want to do this without her. I've run her through it, but I just don't think I've got her over the line. We vote tonight, though. We can't waste any more time. If we are going to do it, we have to launch at the Queentide meeting tomorrow. I need her to agree at our committee meeting tonight.'

'What if she votes against it?'

'She will be outnumbered,' Bodie sighed, 'and we will proceed with the strategy. Helen may come around, or she may leave. It won't be the first friend I've lost along the way. Or the last, by the time this is all over.'

'You will always have me, old woman,' Janet said merrily.

'You may not have me if you keep calling me that.' Bodie laughed, and the friends said their goodbyes.

Bodie put her phone down and looked at the card. Maybe it was time to put it in a frame. It really was looking quite tired now. She hauled herself up and went to the stove, pouring the rich liquid into the ugly cup. She added honey, letting it drizzle slowly from the honey pot. She sat down at the table, wrapped her fingers around the thick pottery and felt the heat seep into her knuckles. When they'd warmed enough to unstiffen, she raised the cup to her face and breathed in the sweet steam. Finally, she took a sip.

It was worth the wait.

Chapter 6

The house was quiet, like the hush that falls after a hailstorm. A stillness before people emerge to check the damage. Lilith tidied and cleaned but didn't disturb the girls' room. Teddy bears still enjoying a tea party, abandoned dragon tails and fairy wings, shipwrecked on the shaggy rug. She wanted them to know that time had stood still while they were gone. They would pick up where they'd left off. They had missed nothing. Neither had Lilith. Make-believe. Let's pretend. Not just a game for children.

Lilith put the radio on as she cleaned the rattling bi-fold windows. The voices let her pretend she wasn't alone. Lonely. She tuned into a talkback show, not because she liked what they said; in fact, most times, she would tut all the way through it. But, comfortingly, they didn't play music. Her heart was too raw for music. Overly vulnerable to piercing voices and plucking guitars.

The broadcaster was interviewing the Prime Minister, someone Lilith had once met at one of Ben's fundraisers. There was a female voice there too, Kathleen Rae, a young MP who'd led a sexual harassment claim against the Minister for Health. Another man she'd met through Ben. An old rugby pal. The one who would put his hand way up Lilith's skirt whenever Ben wasn't looking.

Lilith said nothing. Ben wouldn't believe her. Or would blame her later, when everyone else had gone. It was better to just swat the minister away, pretend it hadn't happened. Make-believe, not make trouble. That was Lilith's motto.

But Kathleen Rae was making trouble. She found five other women who he'd also harassed, who weren't happy to just swat him away. He'd defended himself by saying they were too old or too Black or too gay to interest him. The media was fine with his prejudices, but not with the women's ambition. Was it normal for a woman to want to be away from her family? Was it normal for a woman to not have one?

The media took them down. Photos of boozy nights out. Juicy stories from disgruntled ex-boyfriends. Leaked medical reports of abortions. The rest of the women had dropped the claims, then left Parliament, but the media didn't let them go. After all, they couldn't start something, then change their minds. They were asking for it. One of them committed suicide, eventually. Lilith didn't grieve when she heard about it. That process had started weeks earlier. Inevitability had numbed her to the unavoidable news. When a crack appears in a windowpane, you feel the sadness then. Not when it finally shatters. Sometimes it's a relief when it finally breaks.

But Kathleen just grew stronger in the dirt they threw at her. She fed off it, put roots down in it and let them spread, sprouting in unexpectedly welcoming places. Breakfast television in the UK. Speeches at the UN. Where people wanted to hear what was wrong with Australia. Where people weren't interested in playing pretend anymore.

But this radio show wasn't one of those places. The host, Allan Grieves, kept the charade alive. He propped up the facade of a "fair go" Australia, and he didn't like people like Kathleen tearing off their masks and spoiling their fun.

'Look, it's a fact that you are ambitious, Kathleen. Shadow Minister for Aboriginal Affairs in your first year in politics.

Incredible.' The way he said it wasn't a compliment. 'There's leadership talk now. Loud leadership talk. Some even say that the current leader isn't stepping down – that you, in fact, have pushed him out of the way. I mean, it's really the only way someone like you would be considered for the top job in the Labor Party.' He paused briefly, allowing the audience to decide which part of Kathleen Rae made her rise so incredulous to him. Woman. Young. New to politics. Gay. Aboriginal. Not like the people he liked.

'I'm sure you are happy about that. Can't say the rest of us are,' he sputtered, leaving no room for interruptions. 'It seems this has all worked out rather nicely for you. Nothing like a bit of controversy to get noticed, is there? Bit of a coincidence, some might even say, that a young, inexperienced politician like yourself has become so famous. Famous enough to be considered for the top job.'

'Allan, I'd rather be known for my record on First Nations policy reform than this, for what I have achieved as Shadow Minister.' She kept talking, trying to stop the inevitable interruption. 'It's the reason I entered politics in the first place, to make things better. I'm not pushing anyone out of the way. David, our leader, is retiring. No one is pushing him, certainly not me. I never expected to be in the spotlight over something like this, and I didn't expect him to put me forward as his preferred successor.' Kathleen replied calmly.

'So you are admitting you are after his job? That you're happy to be the centre of attention?' he spat back.

'No, that's not what I'm saying. I don't think any woman is happy when MASC has them in their crosshairs,' Kathleen persevered.

Ben had friends in MASC, more old rugby pals, drinking buddies. Ben said they were harmless. Just a group that was tired of men being mistreated. Trolling women on the internet and sending abortion doctors death threats was all just to get their message out. The patronage of mining magnates and media barons helped, too, as well as friends in the Government. Like Ben. They gave them a patina of respectability and access to policymakers.

Ben had helped them get the family laws changed, the same ones that were tying her in knots now. That had been a big campaign, and Ben threw himself into it. MASC had marched in all the cities, wheeled out crying men who had lost their children. Started a Facebook page recording every male suicide. MASC said too many women claimed home violence in custody hearings after the pandemic – it was proof they were making it up. After all, the police hadn't reported an increase in arrests for home violence, so how could it be true? Lilith listened as Ben recited this to her every night, practising for Parliament or the next television interview. Or sometimes, Lilith thought, just for her benefit.

She listened, never interrupted or corrected him. She didn't tell him what her counsellor had told her. Or that she even had a counsellor, a colleague's daughter. She didn't see the need to tell him that Maud at work had spotted her wrist one day. Bought her a hot chocolate and introduced her to Sally, her daughter, the counsellor.

She didn't tell him that most of the suicides came after the man had murdered his wife and children. Or that the police didn't make that many arrests because removing the woman to a shelter meant less paperwork for them and less pressure on the jails. Or that she knew the word now for the confusion in her head. Gaslighting. She didn't tell him the suspense of not knowing *when* he would hit her was worse than the pain when his hand finally made contact. That it was that stillness, not the explosions, that were the hardest to live with. She didn't tell him any of this.

She just silently made plans to leave and one night found a chance to follow it. No dramatic exit, no screaming or tears. She packed the car in the dark, got the children out of bed and left hours before he was due back from Canberra. For a few blissful hours, the only sound was the rabbit running through Lilith's veins. Steady and calm. Until Ben came back to a silent house. From then on, Ben had filled Lilith's life with a furious wall of sound. Four, in fact, that sealed her in.

'I don't see what MASC has to do with this, Ms Rae,' the host said flippantly.

'They are trolling me on social media. They send death threats, worse, to my office every day,' Kathleen replied.

MASC's new target. Lilith was sure Ben was practising a speech in a mirror somewhere right now.

'You sound a little hysterical here, Kathleen.' He was laughing now. 'I mean, what could be worse than a death threat?'

'If you were a woman, I wouldn't have to elaborate.' She paused. 'You want me to tell you? They send me the items they are going to rape me with until I'm torn up inside. Metal poles. Broken bottles—'

'Ms Rae, please. This is a family broadcast. There could be young children listening.' The host sounded like he was telling off a rude teenager. 'I really don't think it's appropriate—'

'No, Allan, it isn't appropriate. That's exactly why your listeners need to know exactly what this so-called legitimate group is doing. We can't keep hiding it.'

'How do you know it's MASC Kathleen?' The Prime Minister's voice was heaving with condescension.

'What?' Kathleen snapped back.

'Well, not to be blunt, but there are many people who don't like you for many reasons.' The Prime Minister let out a sigh. 'I can even think of a few myself.'

'I know who—' Kathleen attempted to talk.

'Please don't interrupt me, Kathleen.' He continued talking over her. 'Other people might not like you because, oh, I don't know, you are Aboriginal. Or another bloke might not like you because you are a lesbian. A man-hater. How could you ever know what it's like to be the average Australian family?'

She tried again. 'You can't say—'

'These aren't my views, you understand. I'm just saying what a lot of *other* people think about you.'

She kept trying. 'Allan, come on, you have to—'

'So, Prime Minister, you don't think that MASC is targeting Ms Rae here,' the host said. 'You think she is just overreacting?'

'Can I speak, please?' Kathleen said sharply but politely.

'In a moment, Kathleen, I'm not quite finished. I think we need to be fair to Ms Rae here, Allan. She's new to politics. Only been in the job since the last election, a few years ago. She's from a small town. A great little town. Salt-of-the-earth type people.' The PM paused. 'Uncomplicated, you might say.'

'This is getting ridic—' It was as if she wasn't there. She was being discussed as if she were a problem the two of them, to-gether, would solve. She was trying to speak, maintaining a low volume. No one likes a loud woman.

'She's found herself in a new environment, a bit more so-phisticated, shall we say? There's a legitimate lobby group that doesn't like what she's saying. Now I can't speak for MASC, but I think their view is that these policies that Kathleen wants to force on us are just plain unfair. A man accused of harass-ment; I mean, it could be a woman. Still, it's always a man that's accused, isn't it?' He paused, leaving space for people to draw conclusions. 'That accused man has to, according to Ms Rae, be removed from the workplace. With no evidence. Immediately deprived of income. So their so-called victim feels safe. I mean, how is that fair?'

'You are oversimplifying my position—' Lilith cringed at Kathleen's clear, insistent voice. A lyrebird trying to find the right tune, the one that would make them accept her.

'Now, of course, a men's rights group is going to be alarmed at this. Kathleen is misinterpreting their legitimate lobbying for some sort of targeted attack. And, as for these death threats or whatever you want to call them, well, we are politicians love. It's not personal. This is the job you signed up for. Some people get angry, need to let off some steam in our direction. You just have to put up with it. This is how it's always been.' The PM sounded triumphant.

'Interesting point Prime Minister. You think maybe she's too sensitive, too thin-skinned perhaps?' the host said.

'Yes, exactly. Too thin-skinned,' the PM echoed back. 'She's put herself in the spotlight with these overblown accusations against a great bloke. Then she's complaining when a legitimate group has an issue with it. And I am too much of a professional to bring up the accusations she's tried to throw my way in *The Guardian* this morning, twisting my words—'

'They are recorded in Hansard, Prime Minister. The media were in the press gallery. I have twisted nothing. You incited violence against me—' Kathleen spoke quickly.

'Can't you just drop it?' The PM's facade of politeness was falling.

'—you said it didn't surprise you that I'd received threats to strangle me.' Kathleen finished her sentence, finally.

'See? She just can't leave it, can she?' the PM said to the host. 'You must have the last word, Ms Rae, mustn't you? Again, I didn't say I wanted to throttle you. I said I'd understood why others may feel that way. You took my comments entirely out of context.'

The host was making agreeing noises.

'Okay. So let's make sure I've got the right context here.' Kathleen's voice was measured. 'You say that you don't want to strangle me, but you think it would be justifiable for someone else to do it?'

'There is no need to get shrill, Kathleen. You can't just keep interrupting people like this. You can't just throw accusations. It is nasty Kathleen.' He emphasised his last few words.

'So which is it? Am I too sensitive or not sensitive enough? What would you like me to be Prime Minister? What would make me agreeable to you?' She was no longer singing, no longer trying to charm. She was tired. You could hear it in her voice.

'Right now, Kathleen, as it seems you are incapable of controlling your temper, the thing that would make you agreeable to me, and every person listening right now, is if you were silent,' the PM shot back at her.

'Good call, Prime Minister, and I think that is where we will leave it. Let's go to the listeners now,' the host said. 'We have Gary from Baulkham Hills. Gary, how do you think we can shut up Kathleen Rae for good?'

Lilith changed stations before Gary's voice came on. She'd heard enough angry men for one day. She alighted at a news station. They were talking about Monica Gaumond, a woman who had gone missing in Melbourne. Six days now. No trace. Lilith had read all the stories, listened to all the reports. She had two children, like Lilith. In the photo the police released, she'd worn a crucifix with an inlaid ruby, like Lilith's mum had. Maybe that's why she was interested. Something wasn't right, though. Monica was reported missing when she didn't collect her boy from daycare. Every mum had seen the face of their child when they were the last one to be picked up. When they thought they were forgotten. Monica would have arranged for someone to collect him. Unless she didn't know she would not be there. Lilith knew there was an inevitability to Monica's story. She just wanted to end the suspense; she just wanted the cracked window to break.

His car announced itself, three hours later than it should have been, two blocks away. It echoed up against the tall apartment blocks, swept out to Collins Beach and continued to ride the waves on the ocean.

Lilith hated these exchanges. The swapping of hostages. They would be let out of the car, one by one, then a cloud of smiles and bows and sparkles would stampede towards her. His disappointment in their joy would be on display. He wanted them to be damaged. For Lilith to be their wrecking ball. He wanted to punish her with her children's pain. The one injury Ben knew she could never recover from. He had succeeded; he just never got to see it. It came at night, flowing through the tears at bedtime. Unanswerable questions, how could she still love them if she didn't love Daddy? It came in nightmares. The fear they had of Lilith leaving them, even for a second, to go to the mailbox. Worried she wouldn't return. Lilith absorbed it all, held it all in, and then, as soon as they were gone, wrung it out until all that was left of her heart was a crumpled rag.

His glossy oversized SUV reversed off the cracked driveway. Escaping from the tiny house with its creaking porch and tin roof, back to where it belonged among twinkling highrises and houses with heavy Tasmanian oak doors. She didn't miss it, the wealth. She felt more at home in her frayed little house. She was never quite polished enough for Ben's world. Her nails always chipped, dress just a little too ill-fitting. Ben didn't complain, at least not about her appearance, because it meant it didn't draw attention away from him. The journalists barely even noticed her, which was a relief. Every day she had felt like an imposter, and Ben was always ready to confirm her fears.

Here was where she belonged, among the weatherworn cottages and overgrown lilly pilly bushes.

She sighed heavily as she remembered the real estate agent's letter. She could ask Ben for money. She hadn't asked for anything so far. But you don't run out of a bear's cave and then pop back in because you dropped your backpack. You put distance between yourself and the bear and hope he goes back to sleep.

She looked up to see Katy trying to reach for the cookies on the bench. Her eyes were level, but her arms weren't long enough to get to the plate that had been pushed right back.

It would be a long time before Lilith's bear went to sleep. He would be a constant presence in her life until Katy and Hannah were grown.

A clatter came from the adjacent dining room, then Hannah appeared, back first, dragging one of the heavy wooden chairs with both hands, placing it next to the counter. With a rolling wave, she invited her sister to ascend, like Cinderella getting into her glass carriage.

'Why, thank you, kind sir,' Katy said, parroting one of the too-perfect Disney princesses.

'The pleasure is all mine, mademoiselle,' Hannah replied, sounding like one of the improbably kind princes.

Giggles warmed the kitchen as cookies were furtively stuffed into pockets.

'Love you, Mamma,' Katy yelled. 'We're just going outside to play.' Lilith tried to keep a straight face as they headed out to the shade of the mango tree, the only thing about the little cottage that was big. The girls were growing up. Perhaps the shadow of Ben wouldn't be cast over them for as long as she feared.

She began unpacking their little backpacks to get them ready for kindy the next day. There was the usual, unusual menagerie of toys, rocks, a band-aid and three colouring pencils. As Lilith pulled out a bundled-up princess dress from Hannah's bag, a white envelope emerged with it.

Lilith's name was on it, in Ben's swirling handwriting. The envelope was bloated, pushing at the seam. She checked on the girls through the open back door at the end of the corridor. They were holding sticks like wands; their imaginary world would absorb them for a while. She slipped her finger under the seal, painfully slicing the side of it in the process. She sucked it to stop the bleeding, then pulled out the letter. The paper was heavy, official. But the first page was filled with Ben's disorienting, curling script. She rolled her eyes at the first word, 'Lilypad'. A nickname he'd given Lilith on their third date. She loathed it and told him so. Back then, she was braver. Ben laughed at her and called her indignation adorable. Then he used the name more and more. Eventually, Lilypad stopped complaining and accepted that was her name now.

Lilypad

There are court orders for you to sign with this letter. Don't bother getting a lawyer to pick holes in it – you can't afford one anyway – and my father's legal firm has made it watertight. I'm making this easy for you. I'll give you 30% of the house, on the condition that the girls live with me and see you one weekend a month. There's also a non-disclosure agreement. No running off to the papers about this or anything else before you get any ideas about screwing me over.

We both know you aren't coping. I know the owner will not renew your lease. He's selling up to one of my old pals. Small world, isn't it? We both know you are out of options, so I'm giving you one. For the girls' sake.

Ben

Her tears burned blotches on the paper, then some blood from her cut finger transferred onto the page, leaving it dappled pink and red. A repulsive sunset. The panic rose. He had cornered her. The chase was over. His muzzle was in the warren, and Lilith was inches from his glistening sharp teeth. She thought about calling the lawyer, but it was 5 pm, she wouldn't answer her phone to clients now. And, even if she did, Janet De Marco would gently tell her she needed to fight. Lilith was too weak, too wounded. But she couldn't give up her girls. She couldn't only be a visitor in their lives.

She crumpled the blood-marbled letter, and threw it in the bin, put the unread orders in her desk drawer. If she couldn't see them, they weren't real. This, her life, wasn't real.

She splashed water on her face, then went to the backyard to watch the girls play. Sitting on the step, she watched the clouds turn to fairyfloss, forming an uneven patchwork quilt over the hill. Somewhere in among the peeling stringybark trees was Bodie Hughes. Waiting. Expecting.

The girls were playing a game of chase. Rules were being announced as they played. Each of the girls, Katy mostly, trying to get one over on the other. Lilith wondered if she should intervene, ask them to be fair to each other. She didn't. Perhaps this was a good lesson to learn. A new rule was announced, which allowed Katy to get an extra cookie. Hannah was obediently freezing to the spot.

Katy ran over to the step where Lilith was sitting, where the cookies had been haphazardly placed on a leaf, to keep them clean.

'Mamma, what's over there, the place you are looking?' Katy took a bite of her new cookie, spilling crumbs as she shouted to her sister that she still wasn't allowed to move. Hannah looked like she was about to cry. Lilith didn't notice.

'On the hill.' Katy was pointing at one of the old sandstone buildings, part of the army barracks where Bodie Hughes and her community were expecting to see Lilith in half an hour. 'Well, I don't know for sure.' Lilith hadn't worked out how to explain to the girls where they were going. Or if they were going.

'Well, what do you *think* is up there?' Katy asked as she took another nibble, 'Hannah! You have to stay still! You can't cry! It's the rules!'

'Maybe fairies riding dragons.' Lilith didn't know how to describe Bodie and her commune. Besides, Katy loved it when her mamma made up stories.

'I'd like to see that.'

'I would too.' Lilith hadn't decided to go, but curiosity was getting the better of her.

'Hannah! Stop it!' Katy yelled. Sometimes she reminded Lilith of Ben. She pushed that thought down.

Hannah was crying now. Lilith had missed the signs. The change in the game's tone. It was time for it to end. Lilith made her way over to the timider of the twins. She was a mum, Lilith reminded herself. She could make up rules too.

'New rule, anyone crying gets a hug.' She nuzzled the top of Hannah's head, still a little downy, still so young. Still time to enjoy some make-believe. Lilith finally decided.

'Okay, who wants to come and find some fairies in the forest?' Lilith asked the girls.

'Really?' Hannah looked up anxiously. Lilith had to be careful – it needed to feel safe for her.

'Sure, I have a friend who lives up on that hill, in the forest.' Lilith pointed. 'She's called Bodie.'

'Bodie.' Katy turned the name over. 'And she lives in the forest? All on her own? Up there? She must be very brave.'

'She is very brave. But she doesn't live there alone. There are other mammas there, and children too,' Lilith said, 'like us.'

'Wait, there are children who get to live in the forest? That's so cool!' Katy grabbed her sister's hand, freeing her from the game, listing all the things they would need to pack in their backpacks to find the forest children and the fairies.

When they were ready, with torches, crackers and teddy bears packed, the essentials for their expedition, they began walking up the hill. Lilith made up a story to keep them entertained. Bodie starred as a witch who helped fairies with broken wings. She taught them to tame dragons so they could ride them, and it was like flying again.

The girls didn't question how the fairies didn't get burned or fall off the dragons or how something as delicate as a fairy's wing could ever be repaired. They were still young enough to believe in happy endings. Or maybe Lilith was a veteran at making them seem possible, even to herself.

Chapter 7

By the time they reached the sandstone archway, marking the start of Sanctuary Park, there was very little light left. A small, neat row of houses stood silent, just beyond it. Lilith looked at a map at the entrance, working out how to get to Building 1, which stood proudly over a parade ground that hadn't seen a pair of army boots in nearly a century. It was so peaceful. The only sound was a kookaburra, laughing at Lilith's hesitation.

The girls joined him, thinking their mamma was pretending to be scared. They gleefully switched on their torches and ran. Lilith pursued the little fireflies. Trying not to think about the women who had been blamed for walking in dark areas. Here she was, in a deserted park, with her two young children. What would Ben say? Monica from Melbourne hadn't walked in a park, though. She'd disappeared in bright daylight, in a crowded city. Nowhere was safe.

As they turned the corner, a cluster of sandstone buildings was modestly lit with the muted yellow of an iron lamppost, like the one Lucy found Mr Tumnus under. Lilith stopped in front of Building 1. The girls had already found it. Lilith straightened her back to make herself taller, willing herself to be fearless like her daughters. She was about to enter her own Narnia. She didn't know if she would find friendly lions or manipulative witches. She let go of her held breath and stepped through the dark towards her giggling companions.

Sanctuary Park had been built during the war to train soldiers to protect Sydney Harbour. Now the park was protected. A sanctuary for flora and fauna and small businesses looking for cheap and quiet office space. And now, it seemed, for women seeking peace and safety.

Building 1 dominated the quadrant. A checkerboard building of doors and windows, what used to be the dorms for the hundreds of soldiers who lived here, not like the higher ranks who lived in the neat cottages at the entrance. On one side of the large porch, bunk-bed frames and ripped curtains were visible in the dim streetlight. On the other side, neat blinds striped across the upper windows. As they approached the grand columned entrance, Lilith heard a gentle hum of chat and the clink of teacups escape into the evening air and dance across the parade ground. The door was already open, and the girls were running up a makeshift ramp that had been placed over the steep steps.

A woman with greying dreadlocks escaping from her headscarf greeted the two young explorers with a smile. Then she welcomed Lilith, assuring her she wasn't too late. Lilith wondered if she had been placed as a sentry to look out for her and make sure she didn't run away. The woman pointed Lilith towards a table of tea and biscuits and grandmothered the children, ushering them to a corner of crayons and books. A couple of children sat on the floor, playing chess on an ancient-looking set that reminded Lilith of her father. Some others were listening to a woman telling a story.

Lilith felt returned to the old refectory at the back of her mother's church. Walking, unnoticed, among the tweed skirts and kilts, sneaking a gingernut biscuit when no one was looking. She would passively listen to them talking, hearing grown-up subjects that her mother never discussed at home. In the refectory, Robyn Green was someone else, someone Lilith didn't know. Robyn was herself. She talked, knowledgeably, about politics, the women's movement. Boldly retelling the stories of a misspent youth. Laughing. At those meetings, Lilith had wished so hard to be more than ten, to be one of this fascinating woman's friends and not her daughter. She somehow seemed more interesting, sparkly even, when she was Robyn and not Lilith's mum.

Just like at church, Lilith lingered at the back of the room. She poured tea into one of the utilitarian tin mugs, the sort the soldiers probably used when they lived here. No one paid any attention to her but, at the front of the room, a hand emerged over the sea of heads and, underneath it, a face framed with messy silver spikes smiled at Lilith. She noticed an indecipherable tattoo on the inside of her wrist, out of place. Lilith didn't know anyone of her mother's generation with a tattoo. But, then again, maybe some of her friends did, and Lilith was too consumed by her youth to notice.

Lilith raised a timid hand. When Bodie didn't approach, she instead listened to a conversation occurring next to her. The women were discussing Kathleen Rae's radio interview.

'Can you believe he said that? I mean, he was blatantly racist,' the woman said in between bites of a shortbread biscuit, 'and sexist. He's a bloody prime minister. Isn't there a law against him saying that sort of shit?'

'There are laws that let him say that shit, remember? Jesus, if I'd been Kathleen, I'd have decked him. She's here tonight. She's telling the kids a story. I think Insley got her to come,' the second woman replied. Lilith thought she'd misheard. How could she be in the same room as Kathleen Rae?

'If Insley had been there, she would've decked the whole studio!' the shortbread woman said, looking around nervously, as though this Insley would appear. The two women started laughing like schoolgirls at the back of the assembly hall.

'That's all Kathleen needs, her girlfriend starting a ruckus. Especially now. She's going to get it, you know,' the second woman replied.

'What, party leader?' the shortbread woman said.

'Yep, she's got the backing of the caucus, and David.' The second woman was relishing having some knowledge her companion didn't. 'He wants them to win, said she's the one that can do it. If they had any doubt, they just needed to listen to her this morning, how she handled those two arseholes. She's got what it takes. They've done some polling, you know, on the quiet. To see if she's a preferred PM. She's in the lead by miles. She's got something for everyone.'

'Apart from old, middle-class, white men.' The woman finished her shortbread.

'Just as well there's none of those around.' The sarcasm was so sharp it was tinkling, like wind chimes hitting each other in a storm.

'So we just get all the women to vote for her.' She brushed some crumbs off her chest. 'Or kill the old bastards.'

'Cheers to that!' They clinked their mugs together toward the children.

Lilith looked over at the children again. Her girls had been drawn to the storyteller who turned and smiled at the women. It was her, Kathleen. Lilith had seen her on the news for years before Ben would come in and switch the television off. She was always fighting for something, always passionate. Racists in Adelaide who wouldn't sell groceries to anyone who wasn't white. Same-sex marriage. Off-shore drilling. Selling off the health system. Lilith would feel her energy sapped by the injustice when she listened to the reports. Kathleen seemed to be powered by it.

'It just fucking annoys me, you know? If a man disappears, they don't go looking for reasons. It's his fault he's vanished.

They just try to find him.' The women's conversation had moved on to the other big news of the day.

Lilith glanced over to where her girls were mesmerised by Kathleen, mirroring her expressions. It made sense that a politician could tell a good story. Lilith wanted to hear what the children were hearing, the tale that was making them gasp and smile. Not the sad ones the grown-ups around her were telling. She'd had enough of reality. Maybe that's why Kathleen was spending time with the kids. Perhaps she'd had enough today, too.

Kathleen sat cross-legged on the floor, looking out of place in this room, bristling with frustration. She looked at Lilith briefly. Her alert eyes dancing, her mouth spread wide into a smile, mid-dramatic pause – the children were practically holding their breaths. Before Lilith could offer her a thin smile in return, she had returned to her audience, letting them exhale.

People were finding seats, the room descending into gentle murmurs. Kathleen was standing now, having wrapped up her story, and the sentry was herding the children to a side room with promises of hot chocolate. The girls looked back briefly, smiled and waved, then started chatting to a little girl with pigtails who had a fluffy toy cat under her arm. Lilith thought about following them to make sure they were okay.

But Bodie was standing at the front, and without announcement, spoke. Lilith didn't want to make a scene. Bodie spoke in her syncopated way, pausing every now and then, throwing her head back as if looking for a teleprompter on the ceiling, and then restarting. She read out an agenda which surprised Lilith. She had expected a circle of women talking and crying. Lilith felt more comfortable with a list. It was orderly and contained. So she lowered herself in one of the last remaining seats towards the back. She was putting her battered handbag on the ground when she noticed someone next to her, keen to step past.

Lilith apologetically moved her bag and legs to let the person through. The young woman selected a seat, one removed from Lilith. They both seemed relieved to have some space. Lilith leaned down to rearrange her bag. As the person sidled past, she dropped something on the ground. Lilith picked it up, a piece of paper with an address on it. She leaned over to get her attention. It wasn't hard to get – it looked like she wasn't listening to the speaker at all.

'Excuse me?' she said, facing Lilith with questioning brows, one of them pierced.

'I think you dropped this.' Lilith handed her the paper.

'Jesus, thanks.' The woman pushed the paper into the pocket of her leather jacket. 'Don't want to lose that.'

'Sorry to have interrupted you. From listening,' she whispered.

'No need. I've heard it all before.' She stuffed the paper into her jeans pocket, then ran her hand over her closely cropped hair. With no hair or makeup to distract her, Lilith's gaze homed in on the woman's eyes. The woman didn't shy away; instead, she looked right into Lilith. There was nowhere to hide. Lilith felt herself reflected. It felt honest. Unnerving.

'It's my first time here,' Lilith felt compelled to confess.

'I bet it won't be your last.' The woman smiled and stretched out a tattooed arm. 'Insley.' Before Lilith could reply, Insley had turned her head to the front as if she knew the spontaneous chant was about to start. She said the words with a passion that wasn't there when she was just listening.

ALIGN
AMPLIFY
CHALLENGE
CHANGE

It was from the book. Lilith recognised it from the second page. Four words. Written, it looked like a manifesto. Spoken, it sounded like a spell, setting Lilith adrift. Were they launching her into unknown waters or directing her to a safe harbour? She looked around and saw another small grey-haired woman who had lips as still as hers. The woman looked confused too. But irritated, not scared.

The rabbit was telling Lilith to jump. Get up. Leave. She shuffled to the edge of her seat, ready to spring. But then wondered how she'd retrieve the girls. Cornered, she sank back into her chair, allowing its plastic wings to hug her.

Bodie introduced a man to the group. He looked nervous in front of a room of women. Lilith felt a bolt of joy seeing the tables turned, recalling the times she'd seen women in the boardroom at work – some bastards didn't even stop talking to listen.

But this man wasn't one of them, Lilith could tell from his non-smirking face, the way he tried to take up as little room as possible next to Bodie. He looked around, then apologised before he even spoke, like someone used to being rejected. Lilith felt comfortable with him.

She listened. His name was Simon. He ran a support group for transgender kids. There was a helpline. The kids sometimes didn't have anywhere to turn. School teachers weren't adequately trained. There wasn't really any material out there for parents even to help their kids. There was one kid who was now identifying as female, Jodie, who was being forced to still use the boys' bathroom at school. She was scared to go in there, so instead, she was holding it in all day, making herself ill.

As the small crowd made sympathetic sounds, one woman stood up and spoke in a clipped British accent. 'This is wrong.' It was the grey-haired woman who hadn't joined in with the chant.

'We agree. That's what we've been saying to the school. Jodie should have access to—'

'He isn't a she.'

The young man said sorry, but it wasn't an apology. It was a question with an edge. He knew what was coming next. He'd heard it all before.

'These transgender men are still men. They are contributing to the erasure of women, and I won't support it.' She reminded Lilith of the men in the office. Dismissive. Rude.

'Jesus. What the fuck is that TERF doing here?' Insley sat up straight, taking her feet off the chair in front, her Doc Martens boots thudding as they dropped to the ground.

'I don't know what a TERF is, but I know an arsehole when I see one,' Lilith said, flushed. It wasn't in her nature to swear. Ben hated it. But Insley snorted. Lilith felt accepted.

'I'd better make my way down there, just in case it turns nasty,' Insley said quietly. Lilith couldn't imagine a room of tea-drinking women causing a ruckus, but Insley slid down the side of the room anyway. The TERF was still talking about women being forced to share private space with male bodies. The man was biting his tongue so hard, Lilith expected to see blood trickle out of his mouth. Bodie's eyes were burning, but she stayed silent until she found a gap in the woman's tirade.

'Well, that's certainly one end of the spectrum of views on the topic, Sam, one that I haven't heard, in fact, since you last shared it during a Chicago protest in the 1970s.' There was some uncomfortable laughter.

'It's even more valid now, Bodie. My god, what have you become? You were a leader. We all respected you. I think you've forgotten what we were fighting for. The rights of women.'

'You were a good protester, Sam, but a terrible activist.' Bodie was walking up the makeshift aisle now. Almost level with the other woman. 'All those slogans you shouted. All those placards you held. What did they get us?'

'They got us heard, Bodie.'

'Sure. But did it change anything? Really? Are women any

more equal now than then?'

'Don't you try to tell me we achieved nothing.'

'Sure, we achieved some things. For a while. We were the noisy seagulls, and they threw us some crumbs. But instead of going back and getting enough for the whole flock, we started protecting the scraps.'

'When one woman progresses, we all progress. I won't have you say what we did means nothing.'

'It means something, Sam. It unlocked the door. But only for some of us. Then we made for the hills and didn't look back. We should have unlocked all the other doors and taken over the goddamn prison. If we find allies, fight for gender rights, gay rights, refugee rights, First Nations rights, we will have a majority. We will outnumber the guards.'

Spoons were tapped against tin cups, the sound piercing. The old woman wasn't giving up.

'You know my views, Bodie. I've never hidden them. You didn't invite me here to convert me.' Sam looked around the room. 'Am I here to be humiliated? Some sort of plaything for your pack to toy with?'

'I'm sorry, Sam. I know what it took to raise those placards back then. To raise your voice. I know what you gave up doing that.' The old woman's lip was quivering. Lilith didn't know if she was clenching her jaw to hold in anger or sadness. Often, they were the same thing. 'I guess I hoped you'd come here to-night and listen. Maybe I genuinely hoped you would listen to-night. You are a brilliant campaigner. You know how to get the media's attention. I wanted you to help us. And you have. So thank you, Samantha.'

The room was silent. Samantha was eyeing Bodie cautiously.

'You have shown my "pack", as you call them, that our way is right. Queentide is right. Women like you have been doing the patriarchy's job for them. You only think you are free, but you are still locked up. You are just out in the exercise yard, fighting over whose cell is smaller. Who got the smallest serve of slops at dinner.' The room was silent. The laughter of the children next door seeped through the walls. 'If we want to be free, truly free, we have to defeat the entire system. We pull ourselves out of solitary confinement, we open up the other cells, destroy the fucking walls and escape – together. The prison will only cease to exist when it has *no* inmates.'

Lilith knew the woman wasn't about to relent. It takes more than one speech to realise the world isn't what you've constructed. Like removing a virtual reality mask and finding an empty room. Everything you thought you'd felt, touched or did was just a projection.

Insley, at the front of the room, an arm extended in the air, led a chant:

ALIGN

AMPLIFY

CHALLENGE

CHANGE

Her voice wasn't alone for long. Soon, the room was repeating it. Over and over. So was Lilith. Caught in the tide. The British woman turned to collect her walking stick and shuffled out of the room. Her head was high. She paused briefly, turning to look at Bodie. Lilith thought she would speak. Maybe she did, but the chanting was loud, overbearing. Her words wouldn't have been heard. Even the slam of the door barely registered. When she was gone, something seemed to leave Bodie, and she grew smaller. She motioned for the standing crowd to retake their seats and asked Simon to continue. She nodded at Insley, who made her way back to her chair. By the time she was back at Lilith's row, a clipboard and pen were being circulated to an enthusiastic crowd. Everyone was eager to sign. Everyone was keen to not be like Samantha. Exiled from the pack.

Chapter 8

Back in her seat, Insley looked up towards her grandmother. She was getting frail, defying her own and Insley's belief that she would live forever. They would just have to make her immortality happen differently. Legacy.

This plan she had come up with was ridiculous, really. Anyone with even the slightest understanding of how elections worked would see that straight away, like Helen. Jesus, she had about twenty degrees in economics and analysis and shit like that. She hadn't come out and said it at the meeting, but she would know there was only one way for this plan to work. Instead, she had been frustratingly diplomatic, raising objections too small for even Insley to turn into legitimate reasons to throw her off the committee.

Insley looked around at the women gathered in the room. Would they figure it out too?

When a magician announces their next trick – *I am about to saw this woman in half* – you know, of course, they can't do that. She'd die, and the magician would be carted off to jail. But, before the saw is even wobbled, you also know you are about to see the assistant's head and legs sent to either side of the stage. And you will be amazed because you desperately want to believe in magic.

Maybe the women here wanted to believe in that, too. Maybe even Helen did. It's why they were all here, after all. They thought they had found a woman who knew the spells to make the world a better place. They thought Bodie was the Good Witch of the South who would bring colour back into the black-and-white world. And she would. If the plan worked.

But Bodie's plan to sway an election would not be as easy as clicking her glittery heels together. In fact, some things would have to be done that Bodie hadn't even considered. Bad things. Illegal things. Things her beautiful, pacifist grandmother would never consider doing or want her granddaughter to do.

But Insley had considered them and had no problem doing them. They had to be done because they had to win. Her grandmother had to succeed. It was her legacy. Insley would just have to keep it a secret, that was all. No need for Bodie to know *how* her legacy was achieved. It would be worth it.

The women in the room needed a mother like Bodie, kind and encouraging. And basically a saint. But they also needed a mother like Insley, who would yell at them to clean up their mess and would kick the arse of the bully who was making their life hell. Love isn't always gentle – sometimes it needs to be violent. At least that's what Insley had learned, with some regret.

Insley looked over the heads in front of her and found the glossy locks of Helen sitting statue-still. She hadn't stood up to chant. She never did. It was just something that Helen didn't do. Like smiling. Or giving Insley a fucking break.

She'd helped Helen out once. Just after Bodie had got Helen involved in Queentide, when her research started focusing on gender bias in, well, pretty much everything. Insley read all of Helen's papers. She'd never tell Helen that, of course. She preferred Helen to think she was an uneducated oink. Insley enjoyed being underestimated – it was her superpower. It let her get away with so much more. Things people thought she just wasn't capable of.

MASC had gone after Helen when the research started getting media coverage. A woman spreading well-researched facts had to be stopped. Insley found the trolls and took care of them. One was on Helen's research team. When he called to resign from his hospital bed, Helen had been furious with Insley. Sometimes it really is best not to know how the trick is done. And you can't get angry with the magician when you work it out, can you?

Insley hoped Helen would just go along with this. Not make a scene. Insley didn't like her, but she respected her. She'd stood up to Insley, which took a lot of balls, and she had done a lot to help Bodie. It would be a shame if she had to be forced to leave Queentide.

Insley noticed Bodie looking at her, looking at Helen. She scowled gently at Insley and wagged a finger. Jesus, the woman was a witch. She always seemed to know what Insley was thinking. Maybe that's why Insley had become so good at keeping secrets. Not because she didn't want her grandmother to know – she wasn't ashamed of anything she'd done. Insley just didn't want her to worry. Insley wanted Bodie to think she was safe.

Which she was, most of the time. Insley realised pretty quickly that, despite all the tough talk, at 140 centimetres, she was no match for some of the men she'd end up confronting. She needed muscle. Thank god the patriarchy had fucked up as many men as it had. They weren't exactly lining up, but they seemed quite happy to work out their daddy issues by punching some paedophile or woman basher senseless.

And Insley was more than happy to see two men try to destroy each other. In fact, if she was entirely honest, she enjoyed it. Maybe, doing her best to kill them, she still had some daddy issues of her own.

At the front of the room, Kathleen was shuffling through some papers, preparing herself. Insley knew precisely what she was going to say. Insley had been Kathleen's test audience for a few nights now. She didn't mind. Kathleen was worth the late nights and the endless discussions to decide if she was coming across as too feminist or not feminist enough. Kathleen was worth it all, in fact. Insley also wanted to protect Kathleen's legacy. Kathleen's destiny. Insley just knew that Kathleen had to be the next prime minister. The one who would transform the country.

That future was worth all of the things Insley was going to have to do to make sure this election turned out the right way. All the things Insley had done to cover her tracks, so Kathleen knew nothing about the things Insley had already done. Insley was in love, but she wasn't an idiot. Kathleen wanted Insley, but she wanted the top job more. If she thought Insley was a liability, she'd leave her. Jesus, she was still reluctant to even admit she was gay. Apparently, that was worse than being Aboriginal in politics and polls. Jesus, this country was fucked. The sooner it was all over, the better. Maybe then Kathleen could relax and start being herself. Possibly Insley could, too.

It was exhausting, simultaneously playing two tracks all the time. Making sure that Bodie and Kathleen only got to hear the radio edit, even when the explicit version of Insley's life was blaring all around her.

Sometimes Aaron, her best friend, got to hear it too. That's what he got for eavesdropping. It's what he got for being her buffer against the world and the controlled explosions Insley had to have sometimes, just to stop the soundtrack from amplifying in the secret space and making her ears bleed.

He'd known Insley longer than anyone, even her grandmother. He'd helped her crawl under his bed when Insley's mum had told her to run next door and hide. He'd silently watch as Insley punched holes in his bedroom wall and then brought her a bag of frozen peas for her knuckles. The same thing her mum did for her dad after he'd stopped beating her. Aaron's mum never noticed the mini fist-sized holes in her walls. They were usually obliterated by bigger holes made by Aaron's dad anyway.

She never went to Aaron for protection, and he never offered it. He just gave her space to do what she needed to do without judgement. It's what he still did. It's why he was her best friend. But that didn't mean she shared everything with him. There were a few things she kept from him. Like this new thing, this woman sitting next to her. And that wasn't lying. It was an omission. And it was necessary for her plan to work. He'd understand. He always did. It would be worth it.

Insley sat back down and looked at the woman. She was new, but Insley knew who she was before she took the seat next to her. Insley knew a lot about Lilith Green. She'd had a listening device in her old house for months. She knew she was leaving her husband, that bastard Ben Hamilton, before Benny-boy even sobered up enough to realise he'd come back from his fundraiser to an empty house.

Insley had enjoyed listening to him ramble all over the place, looking for her and the girls. Like they were playing hide-and-seek or something. The penny had to fall from a big fucking height. He just could not accept that anyone would dare leave him. Insley was actually a bit surprised herself when Lilith went through with it. Sure, she'd squirrelled money away and snuck off to counselling sessions, but she'd always seemed like a bird caught in a jetstream. Moving, but not in a direction she was choosing herself.

Insley wanted to ask her what gave her the strength to pull herself out. She wanted to know, so she might understand why her mother hadn't been able to do it. But instead, she turned to

Lilith Green and raised a pierced brow.

'I don't know why Bodie bothers with those nut jobs,' Insley whispered.

'She's been before, the ... TERF?' Lilith stumbled over the new term – trans-exclusionary radical feminist. This was probably all feeling very new. Insley had to be careful. Not scare her off.

'Not that one. She's an old friend of Bodie's. I can't even imagine them having a thing in common.' Insley shook her head. 'But there've been others. There seems to be a bottomless pit of them. I was in the UK the other week, and I walked past a group of them protesting the Tate having trans-friendly toilets. Fucking cranks. They make our job even harder.'

'And what exactly is your job?' Lilith said.

Insley was relieved when Aunty Caz turned and said hello to her and then started making small talk with Lilith, asking if she'd found the tea and biscuits okay. She handed the clipboard to Lilith, the beads at the edge of her hair making a clicking sound as she did. Insley didn't join in their chat. She never spoke if she could avoid it. It was the best way to avoid making mistakes, putting on the wrong track.

She glanced at Lilith, who was holding the board limply and radiating indecision. Insley lowered her voice to a whisper, attempting to soften her face.

'You don't have to give your phone number if that's what's worrying you. Look at the list. Plenty of women are just giving first names, anonymous emails.' Insley tried to sound reassuring. 'There aren't many phone numbers on there. A lot of the women here prefer to be cautious.'

'I just don't think I'm going to be much use to him – Simon, isn't it?' Lilith's wrist went even limper. 'I mean, I've got no money, no time, no contacts – what can I offer?'

'Hope,' Insley said. 'You can put your name on there and show him that someone else cares. That the world isn't full of mad Sam's. That gives people the strength to keep going.'

Lilith smiled nervously at Insley and then scribbled her name down, handing the board to Insley. Insley made a big deal of pretending to read her name on the list.

'Well done... Lilith Green. You made a semi-independent decision.' Insley grinned.

There was a jostle at the front of the room. Kathleen and Bodie were both standing up, Kathleen supporting Bodie gently by the elbow. A round of applause went up. Lilith Green looked uncertain but joined in. Insley had done what her grandmother had asked, got Lilith to stay. She had just done it for her own reasons. But Bodie didn't need to know that. Bodie needed to believe in her own tricks. How else would anyone else believe in them? More secrets. More noise to hold in. But it would be worth it. Legacy.

Chapter 9

'Well, clearly, there is no need to introduce our next speaker. Ms Rae has journeyed up from Melbourne today to speak about what our prime minister is now calling his "woman problem".' Bodie's voice sounded jovial.

'You would have heard the outrageous exchange on the radio today. I think you will all join me in congratulating Kathleen on her stately response to their playground tactics.' She paused for the ripple of restrained cheers to subside, then Kathleen stood and hugged Bodie.

Lilith noticed the difference in the texture of their skins, one glossy and smooth, the other so crepey it looked as though she was disintegrating right in front of them. But there was unmistakable synchronicity in their atoms. These two women had fire at their core.

'We have an election coming up, and I need your help,' Kathleen began. 'The thing that makes Queentide strong isn't the values we share. It's the differences we bring. We each come here with the same purpose, to change the system. The system that is repressing women. The very same system that is oppressing people living on the poverty line. And the refugees. And the traditional custodians of this land.' Kathleen looked around the room. 'We each see it in different ways. As middle-class white women. As gay men. As trans women. A woman with a disability. I look at it as a gay Aboriginal woman. Bodie looks at it as an elder.' She turned and smiled at Bodie. Bodie feigned offence but smiled.

'That gives us an advantage. Yes, we are all oppressed by it. Yes, we are all silenced. But if we can all come together, we can surround it. We can outnumber it.' There was quiet approval in the room. Kathleen allowed it to circulate. 'So here's my suggestion. What if, at the next election, there was a choice? Someone other than the two main parties. What if there was a new feminist party candidate on each ballot paper? What if Queentide had a political party? The Women's Party. Imagine that you voted for her and encouraged every woman you knew to vote for them. And convinced all the men you knew, the ones who feel cheated by this shitty patriarchal system we have, gay men, First Nations men, refugee men, just bloody good men, to vote for them too? You'd get enough votes to win a seat. Now imagine that this happened in, say, fifty towns, not that many, right? Fifty. But it's enough. Enough to break the two-party system. Enough to form a government with one of the main parties, which will soon have a leader who shares the same ideals as these feminists. A leader who is also part of Queentide. Me.'

Lilith had been at the periphery of Ben's political circles for long enough, heard enough Machiavellian conversations, to recognise a coup when she heard one. She also had that degree from Oxford. Not that it seemed to matter once she was married. That knowledge was put in the attic, like the antique china plates she'd received as a wedding gift. Put out of reach, so they weren't accidentally used.

There was murmuring too low to be deciphered. Then a woman, dressed in black, stood tall, raised a hand in the air, her single silver bangle hula-hooping down her arm.

Bodie had spotted her as she assessed the crowd in front of her. 'Yes, Helen. I expect you would like to speak?'

'Bodie, I would like to communicate in this public forum

what I said during our committee vote earlier. If you do not object?' She was quietly spoken but not apologetic.

'Of course, Helen. I think it's important that we are transparent.'

'Thank you.' The wiry woman produced a pair of similarly thin glasses, then some note cards from the inside pocket of her jacket. She shuffled them a little until they were perfectly aligned. Lilith heard exaggerated tutting coming from Insley, who was idly knocking the toes of her boots together.

'Hello, everyone. I think most of you know me. I have been with Queentide since the start. When it was just Bodie, me and a few others sitting in a café trying to make the world a better place. I will always support its work for female social and economic independence. I will keep leading research to help. I'll be at the protests, I'll help build safe-haven communities, like this one, across Australia, and I will keep growing the Melbourne chapters—'

'Here comes the but,' Insley said dismissively, just loud enough to be heard, as she rolled her eyes.

'But I can't support this politicisation, this weaponising, of our group. I believe the answer does not lie in the seizure of power. I believe it lies in changing the hearts and minds of those already in power.'

'That's a great idea, Helen, if those in power have hearts and minds that aren't made of granite.' Insley's quip was answered with a cheer from the audience and a reproachful look from Bodie. She mouthed the word sorry at her and then, smiling, looked down at her boots, which were back on the chair in front. She knocked them together like a kid reprimanded for being smart in class. Lilith couldn't help but smile. Insley noticed and winked at her. Lilith's smile broadened. Helen didn't even turn to look at her.

'We respect your position, Helen,' Bodie Hughes said. 'How-

ever, the remaining committee members believe this is a necessary change, and it's time to do it now. We've had six years
of bushfires, floods, pandemics ... they've stopped being one-
off events. We're in a recession. Queentide just opened its
one-hundredth community. That's over two thousand rooms for
women and children escaping abuse, and we still have to turn
them away. We've got kids who've missed years of school because of lockdowns. The food shortages aren't going away. The
backlog for funerals is at four months now ... People are tired.
They want to be cared for. They can see that the current system,
the patriarchy, is incapable of the nurturing needed to get us
back on our feet as a country. A planet. They want a mother
to come along and make it all okay. They've seen how Norway
and New Zealand pulled through, what their women leaders ac-
complished. They want that here in Australia too. This group,
MASC, even they see it. They *know* the time for women to rise
is coming. They know that some men want it. That's why they
are attacking us, threatening us. They are backed into a corner
and scared.'

It was easy to imagine Bodie on a podium, rousing crowds
to action. She was almost too much for this small room. She
seemed to be aware of this and reined it back.

'So, respectfully, Helen, to meet the goals you support, we
have to do this. The system you want to change is broken and
needs replacing. We've got the infrastructure, Queentide has
the connections with other activist groups, the passionate support base I see in this room, we've got the understanding of
what needs to be done, and we've got the skills to fix it. So let's
get this done.' She'd been leaning forward. When she finished,
she slumped back like a clockwork doll in need of winding.

A voice came from the back of the room.

'Is Kathleen going to be part of this new political party then?'

'No.' Kathleen's voice was followed by muttering from the

crowd. She was looking at Insley. Insley made a pushing motion above her head like she was straightening an imaginary crown. Lilith noticed Kathleen smile and sit a little straighter.

'So, let me get this right – you are staying in the system that you say is broken? So all these feminists you are talking about are just taking votes away from the Liberal Party to get you and your party re-elected?' The woman was about Lilith's age. Her accent was sunburnt, weathered.

'The only way to guarantee that the Women's Party gets to form a government is with one of the two main parties – we can't expect to get enough seats to knock them both out of the running. And we can't take any chances. We need to know that the party we go in with has a sympathetic leader. One who is going to be happy to share a platform with them. If I am announced Labor Party leader in the next few days' – she allowed the gentle cheer to settle – 'you know you have me in your corner. You know you have the main party to piggyback off. I don't want this just for me. I want it for all of us. One hundred percent. The job's big enough to share.'

The woman, sated, nodded and clapped. Others followed her. Some looked a little teary, Lilith, too. There was something like hope buzzing in her veins.

When order was restored, Bodie went through the next steps. How people could volunteer what they could do to help. It felt like one of the volunteer drives Ben had attended during the last pandemic. Photo opportunity. He even took his mask off but then ran out of the room as soon as the media went. Leaving Lilith talking to a mother who'd lost her child, sending his adviser to cut the conversation short so they could leave.

But he wasn't there to rush her tonight. She offered to help Insley pack up the chairs.

'Bet you didn't expect to see the birth of a new political party tonight, did you?' Insley had picked up four chairs with ease.

Her thin arms were clearly stronger than they appeared.

'Do you really think she can pull it off? I mean, what she's talking about is pretty hard to imagine.'

'Ten years ago, could you have imagined Donald Trump becoming US president?' Insley gave her a grin. 'Or Kamala being the next VP, right after Pence? Sometimes good, unbelievable things can happen too.'

Like leaving my marriage, Lilith thought.

'Bodie and the rest of us just want to see them happen a bit faster. And a bit more frequently.' Insley grinned again, then moved on, stacking more chairs. The girls came running in holding paper plates with twigs and leaves stuck to them. Lilith gambled on them being dragons and breathed happily when she got it right.

The women were saying their farewells. Some were going out the door. Others seemed to be making their way further inside, where the dorm rooms were. Lilith corralled the girls to the open door. The rain was coming down in sheets, looking like television white noise against the lamplight. Sanctuary Park was at the very edge of Sydney. Beyond it was only the ocean. It was the front line of defence against whatever blew in that day. Lilith reprimanded herself for not making sure there were raincoats in the backpacks among the biscuits and rocks.

'Lilith?' Bodie was at her side. Close enough that Lilith could see the brazen lines on her face, worn like battle scars. It was so rare to see them nowadays. Lilith had forgotten how beautiful they looked, like a mellowing patina on gold. 'I'm glad you came. All of you.' Bodie crouched so her eyes were level with the girls. Lilith appreciated this, taking time to see the world from their point of view.

'Good evening, young ladies.' She offered her hand to the girls. 'I'm Bodie.'

'Are you the Dragonslayer?' asked Katie.

Bodie, showing no sign of amusement, answered them solemnly, 'I prefer Dragon*tamer*. I can't imagine killing a creature. Besides, if you can harness a dragon, imagine the places they can fly you to, the marshmallows they can toast with their breath!'

The girls giggled.

'Yes, dragons, the right sort, can be excellent allies indeed.' While she had been talking to them, she had drawn little dragons on each of their hands in blue biro. She straightened up with a groan. Back into the adult world, where there were worse things than dragons to deal with.

'An exciting first meeting for you to attend.' Bodie's head dropped a little to the left. 'I apologise for not warning you that things may be a bit feisty.'

'Well, I came in expecting to see tears and cuddling.' Lilith smiled gently. 'I thought it was that sort of group.'

'No, not quite.' Bodie smiled, allowing the creases around her eyes to deepen even further. Lilith wondered what she had laughed at, cried at, screamed at over the years to earn her stripes. 'We will no doubt cry and hug for many reasons over the coming year. Just stick around. You can join in.'

'I'm sorry I didn't get more involved tonight.' Lilith felt she had failed this old woman. That Bodie had expected something of her, the woman that read her book overnight.

'You will speak when you have something to say. You listened. That is the first step. Enough for now. It's one advantage women have over men. Good feminists listen. I might print that on a T-shirt.'

'I'm not a feminist.' Lilith blurted the words out, thinking of Insley and how dissimilar they were. Lilith couldn't wear that badge. It came with too much responsibility. 'I mean, I'm not really in a position to go to protests and things like that. I've got a lot going on at the moment.'

'You are facing some challenges?'

'You could say that.' Lilith checked to make sure the girls weren't listening. They had taken the opportunity and run back into the room, playing dragontamers. 'I'm getting evicted. I'm running out of money. I can't get a job. I can't afford a lawyer to fight my ex-husband. He's trying to take the children away from me.' Lilith checked herself. She was oversharing. Burdening this stranger. 'I'm hoping that I can persuade him to compromise.'

'Did he ever compromise when you were together?' Bodie, like the lawyer, didn't need an answer. 'So, a new strategy then. Let Janet do her job. God knows she's brilliant at it. She knows the rules of the game, Lilith. You don't even know how to put the boots on for it. Then you focus on yourself.'

'No, the girls are the only thing that matters.'

'Let me ask you a question, Lilith.' She was watching the girls running around with their paper-plate dragons. 'How will you save your girls if you are suffocating yourself? Remember, we always put our own mask on first.'

Lilith clenched her jaw. She was sick of being told to be strong. To fight. It doesn't help when you are sinking into quicksand. The more you struggle, the quicker you go down. She was just trying to keep her head above ground.

'May I ask what you do for a living?'

Lilith wanted to bolt out the door, but the girls were too far away to summon quietly.

'I'm a secretary. Was. I got made redundant a few months back. Look, I really should get the girls home. It's late. '

'Secretaries are very powerful, you know. They control calendars, budgets, know as much about their boss's company as they do, perhaps even more. They aren't distracted by golf and office wars. I often dream of mobilising an army of secretaries to take over the big companies. And then the world.' She smiled ruefully. 'Can you type?'

It seemed like an antiquated question compared with the vision of a secretary's army.

'Um, sure. My boss was a partner at Macquarie Bank. I took dictation as he was going up and down in the lift on the way to meetings.' Lilith didn't mention that she also did his job when he'd drunk too much at lunch to make any rational decisions. She tried to get the girls' attention so they could leave. So she could escape.

'I'd like to offer you a job as my secretary.' Bodie put her hands to her chest. 'I don't drink at lunchtime, I promise.'

'But you barely know me.' Lilith laughed.

'I know enough. I know you read my book, cover to cover, comprehended it. Called the author. Took a risk, came to a meeting. And didn't run when it got intense. I know you are organised. I know you are intelligent.'

Lilith didn't know what to do with the compliments. It was so long since she'd received any. So she pulled at one of the fairy stickers on her battered bag. 'And I can see that, when your loyalty is fired up, you will stand by your friends. No matter how ill-placed. I want to give you a worthy home for that loyalty.'

Lilith felt lumpy anger in the back of her throat. At Bodie. At the truth. It stopped her speaking. Bodie filled the gap.

'You heard. We have work to do. I'm great at planning new world orders, terrible at organising my own time.' Her rich accent felt like molasses being poured over her. Soothing and irresistible. Sticky. She let her keep talking. She found she couldn't move. 'I'll give you 18 per cent more than your last job. Whatever it was. You can work around the children, work from home. Hell, bring them to work if it won't bore them to tears. As long as the work is done and done well, I don't mind how it got that way. Oh, and of course you can live here. In the community. I loathe the word commune. It makes me remember the dungarees I used to wear and the entire garden I killed in 1982. They don't let me near it here. They tell me it's because of my age, but

...' The old woman shrugged.

'Ms Hughes, this is all very generous, but I can't. I mean, my children ...'

'The children would, of course, live here too. At the moment, we have five families living here. All the children are under ten. The girls would have playmates. They seem to like it here. You'd have support. Company. Or space, if that's what you need. Each family has their own small apartment – we've knocked rooms together – you'd not feel crowded.'

'It's not that. It's just that my ex-husband wouldn't like the girls living here.'

'Or you, I suspect. But it isn't his decision. Or mine. Or your children's. It is entirely yours. What does Lilith Green want to do?'

'I need some time to consider it.' Lilith was already imagining life at Sanctuary Park. Space. The peace. That was what Lilith Green wanted.

'Of course. I'd need to know in the next day or two. We have a waiting list – women are waiting to move in. It's based on need. So, if you aren't able to accept, I'd like to offer it to someone who can. You'd be allocated a space, three dorm rooms, and we'll help to combine them into an apartment. You'd need to decorate, furnish the space if you can. There's a communal kitchen, laundry, garden. We help the Trust with bush regeneration. You come and go as you please. The community self-manages childcare. We all pitch in. There are rules, of course. All societies need those. We aren't a nunnery, we don't expect there to be no men at all in your life, but this place is sacred feminine ground. Or, as your girls may say, "no boys allowed". Women here have suffered because of their assigned or chosen gender. Mostly it's men that have caused the pain. So, we want to give them some breathing space. To feel safe.'

Lilith liked the idea of that. No men. Lilith thought again of her mother's women's group meetings. It would be like those, just longer.

'I will think about it, Bodie.' Lilith already knew she would have to say no.

'Well, how about this? The girls seem to have settled in for the night.' Bodie motioned towards the girls, who were on beanbags in the now empty room, drinking hot chocolate that seemed to have appeared from nowhere. The dreadlocked woman who'd greeted them was singing a song to them in a language Lilith didn't know. 'The weather is dreadful. Why not stay tonight, see how we fit? There are beds made upstairs. We were expecting some to stay after the meeting tonight, but they've headed home.'

Lilith wanted to escape, to run away from this strange place and hide. But her girls were happy and warm. Being fussed over by an older woman. They had missed out on that, with her mother being overseas. So had Lilith.

'Okay, well, the girls have made themselves at home. I think there will be a mutiny if I try to take them outside now. Thank you, Bodie.'

'I'm so glad, Lilith.' Bodie hugged her. Lilith stood motionless. She had only experienced child-sized hugs in recent years. Lilith wasn't sure how to respond anymore. She felt engulfed by Bodie's embrace. But also relieved of some weight she didn't know she was carrying, as though Bodie's touch had just swept it out to sea. 'Well, let's find out where that hot chocolate came from, and hopefully, you shall feel as at home as your children.'

Lilith and Bodie talked until the hot chocolate was cold and the children were asleep. It reminded her of talking to her mother before Lilith had followed Ben to Australia. Leaving their mother-daughter relationship 20,000 feet up in the air and 10,000 miles from any shore. Unable to land anywhere anymore. Forever adrift.

The next day, without asking Ben, but after checking with Janet De Marco, Lilith began packing boxes and cleaning out cupboards, helped by two excited girls who were eager to move to the forest.

This felt right. The rabbit agreed. No leaps. No thumps. They were returning to the warren where they belonged. Finally, across the open field. Finally home.

Chapter 10

Bodie looked around the small circle of women, barely listening to what was being said. She'd had trouble focusing lately. Sometimes she felt there was a clock on her shoulder, stealing away the time she had left to do what needed to be done. It distracted her, made her less productive, not more.

Today, she didn't really need to pay too much attention. She knew their stories all too well. Each was unique, of course, with nuances in time, place, people. But none were new. They all had plots that had been repeated for decades. Centuries, even. Some ended happily, others tragically. For too many years, she'd tried to force a plot twist for every woman who looked to be going down the tragic path. She'd soon learned her lesson. People had to be the author of their own lives, or the story would just come out wrong. So instead, she would just try to whisper to them … What if? What happens next? And let them see there were hundreds of answers to those questions, not just the one they thought they were stuck with.

Bodie's focus returned as her eyes landed on Lilith Green. At least she'd turned up and sat down. She would be the next one invited to speak. Would she? It was hard to tell. She'd been with the community for some weeks now. Had been a diligent worker for the community and for Queentide. She was smart. Knew what she needed to do before Bodie told her. Insley had said something about there being more to her. But Lilith seemed to do it without feeling. Without caring. Most women who came to Bodie, who'd read the book, cared deeply. They wanted to change. Not just for themselves. For other women, too.

What did Lilith want? Bodie hadn't figured it out. Maybe Lilith hadn't either.

'Lilith, would you like to speak?' Anne, the woman leading the circle, asked her gently.

Lilith, who was sitting with her hands underneath her legs, quietly cleared her throat. For a moment, Bodie held her breath, thinking she was about to speak. But then she shook her head, hard enough to make the hair come loose from behind her ears.

'That's okay,' said Anne. 'Becky, how about you?' Anne was respecting the circle rules. No judgements. No responses. No advice. And, after the circle ended, no bringing up anything discussed inside the circle. Spaces were sacred because of their rules and rituals.

'Actually, I do want to say something, if that's okay?' Lilith said. Bodie didn't hide her surprise as Lilith looked over towards her. Bodie smiled and nodded, trying to release the pressure valve in Lilith's face. It didn't work.

'I don't know if this is right. If this is what you expect me to talk about ...' There were no expectations. No right things to talk about. But no one could say that to Lilith. No one was there to talk her down. They were just there to cushion the fall in case she slipped over the edge. Or jumped. To a casual observer, it may appear harsh. To form an arena, to watch someone battle it out with their demons. But the circle wasn't just watching. It was listening. It gave the women a place to be heard by others and by themselves. The answers were usually within. They were just drowned out by the sound of others' opinions and advice, well-intentioned or not.

'It's just that I can't get these thoughts out of my head, you know? About him. About how difficult he has made my life. I mean, I left. That was supposed to be the end. But it's just … it just got worse. He says things to the girls. He sends message after message. Calls. Emails. He's set up camp in my head, and I can't get away from him. Sometimes I wish he was dead. Quite a few times, actually. And I hate him for making me feel that way about another human being. It's not who I am. I mean, what sort of person does that make me?'

No one could answer, but Bodie saw the recognition in the faces. Lilith was in a repeating pattern and was just too close to it to see. The silence became more intense, breaths were held. Like being in a forest, knowing an animal was watching you from the bushes. Trying not to move in case you frightened it. Or it attacked you.

'That's all I have to say.' Lilith put her head back down, forcing her hair behind an ear. So there it was. What Lilith wanted was Ben Hamilton dead. Bodie couldn't blame her.

The women silently dismantled the circle of chairs and stacked them at the side of the room. Lilith chose to bring hers to the same pile as Bodie's.

'Oh Lilith, if I may trouble you. We will have a new guest in the community soon. Sibel Polat and her teenage daughter. She's an author from Turkey, here for a literary festival. I've offered her a place to stay.'

'Is she a friend?' Lilith asked, still diligently stacking chairs.

'Yes,' Bodie replied, 'a dear friend and someone whose work I respect. We share a similar worldview. And ambition.' Bodie smiled. 'I wonder if you could show her around?'

'Of course. Whatever you need.'

'Thank you.' Bodie breathed out. Maybe Sibel, in her quiet way, could help Lilith.

'Bodie, was that wrong, what I just shared?' Lilith asked.

'No.' Bodie smiled. 'The circle is to share what's on your mind, without fear of judgement or criticism. If that is what's on your mind, it was right to share it.'

'I hate him,' Lilith said.

'I know,' Bodie replied. 'It is normal, Lilith, to have thoughts like that.'

During the past few weeks, over their honeyed-coffee conversations and idle games of chess, Lilith had shared a sketch of her before-life. A self-consciousness about her voice, borne from hearing for years how its pitch used to make him cringe. A peacock-green patterned dinner plate, a gift from her mother, that had been thrown. How the sound of a door key made her chest thump because it used to signal his return home. How she would grind her teeth when the girls were loud. Expecting him to fiercely tell her to keep them quiet. It was only an outline, but the picture was clear enough.

'You know, you may be suffering from PTSD, Lilith. After what you've suffered. Just because you're out doesn't mean you will not feel you're still living it.'

'I am still living it. I still have two children that I have to let him see or risk losing them. I have to pretend that he isn't the horrible person he is, in case the courts think I am trying to alienate him from the kids. While he still exists, our lives are going to be entwined. And sometimes it feels like it is suffocating me.'

'Fight back, Lilith.'

'I'm not strong enough,' Lilith said, scraping a chair across the floor towards the stack and heaving it up.

'Then get strong enough. Take the help on offer.'

Lilith stopped and looked directly at Bodie. Steadying the chair that was wobbling on top of the stack.

'I sometimes worry that if I start fighting Ben, I won't stop.'

'How so?'

'If I see him on the ropes, if I get some good punches in ...' Lilith paused, perhaps detecting the concern that Bodie was trying to hide. 'Oh, not real ones. I mean, you know, say I get more custody of the kids, will I be happy with that, or will I want to stop him from seeing them entirely? Will I be happy that the papers stop painting him as some sort of saint, or will I want to tell them what he is really like and ruin his career. I'm worried that if I let enough poison into my veins, the stuff I need to actually take him on, it's going to spread. Consume me.' She shook her head. 'That probably doesn't make much sense.'

'You are a good person, Lilith. The conflict you are feeling is understandable. It's also what many women go through when they leave an abuser. They find it hard to rebel against them. You know, some of the women here, they see a counsellor. I know you said you didn't need to anymore, but I wonder if talking to someone would help.'

'I sometimes wonder if killing him would help.' Lilith smiled wryly.

Bodie swallowed the sentence that was pushing past her teeth. The one she wished she'd said to Insley years ago. But Lilith got there just in time.

'Figuratively, of course.' She picked up the chair and started a new stack. 'I think this one should just stay on its own. It's not safe.'

Chapter 11

She liked it. The community, with its rosters and locks. In this tiny universe, her life had shrunk to something manageable. And she had shifted her star to a smaller constellation, away from the far reach of Ben's galaxy, the place she was only ever classified in relation to her proximity to him. His dowdy wife. His vindictive ex-wife.

In her new place in the sky, she was Hannah and Katy's mum. Bodie's EA. The woman who did gardening duty on a Tuesday and peeled potatoes for dinner on a Thursday. The woman who declined further invitations to attend group sessions. She was an anonymous light among many.

She had learned the dance of her new life quickly. It had so few steps. Mornings were spent with Bodie, ignoring the details of the reports she would file, the documentation of gendered violence that Queentide was compiling. Afternoons she would do her rostered chores, then play with the girls. In the evenings, she would delete the obscene messages and emails that had accumulated during the day and burn the violent images that would be posted to her, denying them a presence in her new world.

On the unpredictable days that Ben would summon the children, she would hold her breath and deliver them to him. When she returned to the community, a pot of Bodie's honeyed coffee would be waiting on a bench for her, alongside a book by Plath or Steinem. No notes. A silent invitation. Alcohol would be discreetly cleared from the communal space. She knew this because the first few times she had gone to get a bottle from the fridge, having placed it there earlier in the day, she'd found it had been removed. She had now been sober for nearly two months. The last traces of alcohol had left her bloodstream as she read Bodie's book.

Lilith watched the twins from the steps, making little stacks out of the gravel in the quadrant. They used the officers' mess for committee meetings. Bodie liked to keep them away from the community block. Everything was set up. Lilith rechecked it anyway. Bodie hadn't given her an agenda to prepare, or a list of names, so she waited at the entrance to see who turned up. Bodie was seated on the peeling Andronicus chair on the lawn in front of the building. She was watching the children as she held the phone to her ear. Lilith approached her.

'I'll finish up soon. The other committee members will get here momentarily.' She'd been on the phone, gradually making her way through a handwritten list, seeking out candidates, offering to help other organisations' fundraising efforts, connecting the dots. Creating a constellation. A Milky Way. A universe.

'Do you know,' she shielded her eyes from the late summer sun that was jealously holding on to its light, 'I wrote *Queentide* as a call to arms, to say to the world, hey did you know that there was another time? Before the rich white men started making the rules, women did a lot of things, and we did them well.' It sounded like a familiar folksong now. Bodie would sing it, often. At the meetings, around the community. And Lilith never stopped her. She liked to hear Bodie's soothing voice.

Lilith shook her head, letting the old woman start the next verse. 'Women were equal. We were involved. We were chosen because women are good decision-makers. We are fair. We fight for the greater good, for others. Not for our own ego. We make damn good leaders because of that. Our ancestors knew it.'

She handed the wad of paper to Lilith. It was a list of names and numbers, neatly written in Bodie's bold handwriting. Lobbyists, activists, support groups.

'There are hundreds here.' Lilith turned the pages, amazed. How long had it taken Bodie to write it out? Why didn't she ask Lilith to put it in a spreadsheet?

'There are thousands, actually. What you have there is just this state. The lists for Victoria and Queensland are just as long. That means there are millions of people across the country, in these groups, singing the same lyrics but to a slightly different tune – *this system does not represent me.*'

'But they want different things, right? I mean, someone who wants equal pay for women, like you, is going to need something different from someone who is trying to get refugees out of detention.'

'Sure, but the way they all get what they want is by a government treating its citizens fairly, with compassion. We can give them that if they vote for us. If they allow the feminine to take root again.' There was anticipation in Bodie's face as she spoke.

She wanted Lilith to raise an arm and pledge her support. Since arriving, Lilith had kept her hands at her sides. She'd accepted the job, the home. Bodie had said it was unconditional; now Lilith wondered if there was some fine print she'd missed.

She was relieved to hear a car approaching, its tyres crushing the heavy silence that had descended between the two women. Lilith couldn't make out the occupants until it pulled up and parked in the space next to the mess. She was confused when they got out – a man with a pirate beard clambering out of the passenger side and Insley emerging from behind the wheel.

'Insley, you drive too fast.' Bodie kissed her on the cheek.

'You will scare the beard off Aaron.'

'He'd better hang on to it. How will we tell him apart from the ladies otherwise?' Insley playfully punched the man on the arm; he seemed to be unprepared for it and stumbled a little.

'Ignore her, Aaron.' Bodie kissed the pirate on a patch of skin available, just above his beard.

'I try my best, Bodie. You look well.' He hugged her briefly, gently, but all the while looked at Lilith. Feeling momentarily brave, Lilith held his gaze, at least until she sensed colour coming into her cheeks.

'Thank you. I've been doing great these past few weeks. I've been taking the doctor's advice, taking it a little easier. This woman behind us has a great deal to do with that. Lilith, come on over, meet our committee members, at least my favourite ones.'

'Lilith Green, glad to see you stayed.' Lilith's blush intensified under Insley's warm smile.

'Of course, she stayed. Who else would be my COO?' Bodie must have seen the confusion on Lilith's face. 'Chief operations officer. Inhabiting these old army buildings, you need a military sounding title.'

'There's no need, Bodie. Titles aren't important to me.' Lilith kept her voice intentionally low. She didn't want any attention, especially from the pirate. Life had been blissfully simple the past few weeks, with so few men around.

'Titles are important, my dear. They should be important to you. So, you've met Insley.' She raised an eyebrow at Insley, then turned to the pirate. 'And this is Aaron Quinn, media adviser and feminist.' The man scowled at Bodie, the way the girls would scowl at Lilith when she embarrassed them in front of their friends. Then he took Lilith's hand between his two paws and shook it, firmly but quickly, letting it go before Lilith's unease could rise too high.

'She likes to do that, introduce me as a feminist.' His smile faded when Lilith didn't return it, but he just nodded and turned away.

'It's better than the token male. Which we all know you really are.' Insley was teasing him, the way Katy would tease Hannah. He responded the way Katy would, with a fake laugh.

'So funny, Insley.' He held his stomach as though he were laughing, 'Is that how you are going to defeat the patriarchy, with burns like that?'

'Please at least try to make a good impression, you two.' Bodie was out of her seat and leading the way into the building.

'I am actually a feminist.' It took a while to realise that Aaron was talking to her. She didn't want to have a conversation with him, but her manners took over, and she turned around, allowing their steps to fall in line. Lilith had heard so few male voices recently. His low voice sounded strange. Not loud, but invasive. He was obviously very close to Bodie. He must be okay if Bodie liked him, not like the others. She decided to try to stay polite. Or at least not impolite.

'I've been involved with Queentide for as long as Insley,' Aaron continued. 'Bodie convinced me to do PR for Queentide.'

'She is very persuasive,' Lilith said, trying to stem the flow of the conversation. She had always found it hard to talk to men. Mostly because she would hear Ben's overpowering voice in her head telling her they were just trying to get her into bed. They had to be. She wasn't interesting enough to talk to otherwise. But it wasn't Ben's voice she was hearing. It was her own. It had been getting louder, filling the silence she was enjoying recently. Right now, it was telling her to be cautious. Telling her there hadn't been a single man who'd ever improved her life. Apart from her father. When he left.

She saw the girls come running over and felt relieved. Her chest stopped thumping.

'Who's this Mamma?' Katy was out of breath – she'd run the whole way. Hannah trailed behind her, then stopped some distance away. Smart girl, Lilith thought. Stay away from them.

Then she looked at Katy's face, knowing she would have to be polite or face an embarrassing public discussion on manners with her own daughter. Katy had a ton of confidence and no filter.

'This is Aaron, Katy.'

'Hi, Katy. Nice to meet you. And who's that over there?' Aaron waved at Hannah; she looked down at her feet.

'Oh, that's my sister Hannah.' Katy sniffed, wiping her nose on her sleeve. 'I think she's maybe scared of your beard. It looks like it's on fire.'

'I'm so sorry.' Lilith shot a reproachful look at Katy, who just giggled as Aaron pretended to extinguish his beard with his bottle of water. Droplets were making their way onto his gaudy Hawaiian shirt. Hannah looked up, smiling, but kept her distance. Lilith's lips twitched, and she tried to swat her smile away. She didn't want this man making her daughters happy or her.

'Come on, you two. I've got to work. Let's get you over to the main house. Sorry again, Aaron.'

'Oh, please. Insley has said much worse to me. Do you want me to wait while you drop the girls off?'

'Oh, um, no. That's okay. I'll be right behind you.' Lilith was already walking the girls over, her sentence marking the distance between herself and Aaron. She thought she heard him say something to her, but she kept on walking until they reached the steps where Aunty Caz was waiting for them. They engulfed the woman in hugs, her dreadlocks tickling their noses, then made their way inside.

Lilith made her way back to the room she had set up for the meeting, thankful that Aaron hadn't chosen to hang around outside for her. When she got there, she was glad to see he'd sat in the furthest seat, next to Insley, who was playing on her phone. The other places around the circular table were unoccupied, with a few people still to come. Lilith took the seat closest to the door, next to where Bodie had placed her strange pottery cup. She was standing, looking out the only window in the room. The wrought-iron grill another reminder of the building's past.

'Lilith! My dear, it is so lovely to see you.' Before she could even stand up, Janet De Marco had somehow managed to hug her. 'It has been too long. Bodie here keeping you too busy to call me, huh?' She tutted and smiled in Bodie's direction, but Lilith knew the friendly chastisement was for her. She hadn't returned Janet's calls. Why would Lilith pick a fight when her retreat seemed to be working so well?

'Hello, Ms De Marco, it's lovely to see you,' Lilith replied.

'Please, it's just Janet. I'm like Beyoncé. I don't need a surname. There's only one of me.'

'Thank fuck for that.' Aaron had stood up and was bear-hugging Janet, his beard resting on top of her head like a red winter hat.

'Naughty boy. Sit back down before I call your mother and demand she come back from Nepal and send you to your room.' She winked at him.

Aaron bashfully returned to his seat next to Insley, who raised a hand in salute to Janet, then continued scrolling and teasing Aaron. Her laughter stopped when a woman who Lilith didn't recognise entered the room. She was a storm of colour and scent. Gucci Envy. The perfume some of the women brokers wore at Lilith's old job.

'What's she doing here, Bodie?' Insley demanded.

'Nice to see you too, Insley.' The woman's voice was as garishly bright as her pink dress.

'She is representing Kathleen,' Bodie responded. 'Obviously, now Kathleen is the leader of the Labor Party, and with the election expected to be called within a few weeks, Kathleen will no longer attend Queentide meetings. I assumed Kathleen had told you, Insley.'

'Kathleen doesn't need anyone to speak for her,' Insley said with a pout.

'Yourself included Insley,' the woman hit back, then winked at Lilith, conspiratorially. 'Hello, I don't believe we've met. Kay Conway. Insley's nemesis.'

She offered her hand to a confused Lilith, who took it but hoped Insley didn't notice. Insley had been kind to her, so she didn't want to offend her.

'Well, that's confusing because I thought that was me. Ow! Insley that hurt.' Aaron pulled a dramatic face at Insley, reminding Lilith of the twins when they fought.

'I'm also Kathleen Rae's chief of staff,' Kay said softly as she took the seat next to Lilith. 'Insley doesn't like how much time I spend with her girlfriend.'

Insley was rolling her eyes in response as Helen, the sleek woman from the first meeting, walked into the room. She tutted at Insley, then said a polite hello to Bodie and hugged Janet.

'Right, let's get started. We've a great deal to get through. Helen, I wonder if, now that you have the room's attention,' – Insley received a stern look – 'if you could take us through your latest research.'

Helen looked relieved that the elephant was being led out of the room. She produced a small set of glasses, the stereotypical kind a librarian would wear. The type that commanded hushed respect.

Lilith looked at the other faces – lips weren't moving, but brains and hands were. Words were being absorbed, questions were bubbling, and notes were being taken to remember to raise their point when she was finished. The board meetings

Lilith had attended at the investment firm were just layers and layers of noise, the loudest voice ultimately winning.

Helen was a data scientist, and she talked in numbers and statistics. But her passion for her subject made them feel alive. She conjured them into real people.

She had become an expert on activism. Analysing the effectiveness of protests. That's how she and Bodie got to know each other. Scientist and subject. Bodie had been a mobiliser of large-scale protests for years. She was an expert too.

Helen had been researching changes in political systems to find out the turning point. She was working for a bank at the time. They had wanted it to feed into their modelling to predict changes in the market. Bodie had convinced her to use the information to improve the world and not a bank's bottom line.

Bodie believed in people, in love, to make changes happen. She'd seen it done in the 1960s and was sure it could work in the 2020s. Bodie had talked to Lilith about her past as she poured Lilith a honeyed black coffee – something she wanted Lilith to love. As she had spoken and Lilith had sipped, Lilith had been convinced about the coffee but not the premise. People had a chance to change in the new world the pandemic had produced. But, shepherded by politicians like Ben, they'd run back to the fold to greedily protect whatever patch of grass they could. Not caring about the higher fences being built around them or the people that got left out in the cold.

Lilith tried to refocus on Helen, who was handing out sheets of paper.

'The tipping point seems to be about 3.5 per cent. If you can get that percentage of the population involved, you have a 60 per cent chance of success. I've a few examples here that you might want to look at.'

Lilith looked at them as they were passed from person to person. Lilith looked at the black-and-white photos of large crowds peppered with placards. An angry girl, her breath fogging the visor of a motionless riot squad officer. A woman holding a flower in front of an advancing tank. Images from a collective consciousness. But one was unfamiliar and looked out of place with the others. A picture of an empty grocery store, fully stocked. Lilith held on to it as the other photos continued their journey around the table.

'Ah, that's an interesting one.' Helen came over to Lilith to see what she had held on to. 'No placards. No shouting and no police. Just a refusal to buy goods. Protesters shout, but money talks. Companies want to listen once their profits are in danger.' Lilith handed it back to her, questions lodged in her throat. But before she could release them, Bodie was thanking Helen.

'So, 3.5 per cent of the population. I don't think it's too big a target to aim for, do you? That would give us enough of a groundswell to sweep the Women's Party into parliament.' Bodie hauled herself to her feet.

'We've been playing around the edges so far – petitions, marches. We need to shout our message so loud that they won't be able to ignore us.'

'We are going to need one hell of a megaphone,' Janet interjected. 'People are a little hard of hearing when you're trying to tell them something they don't want to hear.' She put her hands to her ears, careful not to disturb her hair and mimed a la-la-la.

Insley had put down her phone and was looking at the lawyer.

'That's where I come in,' Insley said.

'Oh, God help us. No offence Insley but, while you are indeed loud enough to be heard all across our country, I think you'd agree you are something of a PR nightmare.' Janet cackled. 'Am I right, Aaron?'

Insley elbowed Aaron before he had a chance to answer, but laughed good-naturedly. 'Don't have a kitten, Janet. I will not be making any trouble, not the way you are worried about anyway. I've got a plan to leverage social media. Bodie has started making connections with all these groups. Between them and Queentide, across all channels, we've got an audience of at least a million people. We flood that with a consistent message. We get people talking. We stage Insta-worthy protests. We make it something people want to be part of. We make them want to hear.'

'And for those of us who are, let's say, more traditional?' Janet asked.

'Well, I know you aren't talking about yourself because I am one of your six thousand Insta followers. Nice feed, by the way ... the cutest dog on the net. Loved the one where he was dressed as Yoda.' Insley waited for Janet's predictable beam and watched her give a proud bow. Lilith recognised the charm Insley had used on her at the meeting, urging her to sign the petition. 'So I'm guessing you mean people like Lilith here.' Her eyes locked with Lilith's. 'People who choose, for a good reason, not to have a digital presence?' Janet nodded once. Lilith lowered her head – she didn't want to be a part of this conversation, however briefly. 'For people like her,' Insley added, 'we have Kathleen. On the radio, on television, saying the same thing.'

'Wait, wait, wait.' Kay Conway's hand was waving in the air towards Insley. 'Kathleen is the leader of the second biggest political party in Australia now. She can't go on national television talking like a radical feminist.'

'I don't know if you've noticed Kay, but that's exactly what she is,' Insley said dismissively.

'That is her personal view, Insley,' Kay replied. 'Her professional view must toe the party line. Do you want her to lose? Do you have any idea how much of an uphill battle it's going to be for her to get elected? She's a woman. She's Black. Add feminist to that, and you've all but made her unelectable.'

'You forgot queer.' Insley glared at Kay. 'Have you got a problem with that too?'

'Bodie, I really don't see any point in my being here.' Kay was gathering up her things, but Bodie was unflustered.

'I believe you studied politics. Stanford, was it not?' She was charming, like Insley. Lilith assumed, in some ways, activists needed to be. To get into places they weren't supposed to be. See documents they weren't supposed to see. Hear thoughts they weren't supposed to hear. But Bodie's charm was more sophisticated. Lilith had watched Bodie speak to hundreds of activists and lobbyists over the last month, and many of them had been hostile to Bodie's suggestion of an alliance, but soon they were under her spell. Bodie soothed nerves. She left people feeling calmer, happier about their choices. She was hypnotic. Insley danced with you, spun and dipped you until you were smiling, but dazed. Not sure if your wallet had just been lifted in the process.

'Yes, it was. I won a scholarship.' Lilith understood the pride in Kay's voice. Lilith had been proud too when she had won her scholarship to Oxford. She studied politics too. Strange, to have something in common with someone so unlike her in every other way. Life had just taken them down very different paths.

'A fine institution. I taught there once. A long time ago. I assume they still teach you about the radical flank effect?'

Lilith remembered. They had done a case study on its use in the Black Panther movement. She wanted to speak up. She wanted a gold star from the teacher. But it wasn't her Bodie had asked.

'Of course. A radical view is pitted against something that seems extreme, without context. You shift what is accepted as the middle ground and make progress towards the radical goals.'

Martin Luther King's success after the emergence of the Black Panthers, the end of apartheid ... the radical flank effect. Lilith understood, but Kay got the accolades.

'A-plus, my dear. Kathleen's job is to talk passionately about equality and equity in society. The things she already does talk about and believes in. Queentide will broaden the spectrum of discussion on these things, so Kathleen's views are no longer seen as extreme. She is dead centre. They will accept Kathleen's commitment to a 50 per cent female Cabinet because we will push for a 100 per cent female Cabinet. They will think it's perfectly reasonable to provide subsidised childcare to every family and build more daycare centres because the alternative we will give them is free daycare for all families. They will happily support Kathleen's suggestion that gender discrimination is outlawed again, because we will be pushing for businesses to be taxed if they don't have a gender-balanced workforce. They will believe Kathleen when she tells them violence against women must be punished more harshly because Queentide will flood social media and the streets with images of the women beaten and killed since the last election. We will make them angry. We will make them want to turn away. And Kathleen will be right there to tell them they can do something about it. By electing her.'

Kay, who still had her things in her hand, sat back. Lilith looked around the table. Everyone was silent. Then Helen's deliberate voice sliced through the room.

'What if she doesn't win?'

'She will win. We will make sure of it,' Insley said. 'There are things we can do to ensure the votes go the right way.'

Lilith kept writing, hoping that no one would see her heart trying to escape her ribcage. No one noticed when she dropped her pen. No one noticed she didn't write a single letter after she picked it back up.

Helen was looking intently at Insley, but her voice was aimed at Bodie.

'I respect you, Bodie. You have done remarkable things for

women, and I know you want to do more.' Insley broke eye contact with Helen and stared up at the ceiling. 'But election fixing? It's going too far.' She turned to Janet. 'Janet, you are a lawyer. Surely you agree with me.'

'Too far from what, Helen?' Janet replied. 'Too far from silent anger? Is it going too far if Queentide actually achieves what we set out to do?'

'What we set out to do was make women stronger, safer, equal.'

'And that's what this will achieve.' Janet sounded impatient. 'Kathleen's election is critical to our success. Her platform is basically the manifesto Bodie wrote in her book. The one that convinced you to set up Queentide, if you recall. Now you are telling me you don't want to see it come to life?' Janet gave her little tut. 'Kathleen is a good woman. She wants change. She wants to bring people, women, up. But she's got to get up the ladder first.' Lilith watched the rainbows cast by the light hitting Janet's emerald as she spun the ring on her finger. She didn't look as confident as she did in her own office. 'I've looked at what Insley is proposing to do. I've engaged some lawyers who specialise in defamation cases and constitutional law. This has my support, Helen.'

'But what we are talking about is illegal. You can't fix elections. It's just not right.'

Insley sneered at the end of the table.

'Insley, we are all well aware of your flexible view of the law.'

'If I wasn't flexible, a lot of things would be harder for a lot of people. You included.' This rattled Helen, but she continued.

'How much has she offered to you?' She had turned to Bodie.

'You should know me better than—' Bodie didn't get a chance to finish.

'Jesus, Helen. This isn't about money.' Insley was now on her feet, a tornado sweeping from one end of the small room to the other. 'If she doesn't win, we have that wanker for another four years. And spoiler alert,' – Insley waved her hands over her head – 'things will be less safe, less equal, for these people you supposedly care about.'

'She's blunt, but she's right, Helen.' Lilith noticed that everyone was surprised to hear Kay speak, especially Insley. 'We've got the last four years as proof that this is exactly what will go down. Except, this time, he's even more confident. He's broken into the henhouse a few times without even a slap on the wrist. God knows what he'll go for next, probably the entire farm. You can't expect us to follow laws that are going to lead to our destruction.'

'Kay, isn't it?' Helen asked with condescension. 'I do not disagree with you. There are homophobic, misogynistic and just plain cruel laws being forced on us and, I agree, this is what we should be fighting. It's exactly the point of my work. But what is being discussed here is the rigging of a national election.'

'It is not rigging. It is nudging. Mobilising Australia's population to make sure we get the right outcome this time. We cannot tolerate those men being there for another term. And if you think the PM will not be doing some underhanded things, you must live in a bubble. He has the mainstream media ready to spread whatever shit will help him thrive.'

'But what you are talking about is exactly the same. We are sinking to the PM's level. We will be manipulating people too. It's just not right,' Helen said passionately.

'We aren't talking about fake news. We're talking about exposing the truth. We want the entire country to want the PM and his Cabinet out of office. They don't have to want Kathleen. They just have to not want them. You know her. You know what she can make possible. She's only been an MP for a couple of years, a shadow minister in her first year, and look what she's achieved from that position. Imagine what she'll be able to do as the leader of the country? Imagine what Queentide can do if it has a seat at the table with these governments, with the UN, the World Bank. She will make that happen for us. But if she doesn't have our backing, she won't win. If we don't get our candidates in, if we don't help crush him, she can't. We are levelling the playing field for her. She doesn't have a network of old school buddies to help her. Or unscrupulous foreign governments. We are just going to give her support. That 3.5 per cent swing. It's not much when you think of it.'

Helen sat back. Kay could have been a politician herself. She had captivated the audience. And it looked like she'd converted Helen.

'And how are you going to do that?' Helen asked suspiciously.

'By showing them up for what they really are,' Insley answered. 'We've already been doing some digging. We didn't have to do much to unearth some skeletons. We need to get some more, though … especially on the Cabinet members, like Ben Hamilton. We think there's enough on him to bring the lot of them down. But he's a bit more cautious than the rest.'

Lilith looked up at the mention of his name, expecting everyone to be staring, but only Insley was looking at her. She felt Bodie squeeze her hand, guiding her back to the surface, out of the wave that had crashed over her. Bodie shook her head slightly. Relieved, Lilith knew she wasn't expected to speak.

'I am in the middle of important research, you know that Bodie. If this gets out, that we did this, I will lose all funding.'

'Helen, if we succeed, you will never need to worry about funding again.' Bodie released Lilith's hand. 'Because the right people will be making the right decisions then.'

Lilith didn't hear the rest of the meeting. It was drowned out by the sound of her little universe exploding, sending her hurtling, unanchored, across the sky.

Chapter 12

Insley followed Lilith out of the meeting room, silently picking up the chair that had fallen behind her as she bolted away from the table. Down the corridor, Lilith's shaking silhouette was visible on the steps in front of the open door. Not wanting to startle her, Insley went via the kitchen. She paused to make tea, something she had always done for her mother when she'd found her crying and bruised.

'Here.' She approached Lilith from the front, hoping her boots crunching on the gravel would be enough warning of her arrival. She leaned down and passed Lilith the mug, trying to use her body to shield Lilith from the sun. 'I made you a fresh one. You left yours behind.' She stood awkwardly in front of Lilith, scraping a rainbow shape in the tiny stones. 'I'm sorry, Bodie is better at this than me.'

'No, you're wrong,' Lilith took a sip. 'Bodie makes terrible tea. This is great.' She gave Insley a wobbly smile. Insley gave her a grin in return.

'I meant the picking up after someone falls. I usually just do the knocking over. I'm sorry. About in there. I didn't mean to ambush you.'

Lilith was looking past Insley over the old parade ground.

'I have to go over there sometimes before the girls start playing. Check for dead rabbits.' Lilith shuddered. 'Or what's left of them.'

'It's a bit grim, isn't it? You can't avoid it up here. There are so many of them. Some are always going to be taken by foxes,' Insley replied.

Insley looked over the wide gravelled area. Remembering how she and Aaron would find bits of fur or entrails. It happened so often they became numb to it.

'Why do they do it, the foxes? Leave them scattered like that? If they want to eat them, why do they leave so much behind?' Lilith said.

Insley had seen so many dead rabbits, she'd never stopped to wonder why.

'Well, I guess they do it for fun,' Insley explained. 'It's in their nature to attack something smaller than them.'

'I don't think it is foxes, actually,' Lilith replied.

'What do you think it is then?' Insley asked. 'Have you been listening to the gossip about feral cats?'

'I think it's a person. I think someone is cutting them up and leaving them there,' she nodded towards the gravel, 'for us to find. There are too many for it to be foxes – ten or twelve every day. And the dead rabbits are always strewn in a circle in the middle of the parade ground. Where we can see from the windows.'

'Any ideas who it might be?' Insley asked.

'Do you?' Lilith shot back. 'What is it you do exactly, Insley? I mean, all that talk about digging up dirt, is that what you do, for Bodie?' Lilith's unexpected question caught Insley by surprise.

There was a steel visible underneath the liquid surface of this woman. Insley wondered what it would take to expose it.

'I do what needs doing.' She sat on the step next to Lilith, deciding not to shield her anymore.

'Some of the women, at the community, they say you're a vigilante ...' Lilith said.

'Do they now.' Insley squinted, the sun in her eyes now. 'I'm not sure they'd say that around my grandmother.'

'Your grandmother?' Lilith said, surprised.

'You hadn't spotted the family resemblance?' Insley turned her head this way and that. Then ran her hand over her shaven head.

'Bodie? I'm sorry, I had no idea.'

'Why would you? Bodie acts like everyone's grandmother. You'd not notice that she is genetically coded to love me.' Insley smiled and sipped her tea.

'Is that what it is, Bodie's friendliness? An act? She had me fooled. I didn't realise all of this came with strings attached.' Lilith wiped a tear from her eye. The steel was starting to shine through.

'There are no strings, Lilith. Bodie invited you here and gave you a job because of who you are. Not who your dickhead ex-husband is.' But that is why I'm making sure you stay, Insley thought to herself.

'I'm finding that hard to believe.' Lilith sipped her tea. 'Is your mother involved in Queentide too?'

Insley tried to stop the reflex, but her muscles tensed anyway.

'My mother's dead. Bodie raised me. At least from when I was about ten. It's the reason she moved to Australia.'

'Oh, I'm sorry. You lost both your parents?'

'Not at the same time. My father killed her, my mum. He died later. Just after he got out of prison.'

'I'm sorry ...' The steel slipped back under the depths, and Lilith became a pool of nerves again.

Insley squinted at the sun, shrugged her shoulders. This was the routine she'd been through many times. She'd found honesty delivered quickly was the quickest way to shut caring people down. Lilith fell into line.

'You can read the articles if you want. Bodie kept them. God knows why. The bastard reporters said it was a crime of passion. I still remember them saying that on the news. There was no passion, just fucking anger. He'd hit her, my mum, Celeste. And me. Loads of times before then. She never reported it. Bodie thinks she kept it quiet to protect her. Couldn't have a feminist activist's daughter being stuck in a violent relationship. I think she was just too scared to go to the cops. Anyway, Bodie came. Saved me. And Aaron and his mum. Bodie helped me find a way to deal, you know? At least until I found my own way.'

'She is an impressive woman.'

'She is, and honest too. She hasn't lied to you, Lilith.' Insley had to stop herself from admitting she had lied to Lilith. And to Bodie. Instead, she put on the track that she had also played for Bodie. 'It was my idea to target Ben after Bodie told me who your ex-husband was.'

'So you want to use me to get Ben?'

'No. I want you to bring that fucker down yourself.' Insley felt good saying something honest. Like she'd just taken a swig of cold water.

'It took me years to get enough courage to leave him. I just want him to leave me alone.'

'And is he? Is he leaving you alone?' Insley knew the answer, of course. She knew what he was up to, knew that it was much worse than Lilith actually realised. She also knew Lilith was covering for him. 'What was it that tipped you over the edge, made you finally leave?'

Lilith didn't answer. She didn't need to – it echoed inside her. Insley could hear it.

'Those two little firecrackers I see running around, right?'

Lilith's hands were shaking. Insley had to hold herself back. It felt like being at a red light, having to stop her foot from pressing the accelerator. She'd been feeling like that a lot recently. Like someone was forcing her to stay still. She didn't like it.

'I'd die for those girls,' Lilith responded.

'And you did, in a way. Lilith Hamilton died for them; you ended that old life for them. The money, the house ...'

'What a hero.'

'Hey.' Insley turned Lilith's chin towards her, the intimacy surprising both of them. 'It took strength to leave that. The love you have for those girls gave you that strength. Bodie sees that in you. You and Bodie have got the same strength. Jesus, that woman would throw herself in front of a truck if she thought it would make the world better. Thank God the suffragettes had the idea first. Otherwise, she might have given it a go.'

'It was a horse. Not a truck,' Lilith said.

'Well, thank you, Ms Feminism 2026. I stand fucking correct-ed,' Insley scoffed.

Lilith smiled briefly, but then her face became steel again.

'This isn't my war, Insley. All I care about is protecting my girls.' Lilith stared back out towards the parade ground.

Insley drained her tea and stood up.

'You're just on a different battleground right now. Believe me. This absolutely is your war. It's every woman's war. When you realise the only way to protect your girls is to get your fuck-ing hands dirty, call me.' She motioned for Lilith to give her the cold cup she was still cradling.

'He never hit the girls.' Lilith looked at her. 'Ben, I mean. And most of my bruises are on the inside.'

'No, they aren't.' Insley shook her head. 'They are on show. I can see them from here. What he has done to you, what he is still doing to you, I can see it. Right now.' Insley walked away. She knew Lilith would start crying, and she didn't want to see that. 'It won't be long until you start seeing it on your girls too. Unless you already have, of course,' she shouted over her shoul-der.

Through the kitchen window, Insley watched Lilith cross

the quadrant and run into the community building. Even from that distance, it was clear she was crying. Fuck. Insley threw the mugs in the sink, hard. One of them shattered. The ugly brown one that Bodie loved. Everyone else hated it, but none of them had the heart to tell Bodie or the guts to throw it out. Insley picked up the pieces and happily put them in the bin. Now everyone could stop pretending. Sometimes things need to be broken so life can move on. She wished she'd done it sooner.

Chapter 13

Lilith had spent the weekend avoiding Bodie, and for once, was thankful the girls had gone to Ben's. She needed time to calm the rabbit down. A few times, Lilith had gone to their living space and packed. Only to realise she had nowhere to go. But it wasn't just that – she wanted to be here. It felt like home, except for tonight. Tonight the small flat felt haunted, two souls not where they belonged. The girls' missingness drove her downstairs, where she wouldn't hear their missing giggles everywhere. It was a Sunday evening, and the common area was deserted. Lilith saw a pot of coffee and a book on the long bench in the kitchen. Before her smile had a chance to fully form, a voice startled her.

'Hi. It's Lilith, right?' Kay Conway smiled from the far end of the bench and closed her laptop. 'Bodie's EA?'

'Oh, I think EA is a bit much. I'm just her secretary, really. I didn't mean to interrupt you.'

'That's fine. I'm happy to have a break. Fuck knows what it's going to be like once the election is actually called.'

'It must be a hard job, being Kathleen Rae's adviser.'

'Ha. Not sure about adviser. I'd like to be, but Kathleen doesn't really need my advice. I tend just to answer her emails, speak to the press when she's too busy. I think our jobs are more similar than you realise. Wine?' She was twirling a glass by its stem, the remnants of wine sloshing precariously against the sides, and a half-full bottle next to her.

'Oh, no. Thank you. I don't drink. Not anymore. There's a pot of coffee here. I might just have that thanks.'

She pulled a fake sad face. It made Lilith think of the girls when she'd say she was too busy to play.

'Oh, come on. I think new friendships should always be celebrated.' Before she could refuse again, Kay had collected a glass from the kitchen and handed it to Lilith, full to the top. 'Cheers.'

'Cheers.' Lilith took a sip. It didn't taste like it used to. It tasted like vinegar, burning her throat. She took another sip. It didn't taste as bad.

'So what do you really make of all this?' She waved her hand around the room.

'The community?'

'Yeah, the *community*.' She made it sound like a made-up word. 'I mean, it's a bit, Jane Fonda, burn-your-bra sort of territory, isn't it?'

Lilith laughed shyly, a part of her ashamed for betraying Bodie. She took a bigger gulp this time. The wine feeling like a warm hug across her chest.

'Not really, it's just a group of women living together. Sharing the burden. It's made my life easier for me,' Lilith said, 'and my girls.'

'You've got two, right?' Kay asked.

'Yes. And an ex-husband.' Lilith fiddled with the stem of her glass.

'Ben Hamilton.' Kay released his name. 'The one crazy Insley wants to go after.'

His name swirled through the room and sobered Lilith immediately.

'You knew, at the meeting?' Lilith asked. 'That I was his wife?'

'Sure. It's my job to know these things.' Kay swept her perfect hair away from her face with a perfectly manicured nail. 'I've seen you around Canberra, actually. Doing the supportive wife routine.'

'Oh, I'm sorry, I don't recall ...' Lilith felt oddly guilty that she didn't recognise Kay.

'Oh please, if you'd noticed me, I wouldn't be doing my job properly. My job is to be the shadow that makes Kathleen shine.' Kay walked over to the fridge and produced another bottle of wine. She refilled the glasses, which had somehow emptied quickly. Lilith's mind was starting to feel soft. Malleable.

'I have to say, it's very nice of you to not go through with the divorce at the moment. It could have looked dreadful for Ben during an election,' Kay said.

'Oh, well.' Lilith sipped the fresh wine. 'I think it's better to try to sort these things out, you know?'

'And there are also the threats you are receiving?' Kay whispered.

'I don't know what you ...' Lilith felt Kay's cool hand encase her own.

'It's okay. I know those dickheads at MASC have been sending you all sorts of stuff.'

'How do you ...'

'They target Kathleen all the time. Jesus, can you think of anything more intimidating for a men's rights group than a gay, female, Aboriginal politician running for prime minister? They were already worked up before she announced she was running for leader. Now it's like we've tipped over the hive. They're swarming all over her. We've been inundated. The police give us briefings on what they've been up to. You got mentioned, not directly, but there are few Cabinet members whose wives have just left them.'

'So the police know about it?' Lilith asked, alarmed. 'About the things I'm getting?'

'Of course,' Kay replied.

'But they haven't spoken to me.' The wine was making Lilith confused. 'And I'm pretty certain I have told no one else about it.' She couldn't have. She had no one to speak to there. The only person who had shown an interest in her was Insley and perhaps Bodie when she wasn't too busy, and neither seemed like the type of person to go to the police.

'Have you been to the police?' Kay asked.

'No, I just destroyed all of the photos, the messages,' Lilith shook her head. 'Blocked the senders on emails. Like I said, I haven't told anyone.'

'Not even Bodie?'

'No, not even before I knew they wanted to go after Ben. I didn't want to worry her. I didn't want her to think I was trouble.'

'Then, if you haven't told the cops, and no one else has either, why would the police come and make more work for themselves? They're barely doing anything to help Kathleen, and she is mad as fucking hell about it. She's getting death threats every day. Sometimes some other fucking disturbed stuff.' She poured more wine and lowered her voice. 'Do you think Ben is getting them to do it? I mean getting MASC to threaten you?'

'You know he's involved in it?' Lilith was surprised.

'It's not exactly a secret, is it? He's their poster boy. He goes sailing with MASC leaders nearly every Thursday. It would make sense that he'd ask them to get a little revenge on the annoying ex-wife. Sorry, but you know what I'm saying.'

'So if everyone knows Ben is involved with MASC, then why does Insley need me to help her?' Lilith was confused. She wished she hadn't drunk the wine.

'What has she asked you for?' Kay asked.

'Well, nothing in particular ... but that comment about dirt on Ben ... I mean, obviously there's stuff I know about that would make the election very difficult for him,' Lilith answered.

'Look,'- she sloshed more wine in the glass, giggling as she missed and poured some on the table – 'from what I can tell, Insley can manage just fine on her own. The police know who the real sick bastards in MASC are, and it isn't Ben. You'd be targeting the wrong person. He might be the one getting them to send you horrible stuff and, if you could prove it, which you can't, it might affect his election chances. Is it really worth letting Insley drag you into the spotlight over this?' She took a sip of her wine and put a hand on Lilith's shoulder. 'I mean, you'd be all over the papers, the girls too. And I don't think it would stop MASC, anyway. Look what happened to Kathleen. She called them out, and it just got worse.'

Lilith shook her head. 'I don't think it's the MASC stuff Insley is interested in.'

'Oh?' Kay leaned in.

'Ben and I, the reason I left. I think maybe Insley wants me to expose him, say what he was like behind closed doors.' Lilith expected a reaction from Kay, but she didn't flinch. Perhaps Insley was right. Her bruises were visible. 'And, you know, he makes a lot of money. More than a politician should. I know how he makes it. I took stuff with me when I left.'

'What sort of stuff?' Kay looked down into her glass, not able to meet Lilith's eye.

Lilith pulled herself back. She had said too much. She had drunk too much. The information was her parachute for emergencies only. She didn't want to pull the cord too early.

'Just business deals and stuff. You know, the usual.' Lilith tried to downplay what she knew. 'I think that's what Insley is after.'

'And you don't want to give it to her?'

'I've told her, this isn't my war.'

'I think you are right. I mean, was what Ben did to you, or the fact he made a bit of money on the side, worth sacrificing your own peace of mind over? I mean, you seem happy now. Your girls do too. Do you really want to make this situation any more difficult by picking a fight with him? Won't that just be worse for your girls?'

Lilith took another drink of the wine. It felt good to be told to go back to her corner, to leave the ring. She let the alcohol blur her memory, allowing her to forget why she was angry and sad. She snuggled down into the cloud that was forming in her brain, letting her float away.

'I have known Insley for a long time.' Kay lowered her voice to a pantomime whisper, 'She's a bitch. Shh! Don't tell the sisterhood I said that – they'll have me whipped. Or at least throw me out.' She started giggling. It was infectious. Lilith felt her lips curl, and a pitchy laugh escaped from her mouth.

'I don't think she's that bad,' Lilith said guiltily. 'She's been nice to me.'

'By asking you to hand over information on your ex-husband? Think about it, Lilith. She's not nice. It sounds like she's asking you to give her stuff she can't access herself. Government records? Bank accounts? That sort of thing. Maybe even stuff tying Ben to the dodgier stuff MASC does. You don't have to tell me.' Lilith felt relieved that Kay wasn't digging. 'But I'm guessing that what you have, you haven't got legally. How would that look? It would make a custody case very difficult. Insley knows that. She's using you.' She topped up Lilith's glass. She really should stop drinking now.

'I ...' The disappointment was too big to articulate. Insley wasn't her friend. Lilith was still alone.

'Oh, don't worry about Insley. She'd throw anyone under a horse if she thought it would help *the fight*. I mean, it's admirable and everything, this suffragette thing she's got going on. This little fairytale she and her grandmother are peddling in

that book is all very nice, makes a good story – a feminist revolution is going to make us all equal. Please!'

'You don't believe it's possible?' Lilith wanted to know she
wasn't the only cynical one.

'It isn't possible. Life isn't like that, is it? I mean, not everyone gets the same opportunities. Look at Kathleen.'

'What do you mean?' Lilith took another sip, forgetting she
was stopping.

'Well, she was the golden girl, especially after she managed
to back the PM into a corner over all this harassment rubbish.'
Kay wafted away Lilith's surprised look. 'It is rubbish. Politics
is a tough gig. If women aren't prepared to put up with a little
harassment, they should do something else. It was sad, what
happened to the other MP, the one who killed herself. But it
wasn't the harassment that killed her. It was the media afterwards. If anyone is to blame, it's journalists like Aaron, who was
at the meeting. Insley's friend? It is men like him who put those
stories out there. People like him are putting these vulnerable
women on a pyre for everyone to throw matches at. Anyway, all
I'm saying is, it didn't hurt Kathleen's position in the party to go
after the PM. She got given an opportunity that most wouldn't.
She's only been around for a few years. It's a bit gimmicky, in
my opinion, putting an Aboriginal feminist up against the stale
white male. I mean, she deserves the recognition, of course. All
I'm saying is that I wasn't given the opportunity. There was no
positive discrimination for me. I couldn't even get preselection
for a seat.' She raised her glass again. It didn't seem to be as
empty as Lilith's. 'But that's okay, you know? I like what I do.
I'm happy to do what's needed to get the party elected. It just
would be nice to get some of that fairness working for me too.'

Lilith felt a little sorry for her, she sounded so bitter, but she
was glad she wasn't as perfect as she had thought. It made her
human. It made it possible for them to be friends.

'So you don't believe in what Queentide is doing?' she asked carefully, not wanting to offend her.

'My job is to get Kathleen elected. I'm good at my job, and I'll do whatever it takes to win. If this group, or movement or what-ever the hell they call themselves, wants to help me win, then great.' She drained her glass. Lilith had lost count of the number of drinks they'd had. She couldn't even remember Kay finishing her last one. 'But I don't have to support what they do. I'm here representing Kathleen because she can't associate directly with Queentide. It would look too dodgy. I'll maximise whatever ad-vantage I can get for Kathleen from the Women's Party, and I'll minimise any damage that Insley might cause. And, believe me, there will be damage. There always is where she is concerned.'

Her new friend shook her head and rubbed her eyes. 'Well, the wine has gone again. And I'm all negative. I don't want to be the one to burst your bubble. Time for bed, I think.' She gath-ered her things together and stood up. 'Good night, Lilith.'

'Are you staying here?' Lilith's brain was hazy.

'Oh! You left the meeting before Bodie made the announce-ment. It's going to make it easier for me to work closely with Bodie if I am here, at least until the election is underway. And I can keep an eye on Insley. Make sure she doesn't stuff anything up. Kathleen will probably be glad to have me out of the way.'

'Well, I'm glad you're going to be here.' Lilith's shyness was drowned in alcohol.

'Me too, Lilith.' She hugged her and picked up her stilettos, walking barefoot out of the kitchen. She turned at the doorway to face Lilith. 'It's not very often I find a woman that I get on with. I find it a bit hard to get on with them generally. A bit too bitchy. But you're different. Night-night.' She blew Lilith a kiss from the kitchen door, then disappeared into the darkened lounge room.

Lilith grinned. Then looked at the untouched coffee and

book. A little wave of guilt took the edge off her wine buzz. She emptied the pot into the sink and replaced the book on the shelf. She didn't need Sylvia or Virginia for company tonight.

She had Kay now.

Lilith woke up the next day with a bad head but felt happy. The way she used to the morning after sneaking into a nightclub when she was fifteen. She went about her day feeling slightly euphoric. Carefree. If Bodie smelt the stale alcohol on her breath, she didn't mention it to Lilith, just the way her own mother had pretended not to notice all those years ago.

Bodie also didn't talk about Ben or Insley. It was as though they had disappeared, allowing Lilith to move through her day without them getting in the way. They were suspended in the space that Kay Conway had created when she put Lilith's universe back together again.

Chapter 14

Aaron was regretting his decision to get off the bus two stops early. He cursed Insley all the way up the hill. Aaron was not out of shape, and he did not look like a gnome in his gym shorts. He pulled his phone out of his back pocket to FaceTime her and prove he was fit. The sweat underneath his beard was making him itchy, and his satirical Hawaiian shirt was chafing under his arms. He was sure the small amount of exposed skin on his face had also got sunburnt. In winter. She'd laugh her arse off if she saw him. She was such a dick. He'd just call her instead.

'Insley, it's Aaron ...' He only realised how out of breath he was when he spoke.

'Jesus, are you okay?' She sounded alarmed. 'What's happened?'

'Nothing ... nothing to worry about.' Maybe calling Insley was a bad idea. 'I'm just a bit out of breath ...'

'Why, what have you been doing?' Insley asked.

Aaron knew he'd regret what he said next, but there wasn't enough oxygen in his head to come up with a convincing lie.

'I got off the bus at the bottom of the hill,' he said resignedly.

'You rang me to tell me that?' He could barely make out the words in between her cackling laugh.

'I rang to tell you I am not an out-of-shape gnome.' More laughter. 'Or something. I don't know. I can't think straight.' Then the snorts came. 'I feel a bit faint.'

'As much as I appreciate you lightening up my day, kinda got things to be getting on with Az, so ...'

'Hang on. There is one other thing.' Aaron ran his forearm over his brow to stop the sweat from falling onto his phone. Fuck, he really was out of shape. 'I'm up at the community to do that interview for Bodie with that author. But, if I see Lilith Green, do you want me to talk to her? See if I can get her talking?'

There was a pause. The noise in the background changed. Insley had gone somewhere quiet. Private.

'She knows something Az, but she's holding back. I don't know if it's fear or some sort of twisted loyalty thing, or some good-girl syndrome ...'

'What if it's none of those things, Insley?'

'What else could it be?'

'What if she's playing us? What if she was planted here by Ben and his cronies to find out what Queentide is up to? What if they know we're planning on aligning with Kathleen?'

There was silence as Insley considered what he had said. She never shut him down immediately, like she did with most people.

'No, not possible. Bodie found *her*, not the other way around.'

'Things like that can be staged, Insley. Jesus, you've done it to other people enough times to know that.' He rarely brought up what Insley did. He was waiting until she was senile and slow and couldn't beat him up. He was going to write about the militant feminist's antics. 'I mean, she's Bodie's EA. She's been welcomed into the community, given protection, but she won't help us go after someone who supposedly abused her?'

'Supposedly? You think she's made it up? C'mon Az, really?'

'Sorry. I didn't mean to sound like a dickhead. It's just...it's not making sense to me.'

'It doesn't need to make sense to you,' Insley replied. 'What you think about Lilith Green doesn't matter.'

'Thanks, Insley,' Aaron said, just a little hurt.

'You know what I mean,' Insley said. 'Lilith is scared. Of Ben. Of MASC. I don't blame her; they are a bunch of crazy fuckers. You would not believe what I found, one of them planning ...'

'I'm still not sure we can trust her, Insley.' Aaron didn't want to let it go. 'What you and Bodie are trying to do—'

'What *we* are doing, Az. You are an important part of this ...' Insley was always quick to affirm his role. He didn't believe her. He sometimes felt like a pompomless cheerleader, but he appreciated her effort.

'Okay, okay, what *we* are doing, it's kind of a one-shot thing. If we fuck this up, if we put our faith in the wrong people, we may not get another chance. It might actually make things worse. I just don't want us to take any risks.'

She was quiet again. This time for longer. How was it possible for her to sound angry when she was silent? What had he said? He couldn't stand it.

'Insley? Are you there?'

'Aaron,' – he was in trouble; she had used his full name - 'do me a favour. Talk to her. Look in her eyes and tell me who she reminds you of. Then let's have this conversation again.'

'I know who she reminds *you* of. And Bodie too.' The line was so quiet he could hear Insley breathe. 'She's not the same woman as Celeste.'

'That's enough analysis from you, Freud,' Insley said, with just a little too much bravado to be convincing. 'Just fucking speak to her, will you?'

'Look, Insley, I didn't mean to—'

'It doesn't matter, Aaron. She's scared, alright? Just like my mother was. Just like yours was. We need her to expose this bastard. Turn on some of that charm everyone tells me you have and convince her this is her war too. She will come around. If she doesn't then—'

'So you can lecture me about trusting her, but you don't have to trust her yourself?'

'I believe that Ben Hamilton is a genuine bastard, and Lilith actually left him and, by some sort of karmic hippie Zen thing, landed on Bodie's doorstep. But I don't trust that Lilith has the strength to pull anyone else into the little warm burrow she's made for herself.'

'So you'll throw her to the dogs? Jesus, Insley. I'd hate to see what you'd do to someone that didn't remind you of your mother.'

'Fuck off, Az. Like you said, we've got one shot at this. I'll do what needs doing. We all have to make sacrifices, even people who remind me of my mother.'

'Insley? She was a good person, your mum.'

'I know. And so is Lilith. But being good isn't enough sometimes, is it? It didn't keep her safe.'

Aaron was relieved when she hung up. There was no point talking to Insley once her mind was made up.

He put the phone away and stood for a moment at the gate to get his breath back and figure out what to do next. He had to do the interview with Sibel Polat today. It would be his second. This time pleading to the public to not let the government kick her out.

Her visa had already expired. It wouldn't be long before immigration came looking for her. They needed to get a campaign up and running before she got sent offshore or sent back to Turkey.

There would be no public shaming this time. No nights to cool off in a cell. Sibel Polat and her daughter would vanish. She'd been all over the internet, in the last article Aaron wrote when she'd first arrived for the writer's festival. The photo of her hands, showing the scars where her hands had been whipped.

For writing children's books. There would be a queue of people waiting to punish her. Some official, some not. Because of Aaron's article. And the Twitter feed. And Instagram. And Reddit and every other means of communication possible because he had to get the word out. He had to show the world how out of balance it was.

Fuck it. Aaron could just go back down the hill, go to the airport and get on a plane to Nepal. He could teach kids English in his mum's school and never write another article or tweet again. At least he might be making someone's life better instead of what he'd done to the women and men he'd written about over the years. Those poor bastards in the spotlight of his writing. A nice clear target for the trolls and bigots and bad, sick people. Maybe Lilith Green would be safer if Insley did her thing. Aaron's way just seemed to make things worse. That poor politician. His article hadn't helped her. He'd just laid down some fresh meat for the hungry press to fight over. She'd been ripped to shreds. Beyond repair.

He plopped himself on the ground and pulled out his notes and a tissue to soak up some of the wetness from his face. The kids from the community were running around the quadrant, flapping imaginary wings. When it was him and Insley playing there, they used to throw the gravel at each other until his mother or Bodie would tell them to stop it. Hippies didn't like conflict. At least not among themselves. He should call his mum. It had been months since they'd spoken. Mobile reception isn't great in the hills of Nepal. Maybe he'd try the school's landline.

He stashed his notes back in his bag and dragged himself up. Time to shake it off. He wasn't going to Nepal. He would not stop writing. There were already enough disillusioned journalists crowding the Himalayas. And this new plan of Bodie's might just work. He would not abandon her, or Insley, now. They needed his cheers now more than ever. Or at least that's what they said, and he needed to believe that.

As he started dragging his legs towards the community build-ing, where Sibel was staying, he saw Lilith Green approaching the group of children. He wasn't ready for this, not today. He'd try to avoid her, go around the back and see if Bodie was in her office. But it was too late. She was herding the kids towards the same place he was heading. They were on a collision course.

She saw him coming over and seemed to speed up. Seemed like she wasn't so keen to see him either. Well, that was just fine by him. He'd interview Sibel, go home and have a few whiskies and think about how to approach Lilith Green another day.

He tried to slow down, to give them time to get inside, but the twins were part of the little cluster of kids. The louder one, Katy, stopped on the stairs. Her sister obediently copying her. Katy started making pirate sounds to her sister and pointing at Aaron. Stumbling around as if she had a false leg. They both giggled and waved enthusiastically at him. Lilith looked over her shoulder and made eye contact. She ushered the girls in and turned to face him.

'Hello. Sorry about that. The girls are a little hyped up today.' It was an apology, but she didn't sound as sorry as the words suggested.

'Oh, that's fine. It's nice seeing more kids around the place.' He tried to sound casual. He didn't. He might have even seemed a bit creepy. Great.

She didn't respond. She was barring Aaron's way in. To the place that used to be his home. He looked her in the eyes. Like Insley asked him to. She didn't remind him of Insley's mum. Celeste had always felt like a dark and heavy rain-cloud, ready to be blown away by the wind. Lilith Green was a rain-cloud too, but not one that would be blown away easily. There was something brewing inside her. She crackled with the threat of lightning. Her thunder was just a little too far away to be heard.

But it was coming. Aaron could feel it. It made the hairs on his arms stand up to be around her.

'Actually, I'm here to see Sibel Polat,' he eventually said.

'Sibel? I didn't know anyone else knew she was here, I mean outside of the community. I thought Bodie was keeping it quiet, given the circumstances.'

'Well, I guess I'm not outside of the community.' Aaron tried not to sound offended, but he was. 'I used to live here when I was a kid. With my mum.'

'Insley mentioned something. I guess that makes more sense.' She moved towards the doorway, and Aaron followed. 'I couldn't figure out why a man was involved in Queentide.'

'What, men can't be feminists?' It was meant to sound smooth, but it came out covered in splinters. It was a sentence he'd dragged out so many times before.

'Not the ones I know,' she replied without turning around.

'Perhaps you've been hanging out with the wrong sort of men.' It was low. He knew it. She stood still, letting his words pass over her head. Her face was emotionless. 'I'm sorry. That was unkind.'

'I've heard worse.'

'I'm sure you have. I'm sorry about that too.' Her face was giving nothing away. He would not be able to charm her. She'd obviously heard enough bullshit in her time to have become immune to it. Maybe he needed to try a different tack. Perhaps he should just be upfront. 'Look, I think we've got off on the wrong foot. Maybe we could grab a coffee sometime. I know this must be difficult for you.'

'What part must be difficult for me?'

'Well, leaving a marriage. Moving here with two young kids. Having to see him being praised in the press for being such a dedicated dad.' Aaron wondered if Bodie still got the paper delivered.

'I saw that this morning,' Lilith said exasperatedly. 'The shots of him in the park with the girls. A bit convenient that the photographer just happened to know he'd be there.'

'You were involved in politics for as long as Ben was. You know how it works. The media, the PR. That's why I do what I do for Bodie. We've got to play their game.'

'I'm done playing games, Aaron. I'm sorry.' Lilith sighed. 'I'm sure you and Insley can find enough dirt on Ben without me.'

'Just because you want to sit this one out doesn't mean they will not drag you onto the stage. That article this morning? That was their first move. They're gearing up for an election. They know they need the female vote. They know they have little to offer women – they have decimated childcare, they've rewound reproductive rights ...'

'Ben helped put those policies in place – how can he possibly help them get the female vote?' Lilith's thunder was getting closer.

'By making women feel more sympathetic towards him. The single dad, juggling a demanding job, raising two cute little girls, left by his wife ... it's a great little story, and he makes the perfect good guy. The hero. And you know what every hero needs? A villain.' He put a hand on her arm. 'And that, Lilith, even if you don't want it, will be you. They will turn a spotlight on you, a bright one to show up all your flaws.'

'I appreciate your concern, but I think you are wrong.' Lilith moved her arm, leaving Aaron's hand dangling in the air. 'Ben wouldn't share a spotlight with anyone. Least of all me, even if it was to show up my flaws. I'm an embarrassment to him. I was even before I left him. He doesn't want me in the papers. He wants me to go away quietly and disappear.' She smiled awkwardly. 'And, for once, we both want the same thing. I'll go get Sibel for you.' She headed up the sturdy creaking staircase. As Aaron watched her, his skin chilled as he thought about how far Ben Hamilton might be prepared to go to make his ex-wife disappear.

Maybe it was this, a premonition of familiarity, a shared fate with her mother, that Insley had seen in Lilith's eyes.

Chapter 15

Aaron went into the kitchen, searching for something to bring some warmth back into his skin. A pot of coffee was on the stove, Bodie's strange percolator thing. It made him remember long nights studying for his university finals when it would appear with a plate of biscuits outside his room. The sound of women's voices floating up the staircase. Insley sitting on the top step, listening, eating a stolen cookie. It was the year she'd shaved her head and dropped out of school. The year of the court case.

He found two cups and poured the viscous liquid, adding two generous spoons of honey from the jar on the counter. The same one that his mother had brought with them when they became the first family to move into the community, along with Bodie and Insley. It had been his grandmother's. The only thing his mother had grabbed, apart from their suitcases, when they ran out of the tiny fibro shack they lived in. Tiptoeing around. His father passed out on the creaking front porch. A potentially deadly game of sleeping lions.

His mother had been Celeste's best friend, the one to summon Bodie from America. She couldn't give Insley a safe place to live. Bodie had to come, or she'd get taken into care. Six months later, she made another call to Bodie, who was now living in Sydney. This time asking if Bodie could give Aaron a safe place to live. Bodie said she could, but only if his mum came too. She had room for both of them in the army barracks she was leasing and was turning into a shelter for "battered wives". That's what people like his mum used to be called.

He noticed there was a game of chess set up on the dining table. It was the same battered old set he and Insley used to play on when they were kids. The one with a missing queen. The pottery woman who had lived there briefly had made a crappy replacement. It was ugly as hell and barely fit on the square. Insley had always made Aaron use it. She told him it was good luck. He never remembered winning against Insley, though. In anything.

As he carried the coffee through to the lounge room, he noticed an unfamiliar scent. It was floral and rich, heavy. But it wasn't the patchouli and lavender that was usually there. It felt manufactured. Modern. Seductive.

A woman was sitting with her legs up on the sofa, rhythmically tapping a pen on a pad. She was singing gently under her breath. Aaron could just make out the black snake of earphone cord underneath her unnaturally perfectly streaked blond hair.

Aaron slowly came into her line of sight, so he didn't startle her. Women were often jumpy at the community, especially when a man appeared out of nowhere. He shouldn't have bothered. Her head lifted confidently, and she smiled. It was Kay Conway. Kathleen's chief of staff.

'Oh, hi!' Her voice was bright and perfect, like her smile and her streaks. She took the earphones out. 'It's Aaron, right?'

'That's me!' he became self-conscious of how he must look. Did he have sweat marks on his shirt? He couldn't even straighten his hair with two hot cups of coffee in his hands. The steam was tickling the whiskers on his chin, and he could feel condensation forming on his lip. 'And you are Kay. We didn't really get a chance to talk at the meeting.'

'Just as well. I don't think Insley likes it when I talk to her friends.' Kay smiled. 'Is she with you now?'

'Ah, no. I'm on day release today.' He was always surprised when everyone assumed he and Insley were joined at the hip. 'Here, would you like a coffee? I'd made it for someone else, but she hasn't appeared yet.'

'Oh, that would be great, thanks. Although I don't think this qualifies as coffee. I'm used to having a latte from the café near my apartment.' Kay took the cup and politely sipped.

'Still adjusting to community life then?'

'Yeah, it's a bit different. I haven't shared a kitchen with anyone since university. And some of the conversations, or therapy sessions, or whatever ...' Kay rolled her eyes. 'It's a little intense.'

'Not surprising, really, when you know why they are here,' Aaron said patiently, taking a seat next to her on the sofa where her feet had been moments before.

'Oh, of course. It's terrible.' Kay shook her head. 'But does talking about it help, really? I mean, isn't it enough to just be out of danger?'

'Well, actually, no. When women get here, they are broken. The community, the place, is really just a space. It's the care they get that puts them back together again. The support groups, the medical interventions, the retraining, all that.' He sipped his coffee. She was staring at him. He tried to subtly wipe his moustache to make sure there was no coffee left behind.

'You really are impressive, Aaron Quinn.' Kay gave him a nudge.

He tried not to blush. Insley would be furious with him right now.

'I don't know about impressive. I mean, I believe in all of this' – Aaron waved his hand in the air – 'everything Queentide does. Why shouldn't women be treated equally? Why shouldn't we have a gender-balanced parliament? It just seems obvious to me.'

'I didn't mean the work you do for Queentide.' Kay grinned bashfully. 'I mean as a writer. A journalist. I'm a big fan.'

'You are?' Aaron tried unsuccessfully to play it cool. 'I didn't know you even knew who I was.'

'Of course, I know, silly boy,' Kay replied. 'I've worked in Canberra nearly as long as you.'

'I'm surprised we haven't crossed paths,' Aaron said.

'Me too.' She put a hand on his knee. 'A little disappointed even.'

Aaron's polyester shirt felt itchy again, his skin elevating just a few degrees too many. He could almost hear Insley delivering a lecture right into his ear, like some shaven-headed Jiminy Cricket. He decided to change the subject.

'So, have you made any friends with the other residents?'

'Not really. I think the women here see me as a bit of an outsider. I think they can tell I'm not, you know, like them.' She twisted her lips. 'I'm trying to stay out of everyone's way. I venture down when I know they'll be in the garden or exercising the children or whatever it is they do. I got chatting to Lilith Green the other night, though.'

'Oh, really?' Aaron was surprised.

'She doesn't seem to want to help Queentide out, does she?' Kay lowered her voice. 'What she must know about Ben – it would be very helpful for that to make it into the media.'

'Sure. We've already gathered a fair bit on Mr Henderson, but it's all unsubstantiated. Now, if his ex-wife were to speak up well ...' He paused. 'But I think she's scared of the consequences.'

'She told me she took a whole load of stuff when she left. Emails, cabinet documents.' Kay leaned in, whispering. Her perfume was making Aaron feel dizzy. 'Stuff that could end a political career.'

'That's surprising.' He was confused. 'That she thought to take that kind of stuff. From what Bodie said, she had very little with her when she moved into the community.'

'It's even more surprising that she hasn't used it. Ben is playing hardball over custody. Why doesn't she just threaten to release all of this stuff if he doesn't play fair? That's what I would do. If she's so desperate to protect her girls, and she's saying that's the reason she won't help you guys out, why doesn't Lilith use what she's got?' Kay wondered.

'So you don't trust her?' Aaron asked.

'Do you?' Kay asked in return.

They both jumped apart as voices drifted towards them from the corridor. Sibel Polat appeared, with Lilith Green next to her. Sibel held her chin high, defiantly. As if she were waiting to be challenged. Her hair was pulled back into a glossy ponytail, lightening streaks sparkling in the sun streaming through the window. She wore a sleeveless top, no attempt made to hide the scars that ran down her arms, covered her hands. Lilith Green stood awkwardly, holding her arms around herself. She kept looking towards the door, but she smiled warmly when she saw Kay. Kay gave her a small smile.

'Aaron, I've been looking forward to meeting you. Bodie has told me much about you.'

'Likewise. I made you a coffee, but ...' Aaron looked towards Kay.

'I'm sorry. Aaron gave it to me. I'll gladly go and get you another.' Kay's voice slipped over Aaron like silk, but it seemed to catch all over Sibel Polat.

'No, thank you,' Sibel replied. 'I think it's best that Mr Quinn and I just get on with our business. It was nice to meet you, Ms ...?'

'Conway,' she replied, 'Kay Conway.'

'Ah, yes.' Sibel thought for a while. 'Kathleen's EA, correct?'

'Chief of staff,' Kay responded. Her smile had melted away.

'I am sorry, my mistake,' Sibel said. 'I hope I didn't offend you.'

'Not at all.' Kay had reassembled her smile but had forgotten the sincerity. 'If you'll excuse me. I have some work to be getting on with. Actually, Lilith, do you think you could help me?'

Lilith unfolded her arms, and she was nodding, but Sibel interrupted.

'Actually, I'd like Ms Green to sit in for our interview, Aaron. And take notes. If you don't mind, Lilith? Bodie tells me you are an excellent scribe.'

Lilith looked at Kay, then nodded at Sibel. Kay shrugged her shoulders and left the room slowly.

'I prefer another person with me when I speak to journalists. And an independent record of what was said. I hope you can understand that.' Sibel spoke deliberately.

'Of course. I mean, you have nothing to fear from me. I'm sure Bodie has explained my position, what I do for Queentide. That this article, like the last one, is being produced to help you stay here.'

'She has. But old habits die hard. Now I think coffee for Ms Green and myself might be in order ...'

'I can get it. I need to grab a notebook and pen anyway.' Lilith was in the kitchen before Aaron could even respond.

Aaron got himself organised. Flicked to the questions he'd already scribbled in his notebook. Tested the mic on his phone a few times before Lilith emerged with three mugs and placed one silently next to his notebook. She sat in an armchair that matched one that Sibel had chosen, the rose pattern faded, pink petals tinged with sepia from years in the sun. He recapped the last interview that he'd done at the writer's festival.

She was a writer and had been arrested and punished many times for just writing stories. Children's stories where the hero was a girl. But then she became a hero herself, saving a woman who had dared to go to a book signing and buy a book. She'd left the store and been set upon by a group of men who were trying to tear the book out of her hands. Sibel put herself in the middle of the ruckus and began swinging a pole at the men to make them stop. They ran away. The bookstore owner told Sibel to get out. And take her daughter, too. It wouldn't be safe for either of them. They hadn't been back since. Bouncing from country to country, landing in Australia. Bodie somehow got a visa, with Janet De Marco's help, for her to attend the writer's festival. Her visa, and her daughter's, had run out a few weeks ago. She was in the country illegally. News had come through last week that her husband had been killed. This was where Aaron stopped talking and waited.

'He was dead as soon as I lifted that pole.'

'Do you regret it now? Was it worth losing your husband? Your country?' These were on his list of potential questions, but he hadn't planned on diving straight into it.

'As you said, I have a daughter. It was her I thought of when I lifted that pole. Not me or my husband. I thought of her and the world she was going to grow up in. A world where she couldn't write a book. Read a book. Buy a book. Where a woman was strong, a hero. How could I let that be? How could I let her grow up thinking women couldn't be heroes? We are all heroes, at least once in our lives.' She turned and looked at Lilith, who was furiously taking down notes. 'Lilith, you have daughters. You understand. At that moment, I would have killed those men if I thought it would make the world better for my child.'

Aaron looked over at Lilith Green. She had stopped writing. Her jaw was clenched.

'I don't think we are the same people, Sibel. I'm not as brave as you. I'm no hero.'

'If we could get back to the interview,...' Aaron gently pleaded.

'I am sure you have done brave things for your girls.'

'I haven't fought for anything,' Lilith replied. 'I haven't changed anything.'

'I picked up a pole one day,' Sibel said. 'You picked it up every day for years. From what you have told me, you fought for hope, for safety. And you've changed your entire world and made it better for your children. They see now that life can be better. You have switched a light on for them, just as I switched one on for my child.'

The light was casting a halo behind Lilith's head, putting her features in the shade. He couldn't see her expression, but he saw her wipe at her eyes with her sleeve. Sibel got up and put her hands on Lilith's shoulders, then kissed her head. She re-took her seat.

'If Lilith is ready, shall we continue, Aaron?' Sibel looked at Lilith, who nodded and then fixed her gaze on Aaron.

The rest of the interview fell into a more familiar rhythm. Sibel recounting what awaited her in Turkey, Aaron prodding, but not too hard at the tender spots, the bits he knew would give way to the universal blood that flowed through a Sydney accountant's veins, as well as a Turkish refugee. For people to help, they had to know that if they were cut, they would bleed the same way. They would feel the same pain. Aaron had learned that the idea of losing a loved one, particularly a child or partner, was the quickest way to make it flow.

He pressed a little harder when he asked Sibel about her husband until the room was filled with her distress, but she did not cry. She was a witness giving testimony. She wanted to be understood. She wanted her words to matter. He asked how her daughter was doing, in a strange country, with no friends, no family or school. He asked how long it had been since Sibel had seen her parents and how it felt knowing she would never see them again. This was calculated too. Since the pandemic, the older generation had regained their revered status. Time spent with them was now seen as valuable – a resource that no one deserved to be deprived of. When he had wrung her out, he asked Sibel to move towards the window so he could take her photo. He moved Bodie's weird framed card, so it wasn't in the shot.

He positioned her in a way that the sunlight lit up the pale scars on her arms, traversing her hands, the raised ridges startling in the plain winter light. People needed to feel the lashes, look down and imagine welts appearing on their own hands. Lilith Green watched from her armchair, wincing. When they were done, Sibel placed her evidential hands on his shoulders as she had done with Lilith. They felt like pincers, narrow and firm.

'Thank you for your time, Aaron,' Sibel said. 'I look forward to reading the article.'

'There will be some posts on social media too. Bodie will talk to you about the Facebook group Queentide is setting up, some protests too ...'

'I have told Bodie I will do what I can. Now, if you will excuse me, I believe I am rostered to prepare dinner. Lilith? Thank you too.'

'Would you like the notes I made?' Lilith held out her notebook, her compact script visible.

'If you have the time, could you read it first and then give it to me?'

'I haven't made any mistakes ...'

'I believe that. I just would like you to read the story you have written.'

'I haven't really written a story,' Lilith said. 'They are your words.'

'Not anymore. I have passed those words to you,' Sibel said as she left the room.

Aaron and Lilith were left alone.

'Well, thanks, I guess, Lilith.' Aaron started to pack up.

'Do you want the notes too?' Lilith offered them to Aaron. 'I can make a copy.'

'No, no, that's okay,' Aaron said, trying to be kind. 'I was recording the interview anyway.'

'You must have so many voices now, saved away somewhere,' Lilith said. She must have seen his brow cross because she continued. 'From all the recordings you must have made over the years?'

'Oh, right! I guess I do. I've never really checked, but it would have to be thousands of people now, all stuck in my hard drive.'

'Do you ever go back and listen to them, the recordings?'

'A few, not very often. It makes me uneasy. Like I'm releasing ghosts.' He laughed, but it fell short. It was too accurate to be comical.

'Some things should be left in the past,' she replied. 'I should get going. Kay wanted help with something.'

'She mentioned that you and she had got talking.' Aaron was surprised to see Lilith smile for the first time, the heaviness inside her seeming to lift.

'Yes, it's been hard to make friends here. It's nice having someone like Kay around. Someone I can talk to.'

Aaron tried to make this conversation fit with the one he'd had with Kay. They were friends? That wasn't the picture he was seeing emerge, but there were still too many pieces missing to know what he was looking at.

'I'm glad, Lilith.' He gathered up his things and slung his satchel over his shoulder. He was about to leave but then turned back to face her, stroking his beard, something he did when he was trying to arrange his thoughts. 'Look, I hear a lot of things in my job. I get tip-offs that sort of thing ...'

She was looking at him quizzically.

'I don't just want to help Queentide. I want to help you. If I find out something that you need to know, I'm going to tell you.

I promise. I want you to be safe. Above everything else.'

'Thank you, Aaron. But, like I said, I really don't think Ben is a danger to me.'

Aaron hadn't been thinking of Ben but, before he could elaborate, Lilith had picked up the cups and gone to the kitchen. The interview was over. Time to leave.

He had intended to walk down the hill towards the ferry wharf, but he found himself ordering an Uber before he'd even reached the gate. As he slipped into the back seat, with its plastic protectors, the driver turned up the radio. They were talking about that woman in Melbourne. Monica. The one who went missing. The husband had vanished now. And the police were calling him a person of interest. Of course he was. Aaron shook his head. It didn't take the journos long to find out she'd told friends she was leaving months ago. Or that there were dozens of police call-outs to their house. But they didn't report that because they'd already cast the husband as the right guy. Aaron couldn't get his article placed, and he wasn't gaining traction on social media either. Except with MASC members, who called him a traitor for stirring up anti-male sentiment with his alternative facts. Wankers.

He put his earphones in and started to listen to the recording of Sibel's interview.

He pulled out his laptop and started typing. He might have it finished before he even got home to the other side of Sydney. He could submit it before dinner. He typed and retyped the first sentence. He watched the cursor blink on his screen, then paused the recording. He couldn't focus. The mismatched conversations he'd had with Kay and Lilith were niggling him. Sadly, he knew why.

He didn't trust Kay.

He pulled out his phone to call Insley. Surely she must have looked into Kathleen's new chief of staff. But before he had a chance to dial, his phone rang. It was a number he didn't recognise.

'Hello? Oh, Kay ... yeah, actually, you have no idea how much of a surprise this is. Sure it would be great to talk about the campaign ... tonight? Well, I've already left, actually. I'm in a car on the way home ... Ultimo. The non-trendy end ... yeah, there are some great restaurants, that's true. I like Bonito's too ... dinner? Well, sure, I mean, I've got no plans ... Okay, see you there in an hour. Bye.'

Aaron looked down at his phone, then smelt his shirt. He had just enough time to have a shower and get to the restaurant. No time to call Insley now – later. After dinner. Maybe.

Chapter 16

The question was about First Nations healthcare. It came after the discussion on compulsory post-pandemic annual testing. Kathleen knew the question was coming from a young man in the audience called Jeremy. Kay had told her to expect it and be prepared. At least that's what she said. What she meant was 'be better than the male MPs on the panel. And the white female scientist'. Don't make any mispronunciations like them. Don't stumble over your figures like they sometimes do. Don't forget to sound fair to everyone, even though they aren't. Sound strong, but not aggressive. Feminine, but not girly. Quiet, but not timid. Be perfect.

When Kathleen went for preselection, they had run a rake over her past to see what it turned up. An Aboriginal woman was a risk. Someone who may not take root with enough voters. They had to know if the earth surrounding her was good enough to give her a chance to grow on the reluctant voters. Best they checked before the other party did. They were incredulous when they found no weeds that would have to be burned.

Kathleen had worked three jobs to put herself through university. Got Honours in Law and Planning to help her mob. She'd had a big extended family but kept a close circle of friends at university and never went out partying. So the only photos and videos of her they could find online were when she had volunteered at the homeless shelter and when she had sung 'Happy

Birthday' to her six-year-old niece.

What they hadn't realised was that Kathleen had spent her life cultivating the land around her, removing any vines before they had a chance to grow and choke her. She wanted to be the prime minister. As simple and as complicated as that. She had been a teenager when Gillard had given her misogyny speech to parliament, and when she'd watched it, she understood that being good would never be enough. She would have to be perfect. She would give them, the party, the electorate, no other reasons to attack her. If they rejected her, it would only be for her gender, her sexual orientation, her skin colour. Their prejudice. Their flaws. Not hers.

And she would point that out to them. Loudly. It's not me. It's you.

She told the selection committee she was gay. They told her to keep it quiet; she did. That was a mistake. The only one she'd ever made. She swore from that point on that no one else would ever edit her story.

So here she was, a gay Aboriginal woman. Kathleen Rae, leader of the opposition. Being faultless to make up for others' flaws. She was so tired of it.

The host asked Jeremy from the studio audience for his question. The young, slightly hipster man, a typical member of the audience, asked his question. 'How can the government's new policy on First Nations healthcare not amount to forced removals?' Kathleen could give a two-word answer – it can't – but instead, she had to position her party's policy. She had to state the obvious. Kathleen had to expose this new policy for the cruel and ill-conceived disaster it was. She almost launched straight into it, thinking about how to make it sound not practised but perfect. Then she realised, just in time, that the question had gone to another person on the panel. The political cartoonist, Tazza. He looked surprised. Kathleen was aware her mouth was as wide open as his, and she closed it.

He babbled about the Stolen Generations. At least he was sort of on the right track. Then he scanned the faces of the panel – she could almost hear him ask himself if it was okay to ask Kathleen her opinion. *Would that make me racist for assuming she'd have the answers?* She caught his eye, nodded encouragingly. Then he was interrupted by Ben Hamilton, the new Minister for Health. The previous one had finally stepped down. No need to apologise for all the sexual assaults Kathleen had lodged complaints about. They didn't even ask him about the accusations before handing him the keys to his new office at the bank with a pretty young secretary sitting inside. She'd been told that he and Ben Hamilton were heard joking that they both wanted to buy Kathleen dinner to thank her. Wankers. Kathleen reminded herself to be careful what she wished for.

Ben Hamilton was polite, of course, on television. Enthusiastic, even. Talking about his shiny new government policy. The millions of dollars for Aboriginal people. Spent on childcare clinics in big towns. It made economic sense to concentrate the services – more people could be seen. Kids got eye tests. Dental. All for free. Yes, there would be some disruption. Yes, children may have to be left in the centre's care or local social services, or even foster families, if their parents had to go back to the remote communities. But, ultimately, it was for their own good.

Kathleen looked towards Kay, who was furiously shaking her head, like a dog trying to get rid of a fly. Kathleen bit her lip. Waited for the host to turn to her. Surely he'd have to. She was the leader of the opposition. Her family was directly affected by this policy. Surely her opinion was relevant here? Or were things really that fucked up now?

'Okay, thank you, Minister Hamilton. So, moving on to Jackie with a question about electoral boundaries ...'

'Actually,' Kathleen looked over to Kay, whose hand was making its way to her forehead. 'I don't think we've quite finished on that one, Tony.'

'Oh, Ms Rae, you have some comments you'd like to share?'

'In fact, I have some questions for Minister Hamilton. I'd like to hear from the minister what consultation was carried out with the First Nations community before this policy decision was made. Have you thought about the logistical difficulties of families flying, or driving, into Darwin just for eye tests and dental appointments?'

'Well, if it were my children, and I can only speak for myself as a single dad, I would move heaven and earth for my girls. I'd move closer to a place with accessible healthcare, state-of-the-art equipment.'

A smattering of applause went up from the audience.

'With all due respect, Minister, your opinion as a middle-class white dad from Sydney, with shared custody of his children, has very little to do with a debate about *First Nations* communities, not just *Aboriginal* communities for the record Ben, and their right to remain on country. At least include all the families being ripped apart by this terrible policy.'

Another round of applause, this time, a little more enthusiastic.

'I don't think there is a debate, Kathleen. We are supporting Aboriginal communities,' he subtly emphasised the word she'd corrected, and was that a wink she saw? 'We aren't forcing them to move into well-equipped towns. I'm simply saying that most parents would want the best for their children. But, given your lifestyle choices, I don't suppose you know much about that.'

'Well, we might go to another question. I think we have a question from Greg via Twitter about the new offshore drilling ...' The host looked towards Kathleen, who avoided his gaze.

'So because I'm gay, I can't understand what it's like for a First Nations mother or father to raise a child? But you can?'

'I was referring to all parents. Not just Aboriginal parents. Look, if you are going to start playing the race card ...'

'We might just move on, folks ...' The host was trying to restore order, but Kathleen saw in her peripheral vision that the producer was signalling to let Kathleen continue.

'You want to talk about cards, Ben? Great. Because I've got the royal flush. Here's my First Nations card. Let's start there. I am a proud Kaurna woman from the Adelaide Plains. I know what it is like to walk in this country, where my people began and made to feel that I do not belong. I know what it is like to have different skin from most people on the street, even though my heritage on this land stretches back thousands of years. I know what it is like to be looked at funny when you walk into a shop. Have people hold their handbags just that little closer when you get on the train. I know what it's like to have people like you tell us you are "caring" for us. We aren't your pets or cattle. Talk to us. Ask us what we need. We can care for ourselves if you'd just bloody let us.'

Kathleen took a sharp breath when she realised what words were forming in her head and that she was damn well going to say them. She purposefully avoided looking at Kay.

'Here's my gender card ... I am female. I know how hard it is to make your way in a world designed and built and maintained by men. I am not "anti-men", as some people assume. Men are valuable. Men, of course, are needed in society. They just aren't more important or more necessary than women. Do I intend to stack my Cabinet with women? Hell yes. I want to make balanced decisions. A room full of men can never understand the impact of their decisions on women.

'Here's my LGBTI card. I am gay. I can't change it. I don't want to change it. And who I am attracted to or fall in love with is none of your goddamn business. As long as I treat them well. Being gay doesn't mean I don't understand what it's like to care about family. It means I know what it's like to try to get a job to support them and be turned down on religious grounds because the business owner is Catholic and thinks you are a sinner and going straight to hell.'

Kathleen was gathering up speed, like a train hurtling down the tracks. And she was focussed on running right over Ben Hamilton.

'Here's my working-class card. I grew up with two parents who'd come home exhausted every night from working fifteen-hour days, who still worried about having enough money for food and electricity. It wasn't just their hard work that got me to university. It was also bloody good luck. Something finally going my way. A scholarship that just happened to be taking applications that year. Not everyone gets the chance that I did. My sister didn't. Even if they deserve it. Even if they work hard.

'This "fair go" your lot keep going on about? It only exists for people who can get up onto the platform in the first place. If we don't put a ladder down the side for those who are still trying to get up, they won't make it. They'll get hit by the train. There are too many people on that platform who are too scared to put the ladder back down in case there's not enough space for everyone, and they'll get pushed off the edge. If we help them up, they might just be able to help us build a bigger platform so everyone can fit on. That would be a fair go.

'And here is my human card … And I can't be blunter on this one than I'm going to be right now. It is inhumane to separate children from loving parents. It is inhumane to allow a computer to decide if a person needs benefits or not. It is inhumane to keep people in offshore detention for a decade, not allowed to enter Australia, not allowed to go anywhere else.

'It is inhumane to treat people differently, according to whatever cards life has dealt them. I understand the people of this country, the ones who aren't white, or aren't male, or aren't straight or aren't rich – the majority of people – because we're playing with one card less than everyone else. We know the game is stacked against us, and we know our opponent is someone like you.

'Now, Minister, let's see what hand you are holding.'

A wave of claps echoed into the black space of the studio, beyond the cameras and bright lights. Kathleen felt drained, exhausted. She couldn't remember what she had said, and that left her feeling exposed. She very rarely said anything in public that hadn't been practised to perfection. To make sure the words were the right words. The tone, the right tone. To make sure it was perfect. What she had just said was her unfiltered view. Her anger finally allowed out to play after so long in confinement. She wasn't sure she'd ever been able to persuade it to come back in again. She looked over towards Kay. Her anger was clearly out dancing too, but to a very different beat from Kathleen.

Ben, at the other end of the semicircle table, was sitting back, grimacing. He had screwed up the piece of paper in front of him, and his pen looked broken. She had got under that watertight skin of his. He didn't know how to react. He was wavering between anger and frustration, that place of inertia where no move seems like the smart move. Good. He could squirm there forever as far as Kathleen was concerned.

The host saved him by calling for some quiet, then invited Tazza to reveal the cartoon he'd been working on. It flashed up on a big screen behind the panel, exaggerating even further the caricature of Kathleen, a borderline racist profile of her features. Cartoon Kath was flicking a full deck of cards in a distorted Ben's face while he sat crying crocodiles into his empty hands.

The audience cheered. Ben quickly pulled off his microphone and walked out of the studio, but not before the camera operator followed the director's instructions and trained the camera on him. Kathleen wondered how much trouble the ABC would get into for that. The PM would be furious that his golden boy was caught on film being less than perfect. He'd probably try to accelerate the bill to sell the national broadcaster off before the election. Kathleen would have to fight that one hard. Australia would lose its last independent news channel.

She was already working on what strategies to use as she made her way off the stage into the blackness, where Kay's voice barked at her.

'How could you fucking do that, Kathleen?' The crew packing up around them turned and seemed amused to find the voice belonging to a tall, stilettoed blond. 'We've worked so hard to make you likeable.' Kathleen had hoped Kay would have clicked her heels in a storm of rage and disappeared. No such luck.

Kathleen was out of patience today. And Kay was the last person she felt like explaining herself to. Or being polite to. Kay wasn't her pick. It wasn't who Kathleen wanted as her chief of staff. Kathleen wanted the young bloke from Redfern. The one who went on the LGBTQI+ march with her. Bodie had ended up employing him to help Insley organise the Million March they had coming up. He'd do a good job. She was glad in a way that he'd be doing something more useful, but she wasn't happy she was stuck with this woman. Kay had been forced on Kathleen by the party, or at least someone in the party.

'And what I just said will make me less likeable? Describing myself, speaking my mind, makes me less likeable?'

'Yes, it does. To voters who don't want a woman. Who don't want an Aboriginal prime minister.' Kay's vowels were becoming elongated, her words stretching out and sagging just a little in the middle. She had a habit of forgetting to hide her west-Sydney accent when she got angry. It wasn't as easy to hide as the ginger hair she covered with dye or the freckles she covered with makeup – Kathleen had spent a lot of time on the road with

Kay, enough time to see her unpainted and between trips to the salon to hide her roots.

'So if I'd stayed silent, they might not have noticed my breasts or skin?' Kathleen let out an exasperated laugh. Kay didn't even smile.

'I wish we lived in a world where gender or race didn't matter in an election, but we don't. They do matter.' She said it with a straight face, causing Kathleen's face to twist.

'Are you seriously going to lecture me about racism and gender inequality?' Kathleen was incredulous. 'You are right, Kay. They do matter. Not just in elections. You think I haven't noticed that, growing up as an Aboriginal woman in this country? Maybe the reason things haven't changed, the reason things have got worse recently, is that some people have been pretending they don't.' Kathleen ignored Kay's eye-rolling, the same eye-rolling she got whenever she talked about Queentide. Or feminism. Or gender equality. Kay Conway was a successful woman. Her gender hadn't ever held her back. In fact, it had helped her. If the rumours were to be believed, the fact she was a beautiful young woman had helped her career along quite nicely.

Kathleen checked herself. Kay's sex life was none of her business, but her attitude was. That was the problem.

'The fact is I will be a better prime minister because of my gender and my Aboriginality. And I think it's about time we started acknowledging that. If you aren't comfortable with that, then maybe this isn't the campaign for you. I know I wasn't the person you expected to be working for.'

'I didn't take the job because I had to. I took it because I wanted to.' Kay sounded sincere. Kathleen tried not to think about the rumours, the innuendo when she'd been 'advised' by one of the senior party men not to fight Kay's appointment. Kathleen wondered what advice he'd given Kay over the years. Kay's preselection for a local seat had failed a few years back. She'd been told by one of her mentors that a few of the women had reached out to her beforehand, tried to get her to come along to the Women's Electoral Lobby. There was a network of support just waiting to help her. The Labor Party was still working towards its quota. She said she didn't need it, didn't want to be seen as a 'feminist'. She lost to another female candidate. Kay's gender was never the issue. Kathleen wondered how Kay Conway wanted to be seen now. Kathleen looked at the made-up face in front of her. It was flawless, almost like a mask. She was so hard to read. Perhaps Insley was right about her.

'Look, Kay, you are good. I mean it. You've got a knack for politicking. I don't deny it—'

'Then let me do what I'm good at. Please. I know how to get these people to vote for you. I know how they tick.'

'And so do I, Kay, the ones who vote for the Ben Hamiltons of the world or call those awful talkback shows. They will never vote for me or anyone like me. It doesn't matter how perfect my speeches are, how well modelled my economic policy is, how much they will benefit from an intersectional government. They will never vote for me.'

'Kathleen, come on, I think you are being pessimistic. You've got to stay positive.'

'I think you've misunderstood me, Kay. I'm not sad about it.' Kathleen leaned closer to Kay. 'I'll let you in on a little secret – they are the minority. We don't need them.'

'Kathleen, be serious,' Kay responded. 'The polling we have done ...'

'I am serious. Talk to Helen at Queentide. She'll show you the stats if you'd rather put your faith in numbers than in me. The power those people have, the ones who don't like me, they get their power from acting as if they represent the majority of views in this country. So it's not worth fighting because you will never win. They keep the rest of us separated into our own little camps. But if we made it one big camp, brought everyone into the same tent? If we get the female vote, the Black vote, the working-class vote, the gay vote, the vote of all those people who feel marginalised, ignored by this government, we get the majority. It's the same strategy Queentide will use to get their candidates elected. And I'm going to follow the same strategy, Kay, and I want the rest of the Labor candidates to do the same.'

'We will lose seats, Kathleen,' Kay said.

'No, we won't,' Kathleen quickly replied. 'Queentide will put up candidates in every seat too. If we can just draw the votes away from the Liberals, make sure we've got preferences set up, it doesn't really matter if Labor gets the seats or the Women's Party. We end up with a government that will represent the people it works for. All of the people.'

'You can't be closely associated with Queentide. It's a bloody group of activists, Kathleen. How will that look?'

'It will look like I'm supporting a feminist movement.'

'Exactly.'

'That's not a story that's going to sell Kathleen.'

'Well, it's the only one I'm selling Kay,' Kathleen said. 'So I guess the question is, are you as good at your job as you keep telling everyone you are?'

It was unfair, and Kathleen knew it, to ask Kay to sell something she didn't believe in. But she wasn't going to let Kay or anyone else ever edit her story again.

Her mobile buzzed. It was Insley.

'Hey Ins, I'm still in the studio. Can we talk when I get home?'

'You need to stay there for now.'

'What are you on about?'

'There's some stuff come up online, threats. The MASC boys aren't the brightest, but they are fast. There's a crowd of them gathering outside, waiting for you to leave. They're a bit upset about you attacking their poster boy.' She laughed. 'I'm bloody proud of you, though. Look, it's probably them just sounding off, but let's just not take any chances, okay? Is Kay with you?'

'Yeah, she's right ...' Kathleen looked around. 'Shit, she must have left.'

'Okay, I'll call her. I'll try Aaron too. She's probably on the way to his place. It's just around the corner, and those two are pretty much attached at the groin these days.' Insley laughed again.

'God, Insley, that's disgusting.' Kathleen managed a laugh too.

'Tell them that, not me.' Insley's voice had sharp edges to it. Kathleen couldn't tell if it was the thought of MASC protesters or her best friend shagging someone she hated. 'Ask one of the security guards to take you another way out. And ask the producer to get a car for you. You can't get in an Uber. Not tonight.'

'Insley?'

'Yeah?' she said.

'Did I fuck up tonight?' Kathleen closed her eyes. Insley would tell her. 'Did I go too far?'

'No. You went where you needed to go.' Insley's voice was muffled by the sound of a passing car.

'Where are you? I thought you were at home.'

'No,' she said distractedly, 'I'm taking care of something for Bodie. Call me later, yeah? Let me know you got back okay.'

Before Kathleen could tell her she loved her, Insley had hung up. She wouldn't have said it back anyway. Insley I-love-yous came as warnings about MASC, unexpected cups of tea in bed, and loyalty that was so fierce it almost burned you. You didn't hear her love. You felt it.

Kathleen started walking down the corridor with its threadbare carpet and age-creamed walls. It reminded her of her aunty's front room, cosy in its slumped overtiredness. She heard voices coming from one of the side rooms and recognised Steven's laugh, the kind producer who'd given her a platform when no one else wanted to hear a junior politician complain about sexual harassment. As she came into the room, she saw he was perched on the desk, sharing a thermos of tea with a security guard. After relying on Insley's message, the security guard left her with Steven to check the front of the building. She sipped the tea Steven had poured into a champagne flute, the only other drinking vessel in Steven's office.

'You are using the right glass there, my love. You should be celebrating.' Steven raised his thermos lid towards her and winked.

'Celebrating that there's a bunch of men's rights activists outside eating to beat me up?' Kathleen raised her glass.

Steven had his pointed brogues resting on the swivel chair below him. He swayed it back and forth.

'If they are outside, less than an hour after we broadcast, then Ben Hamilton must think you are a threat.' He tapped his toes together.

'Oh, I'm more than a threat. I'm a promise,' Kathleen said.

'I'll drink to that. Cheers,' Steven said. 'You know Bodie Hugues, right? The Queentide woman?'

'Yes, I do. But I'm surprised you do.' Kathleen felt her guard go up. He was a nice guy, but he was still the media.

'She's becoming quite the underground celebrity, is old Bodie. I'm involved in a few activist groups. I don't tell many people. You know, you can't have political views, or any views actually, when you work for the national broadcaster.' He rolled his eyes. 'Anyway, she's been coming to a few of our meetings.'

'Yes, I know. Bodie is forming a coalition of the pissed-off.'

'Indeed she is.' He paused. 'It's going to work, you know. Her plan.' He nodded at Kathleen. 'It's going to work because they think we are still drinking the Kool-Aid. They don't realise an old woman has whispered to us all that it's poison.' He swigged down the last of his tea just as the security guard came back in. She couldn't walk out the front. There was quite a crowd. More than the guard could control on his own. He'd called the police, but they might be a while. A car was waiting in the basement.

She thanked Steven for the tea. He raised a solidarity fist.

The car had tinted windows, sapping the colour from the placards that the shouting men were holding. The tint couldn't turn down the violence, though. There was Kathleen's head, beneath it two hands clearly around her throat, and beneath that a lifeless rag doll body. "Here's our hand Kathleen", scraped into every placard.

Fists appeared on the windscreen, banging the glass, startling Kathleen, sending an unfamiliar tremor through her hands. She was scared. Irrational thoughts entered her mind. The driver, who had been silent, made some noises under his breath, then revved the car. Driving it forward. The men scattered like rats. The driver drove forward fast, catching a few of the stragglers off-guard, some of them falling on their backsides as they scrambled.

Kathleen let out a small laugh; the driver took this as a cue to speak.

'I'm sorry, Ms Rae. You shouldn't have to put up with that. You know we aren't all like that. Men, I mean. We don't all think like that.'

'I know. Some of my best friends are men ...' She wasn't sure if he realised it was a joke, but he laughed.

'I've got two girls. A wife. A mother. How can I stand by and let any woman be treated like that? You know?'

Kathleen smiled. 'I don't just know. I'm counting on it.' She looked out of the window. She hoped Kay was okay. How had she got through that crowd?

The driver put the radio on. The ten o'clock news was just starting. Kathleen thought about asking the driver to turn it off, but then she heard Sibel Polat's name.

'... Sibel Polat, the Turkish feminist writer, has tonight been taken into custody after an anonymous tip-off to Border Control. Ms Polat, who had overstayed a visitor's visa, was found to have been staying at a women's shelter run by prominent activist Bodie Hughes, who is also now being questioned by federal police. Ms Polat's teenage daughter, who is also believed to have been staying at the shelter, has not been located.'

'Can you turn around, please? Towards Ultimo? I'm going to drop in and see a friend.' Aaron would know what was going on with Sibel and, if Kay was there, all the better. They could work out how Kathleen should respond and get something ready for the journalists who would be calling very soon.

As the car swung around, Kathleen thought she saw her. But it was better if she told herself she hadn't. Better to believe that it wasn't the woman whose frame and gestures Kathleen couldn't mistake, even in the dark. Best to keep playing along and pretend that she didn't know what Insley was up to. At least for now.

Chapter 17

In her holding cell at Manly police station, Bodie recalled the king tide that had engulfed the nearby beaches over a decade ago. She had taken Insley with her – she still had hoped back then that time in nature would calm the storm in her granddaughter. It only added to her intensity when Insley understood humans had caused so much destruction.

They had gone to Collaroy, the epicentre of the storm. A low-lying suburb where houses had been arrogantly built right on the beach in the 1970s. The houses were now in the king-tide's path.

The authorities had known it was coming. Warned the residents in plenty of time. After all, king tides don't rush in. They gradually surge. There are signs of the tide's imminent arrival if you choose to see them. You have time to get to safety and let it run its course. But some people will try to deny reality, even when it is drowning them.

Bodie and Insley had stood on the hill with the residents as the tide insisted on coming ashore, overwhelming the beach, drowning roses in oceanfront gardens and eventually easing its way into houses.

The water level stayed high for days, eventually leaving, like a party guest overstaying their welcome and leaving behind a house full of mess and disruption. This unwelcome guest also stole some things when it went. Some of the shoreline. A few of the buildings. It washed the coast clean and gave everyone a new landline to navigate and a new appreciation of the power of the ocean.

Not all the residents were on the hill with Bodie and Insley that day. Some were down below, denying the king tide's promise. They put up sandbags, moved furniture and valuables to a higher level. They did everything they could to protect their coastal dream. The one built on sand, where they knew, in their heart, it didn't really belong. They covered their pool, the one built over the ocean, an insult to nature, asserting, as they did, that chlorine and tiles were better than what she had provided them for free. They had played God. And now some, those who were that way inclined, prayed to one.

Bodie recalled a man with a bucket in his hand. A pathetically heroic defence against a giant. He had yelled at it to go away. He looked shocked, genuinely shocked, when it didn't listen, and instead kept coming until it covered his frangipani trees and reached his front door. Bodie had found it comical, laughed even as he held up his useless bucket, finally finding a match for his loud yells and anger in the ocean's roar. He eventually ran down the side of his house, where he was met with pats on the back. Because the man had gone down fighting. Because he had given it a bloody good go. Because that's what blokes do, that's what had been expected of him. To fight it. No matter how pointless it was.

☿

Bodie thought about the man and his bucket as she pondered who had tipped off the police. Who was so scared that they'd grabbed their bucket and started yelling at the tide to turn back? Whoever they were, they had achieved nothing. Queentide would continue to surge forward.

Janet De Marco would have Bodie out in no time. Hell, Janet already had some strategies developed to oppose Sibel's deportation. They were prepared for this. They knew there would be sandbags to overcome. Bodie did not expect them so early, however. Aaron's article hadn't been published yet. Aaron had been knocked back by his editor twice. Wanting more revisions and fact-checking. So Queentide had held back its storm. And Bodie had hidden Sibel and her daughter in the community. To wait for hell to break loose.

Sibel was having a cup of tea with Bodie when the authorities arrived. Bodie didn't know where Sibel's daughter was. And that's what she told them. They took Sibel and Bodie and then swept through the rest of the house like a swarm of locusts. The women and children had been so scared. Men. Loud, clumsy men. Knocking things over. Demanding answers. In a space, the women had been assured was safe from reminders. Safe from trauma. It was as if a grenade had gone off. The women and children scattered in all directions. Bodie didn't know who to try to save, who to run after. She didn't get a choice. She was hauled up from her chair and led out of the door.

The last face she saw was Lilith's, who was on the middle step, the one that creaked. Clutching the railing. She was silent, perhaps taking it all in. Maybe scared out of her head. It was hard to tell. Before Bodie was out of the door, she saw Lilith run up the stairs, taking two at a time. An officer was directed to follow her.

It had been a long time since she'd been in a police cell. The steel seats felt colder against her thinning skin than they used to. Back then, of course, she wasn't alone. There would be around fifty of them, all taken downtown together. They would sing and chant. Discuss the protest, which police officer seemed the most sympathetic. There was always one. Usually the youngest or oldest. The ones with less to prove or little to lose. They would slip them hot drinks through the bars. Bread rolls. There were always good men, if you let yourself look for them. Some of the women wouldn't let themselves look.

And that was a choice Bodie respected. After all, if someone had lost a limb to a shark, no one would question their fear of the ocean. No one would say 'but not all sharks …' Their fear would be respected. So that's what Bodie gave them.

Bodie's daughter had only been locked up with her once when she was in her teens. Celeste had joined her, reluctantly, on a march to Washington. A few hours in a cell made damn sure it would never happen again. Celeste had been afraid. She worried about her permanent record. Concerned it would ruin her future, despite Bodie's assurances that it would not, that this was her right as a citizen. Instead, she had politely always been busy when there was a protest on. Had college applications to do, then job applications, then internships halfway across the world. She had called Bodie every day at first, then not so often as the years went by. Bodie had assumed Celeste's life on the other side of the world had just got happily busier. With work, friends and parties. Then a boyfriend and a surprise baby.

Celeste still asked her mother if she was okay, not getting arrested too many times. Bodie would assure her she was in no danger. It never occurred to ask her daughter the same question. She was too smart, too cautious about being anywhere there was danger. Bodie never suspected a thing.

'Ms Hughes' – the young voice, prematurely heavy with authority, startled her – 'you have a visitor.'

'If it's the Feds, tell them they are too late. I'm an old lady, and I've already forgotten who Sibel Polat is.'

'It's not the federal police, Ms Hughes – I doubt we will see them again this evening. It's your lawyer.' He pulled the retractable cord on his belt, fanning out the keys. 'Come with me.'

'That's a lot of keys you have there. It must be difficult to keep track of which one you need,' Bodie said.

'Nah, only one of them works. The rest are just to make a nice sound when we walk. Let people know we're coming,' he said with a wink. 'I'll get you ladies a nice cup of tea.' Bodie put her hands on her knees and sighed as she pulled herself up. There were always good men, and Bodie always looked for them.

They walked into the windowless room, and there was Janet De Marco, looking pristine. A remarkable feat at one in the morning.

'Oh my god, Bodie. Are you okay?' Janet's arms were already around Bodie before she had shuffled into the room. 'You look terrible.'

'I always look terrible.' She moved out of Janet's embrace. Bodie didn't want her friend to see how much this had taken out of her. Her chest was tight. She needed to lie down, hopefully soon. 'How did you get here so quickly?'

'Lilith called me as soon as the police left. She's here. She's waiting outside. They wouldn't let her in to see you, but she insisted on staying.'

'What is she doing out there?'

'From what I can tell? Working the phone. She's trying to find out where Sibel has been taken. She's working through your contacts. She's found some people in the refugee network who might know. I've told her when we know that, we can start working out our next move. I've got a human rights lawyer onto it. She's from Melbourne. She's the best. She got that Sri Lankan family home last year.'

'Here.' Janet slipped Bodie a bar of expensive chocolate across the table. 'The young officer out there said it was fine. It will go well with the dishwater he's bringing in.'

'Where is Sibel's daughter?'

'Honestly? I don't know. I asked Lilith. Lilith won't say. Just that she is safe. I'd rather not know. It makes it easier to defend you both.'

'Both?'

'You and Lilith.'

'Lilith? But she hasn't done anything.'

'Nothing that they know about. Yet. But Lilith is hiding an illegal immigrant from authorities.'

'Jesus.'

'She would lose the custody case. No question.'

'Tell her to stop. She can't risk the children going to that man.'

'She's aware of the consequences, Bodie. This is her decision.' Janet leaned over and snapped off a square of the chocolate. 'You wanted her to fight – well, she's fighting.'

'I wanted her to fight Ben. I wanted her to fight for a better life for those two girls.' Bodie bit into the square of chocolate that had started melting in her hands.

Janet smiled and reached over the table. To Bodie's surprise, she ignored the sticky fingers and held her old friend's hand and almost whispered, 'Isn't that exactly what she's doing?'

Chapter 18

Before Lilith's father had left, he had taught her to play chess. They would play in the garden – the smell of roses became entwined with her father's cologne whenever she tried to remember him. Lilith had been quiet but competitive as a child. Chess, played in a silent and private arena, suited her, but, early on, it had frustrated her. She couldn't ever seem to beat her father. He always outmanoeuvred her before she could get her king even a few squares across the board. One late summer afternoon, with her father's checkmate ringing in her ears, she had angrily hit the board, sending the pieces tumbling to the grass below.

Her father dug the queen out of the blades, cleaned it and gently placed it in Lilith's hand, closing her finger around the small bumps of its crown, its black base digging into the bottom of her hand.

'You are looking for power in the wrong place,' he said. 'It is the queen who will win you the game. She can move wherever and however she wants, except for the knight's move, of course. She is unpredictable. She is a game-changer. If she is lost, the game is lost.' He squeezed his hand over hers, the bumps pressing further into her skin. 'Protect her.' A few months later, he was gone.

It was risky, organising this from the police station. It was risky organising this at all. But Lilith had to protect Sibel. She had promised her that her daughter, Akara, would be safe.

She looked down the list of names she had made. Janet De Marco had assumed she was using Bodie's contacts. But these were Lilith's contacts. The other politicians' wives. She had no idea if they would even talk to her, let alone help. Their husbands were friends with Ben. But most of the wives weren't friends with their husbands. And that's what Lilith was banking on.

She looked down the list carefully. The first one, the one Lilith would call, was critical. It needed to be a woman the others respected or feared. One they would follow.

Desdemona Matthews. She had once made an impromptu dessert in Lilith's kitchen out of coffee, whipped cream and sponge fingers after Ben had thrown Lilith's trifle against a wall at one of their uncomfortable dinner parties. Desdemona had walked in to find Lilith shaking in a puddle of broken glass and jelly. Without making a comment, she cleaned and prepared, using a damp cloth to get the cream out of Lilith's hair and off her blue velvet dress.

Desdemona never spoke of it at the various fundraisers and parties, but she always seemed to be reassuringly close by. Ready to be of use, an alarm on the wall – break in case of emergency.

Tonight, Lilith was going to break the glass and call the Prime Minister's wife, ask her to help hide an illegal immigrant. But only for a day. Then she was going to ask the Prime Minister's wife to get another politician's wife to do the same. And get that wife to get another to do the same. And another. And Another. Until too many Canberra wives were involved for the government to do anything but stop Sibel and her daughter from being deported. To save their collective skin.

They all had holiday homes. Sibel's daughter could easily

move between them, with some help from a sympathetic wife and mother, and remain undetected for a few weeks. Long enough for the politicians to realise they were all in this together. They couldn't dob in a colleague's wife to the authorities and hope it would all go away because their wife had been as unpredictable as his. They would whisper in the corridors and realise they had been outmanoeuvred.

Lilith opened her phone and looked up Desdemona's number. Lilith had never called her before. Desdemona wouldn't even recognise Lilith's mobile. Lilith dialled before she could think any more. It rang once, then the smooth voice of Desdemona Matthews answered.

'Lilith Hamilton. I was hoping you would call. I've been thinking of you a lot recently.'

'It's Lilith Green now,' Lilith said.

'I like that better; Hamilton was never a good fit for you. A bit stuffy, I think,' Desdemona said. 'How have you been? Are you holding up okay? And the girls?'

'Yes, we're staying in a community at the moment, in Manly. Run by Bodie Hughes – you probably don't know her.'

'Oh, I know *of* her. She is the talk of Canberra at the moment.'

'You mean because of her arrest?'

'Oh, Lilith. You always did try to stay above the politics, didn't you?' Desdemona said. 'She was making waves before that. This Women's Party she's registered. It's got a few of the old boys worked up. It's wonderful!'

'I'm working for her,' Lilith said, some pride bubbling in her voice.

'I know that too,' Desdemona replied. 'You are also the talk of Canberra, at least in the closer circles.'

'I'm sure Ben has been saying many things about me.' Lilith sighed.

'I meant between the wives,' Desdemona said with glee. 'We

are proud of you, Lilith. You did the right thing. I know that it cannot have been easy. And the press recently ...' Desdemona's voice trailed off.

Lilith became aware she was holding her breath. She let it go.

'I'm sorry I didn't do more,' Desdemona continued, 'to help you.'

'You let me know I was visible. That I mattered to someone.'

'Everyone deserves that.'

'I agree. That's actually why I'm calling you.'

'Oh?' She sounded intrigued.

'I need your help. Again,' Lilith continued. 'It's someone I know, in fact. She needs someone to step through broken glass for her.'

'Is it Bodie Hughes?' Desdemona sounded almost excited. 'I'm not sure even I could persuade Howard to intervene there ...'

'No, Bodie can look after herself.' Lilith smiled. 'It's a young girl, Akara. It's your help she needs, not your husband's. In fact, I need your husband to not be involved in this. I need you to not tell him about it,' Lilith said. 'At least not yet.'

Lilith explained her plan to Desdemona, trying to stop the rabbit in her veins from shaking the phone out of her hands. There was silence for a while, and Lilith began to panic. Had she made a mistake? But then Desdemona said, 'Thank you, Lilith.'

'What for?' Lilith was puzzled.

'Most people only see me as a door to Howard. It's very rarely me they need. Thank you. For making me feel useful,' Desdemona said. 'I'm in.'

Checkmate. God save the queen.

Chapter 19

Kathleen Rae was getting used to being seen. It was a new feeling. Even though her skin colour made her stand out in the sea of white skin that flooded Australia, it made her invisible to most white people. They would look right past her. People on the street, teachers, colleagues. They would look right through her as though she just didn't exist. It was like that game kids play. When they are mean to another kid and want them to feel left out.

Sometimes she felt observed but still not seen. In shops, on the street. They'd look at her with caution, suspicion. At least that was better than the hatred that came in hurled bottles, rocks and words. Each hitting as hard as the other.

Her parents hadn't been shy in telling Kathleen life was going to be difficult. They told her the truth. She deserved to do well, and she would do well. But she was going to have to fight. They helped her understand that feeling of not-belonging, in the country her ancestors had walked on for 65,000 years, was manufactured. It wasn't real. Someone had just invaded her home, moved all the furniture around and changed the locks. She did belong. This was her home. Those people making her feel out of place were the visitors here, not Kathleen.

Even as a kid, she felt the injustice, like two ropes pulling her arms, one stretching back into a time before she existed, the other pulling into a future that would exist long after she was gone. The removals, detentions. Heritage blown away or exploited. No reparations. Apologies so thin they'd vanish before they reached your ears. Lack of First Nations people on the television, in parliament, in business. In their own country.

She figured out when she was still young that if she didn't do something, it was going to pull her apart. Community and activism were Kathleen's path to politics, deciding she had to be in the broken system to see what bits needed to be redirected and reconnected.

Kathleen had attended many protests. She'd even organised quite a few. There had been a hiatus. People had favoured online petitions and memes to express their anger – they were too busy tweeting to notice the government sliding their right to peaceful protest away.

Kathleen was already a seasoned activist when America happened. It sparked a new wave of protests. For a little while, it became a trend to get involved. People eager to get their equality cookie volunteered to make placards and hold up the Aboriginal flag or protest the latest attempt to rape the Australian soil to get some gas.

The protests were usually peaceful. The government's response was typically heavy-handed. They had new laws they wanted to try out and some new tactics to enforce them. Kathleen learned how to treat tear gas in the eyes. How to position herself so rubber bullets didn't do any damage. Learned how to speak to a crowd without a megaphone. Knew the law – what the protesters could do, what she could do, without being charged – she wasn't about to let them turn her into a criminal. It's how she first met Janet De Marco. She learned what the police couldn't do, but did anyway. She held the line. She stayed calm. Never gave them a chance to call her a hysterical woman. A violent Black woman. She knew even then the path she was on.

And she wasn't going to give them any excuse to put up a 'No Entry' sign in front of her future. Her destiny. Her fucking right.

When the anti-disruption laws got passed in 2023, just before the last election, it became hard to find someone to paint a placard (hefty fine), almost impossible to find someone to hold it (six months in prison). They had Kathleen's back, they promised. But, really, was a load of people gathering together, maybe all spreading god-knows-what virus to each other, going to change anything? What about the economic losses? The country couldn't afford to be unproductive anymore.

They would declare that the time of the protest was gone. There were better ways. The government hadn't outlawed petitions or sharing knowledge. They would do that. They promised. Then they posted a picture of Mabo before looking at the cat dance on TikTok.

And so most of the electorate went back to sleep, to the soporific sound of the government's lullaby. The ones who heard the subliminal message forced their eyes open. Took the fines, took the sentences, kept on going. But there weren't enough of them. Easily dispersed or gathered up and moved on. Not big enough for media attention, too uncomfortable for most people's attention. They turned away, just like when she was a kid. Invisible.

But not today. Today, there was a protest. And they were thousands-strong. Bodie had done it. Here was her coalition of the pissed-off. There were no placards to identify which group they belonged to. First Nations rights. Women's rights. LGBTQI+ rights. Refugee rights. Environmental rights. There were no placards today. There was no cause today. There was just a message that the women gathered today would deliver, Kathleen included, on behalf of all women, whatever skin tone, however they arrived at being a woman, whoever they chose to love.

And this time, she wasn't the leader of a social justice movement shouting through a megaphone or the university student president organising banner carriers. Today she was marching as the leader of the second biggest political party in Australia. As the woman who was asking the country to make her their first First Nations prime minister. She was doing it without telling her advisers or party, the tingle of freedom and memory in her veins as she made her way to the assembly point.

The air in Australia had become dry. MASC had laid enough kindling with their threats to women journalists. The government walked around with torches lit with bills and rhetoric designed to make women get back in their place. It wasn't going to take much to set things off. Sibel and her daughter being granted asylum was like a westerly picking up sparks and starting spot fires all over the place. No one could understand why the government had done a backflip, Ben Hamilton least of all. He'd made a few missteps in the press. Forgetting his place. Criticising his boss. Then he went silent.

He must have found out what Kathleen already knew. She could have scored a few political points by explaining it to everyone. Why suddenly, the government wasn't interested in further detaining Sibel and Akara Polat or in prosecuting Bodie Hughes. But this was better. Sibel and her daughter were safe. Some women got to understand the power they had.

There was always going to be a backlash, though. The boys would have to puff their chests out somehow. Show they were still in charge. MASC and the government, it didn't matter which – they were merging into one.

The trolls had been getting more active, more women journalists were getting death threats. The addresses of women's shelters were being shared online. Abortion clinics were getting cows' blood pumped under their doors.

The government was on the attack too. Putting criminalisation of abortion on the election table. The PM was concerned about the high number of terminations. During a live debate, he asked Kathleen how many abortions she'd had. She had refused to answer. He demanded to know what she was hiding. Dunked if you denied, dunked if you told the truth. Kathleen had wanted to answer. She wanted there to be no shame. But Kathleen had listened to Kay. She still wasn't polling well in some strongly religious areas. Kay said she needed to stay quiet. Big mistake. 'What is she hiding?' was the PM's campaign calling card.

Queentide had been prepared for attacks from incel groups hell-bent on blaming women for their plight of celibacy, white supremacists, misogynistic-leaning journalists. But now, some women's rights groups, despite Bodie's best attempts, were criticising Kathleen. The Prime Minister had found a way to destabilise her base.

Today, she was planting her feet firmly back on the ground, right in the middle of her base. Even if Kay didn't like it. Kathleen had nothing to hide.

Insley had planned the logistics to the last detail. Bodie had got every interest group to back the protest. Hashtags and tweets were used like targeted missiles deployed in the exact location to gain willing volunteers. Helen's data had helped them work out who to get on board, and when to do so, what they would respond to, what call to action would work best. Janet De Marco had issued directives on what could get them into trouble and what they needed to do if they were arrested. Lilith Green had volunteered to lead the aid team, helping any protesters who were injured. Aaron had independent journalists primed and ready to go. Positioned in the place to get the best shots – the Opera House steps. Kathleen had joked it was being staged like a product launch.

Insley joked it was Queentide's patented patriarch repellent.

Kathleen shivered. She wondered if she should have told Aaron she'd be here. It might have secured some journalists from the networks more publicity. Too late now – they were counting down. Her arms wrapped her winter coat over her naked body. Waiting to feel the buzz in her pocket from her phone. They'd see her soon enough. Kathleen Rae would be invisible no more.

Chapter 20

Lilith had left the girls with Bodie. They would watch together on the television, later. Lilith wanted them to see what it looked like when women didn't back down. Lilith had read Janet De Marco's briefing. If Lilith was there as part of a medic team, if she was only administering help, she wasn't doing anything illegal. Nothing that Ben could throw at her. Lilith wasn't an activist. Just an observer. Someone else was pulling the pin. Lilith was just there to sweep up the debris. Yes, she had organised transport for the protestors. Yes, Lilith had gone with Bodie to negotiate with sympathetic groups who could help with Insley's logistics and media coverage. Yes, she had been given access to some private diaries to make sure certain people would be in Sydney to witness this, thanks to the wives. But that was just her job. It wasn't illegal to be a secretary, was it?

It was unnoticeable at first. From Lilith's higher position, under the Opera House's sails, which had been designated as a medic stand, they were just spots in the multicoloured crowd. Dark grey and black hoods attached to each other like scattered storm clouds forming an ominous mass. The people caught in the middle of it didn't notice. From her vantage point, Lilith could see the clouds swirling in between people who didn't even feel them passing by. They were too busy with their own lives, heads craned towards their phones, missing history brushing right past them. That would change in a few minutes, Lilith thought. Their phones would soon be focused on the strangers engulfing them. Photos would be on Facebook. They'd tweet the hashtag, showing everyone that they were involved, that they were part of something big. The question was whose side they would be on.

Bodie's idea was so simple, Lilith wondered why it hadn't been done before. So many people had suffered because of the patriarchy. It really wasn't too hard to find sympathetic groups and unite them under one cause, change the system. All the groups there had been held down in one way or another. Now, side by side, they were merging and distilling into something powerful. Bitter. Now it was time for them to taste it.

It was a Tuesday morning, quiet. Ibis plodded in the waterfall a little in the distance. Tourists took pictures of the Harbour Bridge under the shade of the grand structure. They didn't notice the hoods behind them take their places. Soon it was impossible to see the steps. The women who couldn't make it up the steps were helped to find a place at the front. Then the dark-toned cloud settled like a blanket, rippling like an ocean beneath the sparkling sails of the Opera House, their backs to Lilith.

Lilith's phone buzzed. The photo was a mirror image of what she was looking at, taken from the front of the steps. She could just make out faces underneath the hoods and scarves. She knew her own face was there, somewhere in the far-off blur, but, despite looking, she couldn't make out even a shape that was a suggestion of herself. The pings kept coming with more notifications. From all the social channels. Similar-looking photos, but all from different angles. Lilith looked down. Each of the hoods was holding a phone. They all had the hashtag #nothingtohide.

In the time it took to put her phone back in her pocket, the clouds opened. Dark hoods were dropped, revealing the defiant and silent naked women they had been shrouding. Every shade of skin was on display, shoulder to shoulder, their chins held high. Some held hands, some didn't. Many had shaved their heads. Had Insley suggested this? Lilith didn't remember it being discussed as a tactic, not seriously. Insley had said she kept hers short to not give anyone a handle on her, something that could be grabbed and pulled. Ben used to wrap Lilith's hair around his fist.

Maybe there was just a collective consciousness, some sort of synchronicity to reject things that felt like chains. Hair. Expectations. Toleration.

They stood and sat like sentries, nothing to hide or say. The tourists and even the ibis fell silent and watched. What was happening? Was it a television stunt? They looked a little afraid. Was anything more terrifying than women who refused to be ashamed?

They were to all stay still. Naked. Apart from Lilith, whose warm winter clothes were feeling claustrophobic. Why had she worn so many layers? She undid the bottom two buttons of her parka. She had water and blankets ready. And the paint. She handed some tubes and tubs to the back few rows. She watched as they dipped and smeared hands with crimson acrylics, then placed their own hands around their necks. Paint oozed out from under fingers, creating creeks and brooks of crimson over the shoulder blades and collarbones of women of every configuration, every shade. Silent. Choked. The few police officers who were on patrol at the Opera House didn't seem to know what to do. They watched with everyone else, talked into their radio. How were they going to respond to this?

Lilith retreated to her post. Checked her kit over again. Checking in with the other medics, who had been posted to various spots around the forecourt. Office workers had now come out and joined the tourists and ibis. The clouds of women were observed, like art in a gallery. A novelty, something to be deciphered. Cameras were being held up.

Some gazes seemed a little too intense. A white-haired woman in the back row rolled her eyes at Lilith when they both noticed the group of young men sniggering and pointing, probably zooming their cameras in.

A woman who was halfway through gender reassignment shifted uncomfortably, more exposed than most. Revealing not just their skin but their private transformation.

'Let them look, honey,' the white-haired woman said. 'Be proud. They need to see what real women look like, the scars we carry for being women. Some of us have lost breasts to cancer, some of us have lost the fight against time, some of us have given birth to children. You are giving birth to your own body. Wear that proudly, dear. Every woman's body is constantly changing.' They held hands and faced forward.

Lilith's phone pinged. Aaron had tweeted the first set of naked photos, adding another hashtag #nostormstayssilent. Within minutes, it was liked and retweeted and spread on other media platforms. Bodie's alliance of the pissed-off was doing its part.

It was like watching a fire take hold. But there was still no sound. No chants. No songs. Just silence. Soon, embers were flying and setting off new fires. Still, the women stood silently. In the distance, Lilith heard police sirens. She flicked between feeds, watching them fill with women and men at home, red hands around their necks. Lilith pulled at the wool scarf around her neck. It was constricting her. She uncoiled it and threw it on top of the cases of water she had at her feet. She could see the police coming through the park on the left and from the narrow approach to the Opera House steps. Lilith looked up – helicopters. Television crews were hovering, recording. Some news vans were pulling up in the distance. It was time.

Lilith sent the message she had been asked to. Her job was done. She took the woollen hat off her head. It was so hot.

For a moment, the city seemed to stop and take a breath before deciding what to do. Before it could breathe out again, a voice broke the silence, addressing the news crews who had arrived with the dozens of police in riot gear. But it wasn't the voice Lilith was expecting to hear. Instead of hearing Insley echo across the forecourt, the voice was Kathleen Rae's.

Then her image appeared to accompany it, projected onto the high walls surrounding the iconic building. It was shaky. No doubt someone just holding a camera phone. Kathleen wasn't supposed to be here. Kay had said she would be in Canberra, away from it all. But there she was. Naked, the potential future prime minister, holding the hand of a girl with a shaved head, at the very front of the crowd. Both of their necks adorned with bright red dripping hand marks. The bloodlike necklaces of the women behind them blared against the dazzling cleanliness of the Opera House sails.

Lilith unbuttoned her coat, shrugging it off onto the cold concrete. Why had she worn such heavy clothes? It was too restrictive. She couldn't breathe.

Chapter 21

'As a proud Kaurna woman from the Adelaide Plains, I wish to acknowledge the custodians of this unceded land, the Gadigal people of the Eora nation and their Elders past and present. I acknowledge and respect their continuing culture and the contribution they make to the life of this city, this region, this country and this world. We have survived. They have tried to silence us for centuries. Denied us our history. Stifl ed our voice. Stopped us from sharing our truth with one another. My people. My First Nations brothers and sisters. Then there are my other sisters whose ancestors walked on lands far from here. There are my gay friends. My trans friends. My refugee friends who have been driven from their homes because of war and haven't found a safe harbour here either. My friends living with a disability. My friends on the poverty line. They've stopped us all of you from speaking too. From sharing.'

Kathleen paused, drew a long breath. Her eyes were full of fi re and tears.

'They are trying to deny that any of us exist. They are hoping we will stop existing.' Kathleen's voice cracked slightly, but she didn't miss a beat. She was proudly letting her emotions show. 'But we do. And there's a lot of us. Millions, in fact. And we are sick of being silenced, held down. Subdued. Squeezed. Detained. So if they will not help us, why don't we help each other? We can pry their grip off each other's throats and help each other speak. They will choke me no more, or you.'

Bodie watched the live feed Aaron had made sure was being broadcast everywhere. The children were playing dragons outside. They did not need to see this today. There would be time, later, for them to fight real enemies. Kathleen Rae raised her hand, stained from the paint, which was still holding Insley's hand. The paint was still wet enough to run down her arm.

'I have nothing to hide. I am not ashamed of who I am, of what I stand for. Or of who I stand for.'

Kathleen turned and lovingly kissed Insley. Then the kiss was then passed from cheek to cheek, like a Mexican wave. This wasn't part of the meticulous planning. It was better. It was human. Bodie thought of ringing Janet to check if this changed things, then realised Janet would already be working on it.

For now, they all stood in an empty space. The protesters had reached the end of something, like the credits rolling on a movie. The police would have to move soon. There was a vacuum developing. It was time. Bodie sent the message. But before she could press send, the chants started. Not from the protesters, but the crowd.

The protesters didn't flinch. It was the soundtrack to being a woman. Like songs played on the radio in the warmer months. 'Summer of 69', 'Boys of Summer'. Overused. Overheard. So wrung out that there was no emotion left in them.

There was a noise, and Kathleen flinched. When her head became still again, red was trickling down her cheek. It was not paint. They had thrown something at her.

Then the camera was on Insley. Or at least a blur of Insley. Her rage was palpable even through the screen. She broke through the crowd, laser-sighted on the man who had made the mistake of his life. Unrestricted by reason or clothing, she ran. Jesus, Insley. Bodie hoped the live feed would stop, but it didn't. Bodie did not want to see this. She knew what Insley was capable of. Now, it appeared, everyone else would see it too. Kathleen included.

The camera obediently retrieved Insley, just as she caught a man by the throat and pulled him down to the ground. The crowd separated, forming a circus ring around Insley. Bodie ran a hand through her hair, lodging it in her spikes, wanting it to somehow restrain her granddaughter's hands. Insley was filling the vacuum. Bodie realised the police in the background. They were edging in closer, but they looked uncertain.

They would all be men. Women had been edged out of frontline service when the new equipment they started carrying was made just too damn uncomfortable and impractical for a woman's body. These officers wouldn't know where to grab Insley without risking being dragged into some media storm or other or sparking a riot. What would they do with thousands of naked women? They would call for backup. Women. The officers they usually just sent to domestic disputes because they weren't as dangerous. Apparently. Bodie watched on as Insley erupted. She was primal, a force of nature that was going to have to be allowed to run its course. The surrounding people sensed it. No-one intervened. No woman wanted to stop her. No man knew how to. Bodie heard the notes gathering inside Insley, working their way up to a crashing crescendo. Bodie listened to the girls squealing and laughing outside in the courtyard.

The man underneath the crest of Insley's rage was laughing. Out of embarrassment or genuine amusement, it was hard to tell. Insley was laughing too, but at a different, much more bitter joke. He didn't get up. The man probably didn't think it was necessary. He was playing to the crowd, this tiny little naked girl standing over him.

His lips moved, and whatever he said made Insley grow. She filled the space above him. He kept talking, and Insley just got bigger. Outgrowing the area she was in. Insley wasn't Bodie's

granddaughter anymore. She wasn't Kathleen's girlfriend anymore. She had gone, become a creature, bouncing from one
foot to another, growling at the man beneath her on the ground.
Then she was movement. The man was too far into his charac-
ter of amused-man-too-strong-to-worry to get out of her way.
Insley's fist came down with force. Every single muscle of her
glistened in the morning sun. All working as a single machine,
built to take things apart.

Not amused anymore, the man started fighting back. Using
his entire weight to push Insley hard against the chest. Bodie
winced as Insley skidded across the concrete. He started yelling at her, then turned around to walk towards the police, who
were now holding their reinforced shields in front of the crowd.
It wasn't clear who they were protecting. The camera caught
a flash of her back, shaved of skin from the gravel, just before
she jumped on his back and started hitting him in the side of
his head. He spun around, panting. Probably surprised by how
heavy this little girl was. Finally, a uniform broke through the
circle. A female officer had arrived. She wasn't wearing riot gear
but moved as though she was armoured. She stood, let Insley
get in one more punch, then threw a blanket around Insley and
dragged her back through the line of tooled-up police officers,
Insley's limbs still fighting a battle that was over. The crowd
was confused. Some were cheering. Others were stunned. Another vacuum.

Bodie grabbed her phone. Pressed send on the message she
wished she'd got through. STOP.

On the screen, just as officers moved in with gas canisters,
the women put on their coats and made their way back to their
lives.

Bodie could see the police reconsidering. The crowd was
dispersing. If they took action now, it would play out badly. So
they watched them leave. Before, they had just been protes-

tors, without labels, but now they went back to being mothers, grandmothers, accountants, nurses. As if it hadn't happened. But it had happened. In Bodie's experience, for every action, there was always a reaction. Personal and universal. Immediate and delayed. She closed her eyes for a second, then went out to play with the girls.

Chapter 22

'What the actual fuck did you think you were doing, Insley?' Kay was on her feet within seconds of Insley walking into the common room with Bodie.

The bruise on Insley's temple was still pulsing. The cuts had been cleaned up by Bodie when she came to pick her up from the station. The paint around her neck was flaking and dry. It felt itchy. Insley wanted a shower, and she wanted to see Kathleen, to know she was okay. The last thing she wanted was a lecture from a Barbie doll. Bodie ignored Kay and crossed the room. Insley sat on one of the plastic chairs that hadn't been stacked away. She leaned back, then leaned forward quickly. Her raw skin rubbed angrily against her T-shirt. She was a mess.

'She didn't think, clearly,' Kathleen said from a corner of the room, rising from the armchair that Insley always favoured. She greeted Bodie warmly as Bodie dropped herself down into the sagging chair. It made her look so old, so small. She had been so quiet on the way over. It wasn't like her. Insley smiled, but Kathleen didn't. Danger. 'But she hasn't caused any real damage, Kay. Give her a break.'

'She hasn't caused any damage?' She flung the day's newspapers into the centre of the room. 'Look at these photos! She looks like a goddamn reject from *Mad Max*.'

Aaron emerged from the kitchen, holding out a steaming cup to Insley. He stepped over the newspapers. Insley could see the smile he was trying to hide under his beard. She took the cup, returned the grin and sat down near Kathleen but not too close. There was a barrier up. Insley could feel it. Aaron went to the lounge, beckoning Kay to sit next to him.

'She's gone too far this time, Aaron,' Kay snapped.

'I am here, Kay,' said Insley, stroking the bruise that was erupting into a massive bump. She couldn't stop prodding it, even though it hurt. 'You don't need to report to your boyfriend.' Aaron rolled his eyes at Insley, but she didn't care. She hated that woman. She was so self-righteous.

'Yes, apparently, I do. Because you don't listen.' Kay shrugged off Aaron's arm, which he'd tried to put around her shoulder. Why was he even with her? 'I told you that Kathleen couldn't be associated with this shitshow today.'

'Shitshow?' Insley had run out of the last little bit of patience she had. She stood up, maybe a bit too quickly. She felt dizzy. 'Have you done your job today, Kay? Have you read what the papers are saying? Have you seen Insta? TikTok? Women are sharing their stories of male violence. Men are sharing their stories. We've got the conversation going. That was the whole point of today.'

'And dragging Kathleen into it? Was that the point of today too? Were you just using her to get some attention?'

'She didn't drag me, Kay,' Kathleen retorted. 'I can make my own decisions. I—'

'Well, from now on, maybe you should run those decisions past me first,' Kay interrupted, taking back the stage. 'Kathleen, the plan was that this lot was supposed to make you look like the safe choice, compared with them. Remember? They act all crazy,' – Kay looked at Insley when she said it – 'demand all these radical things, then you ask for the same thing just in a nicer way.'

'Is that how you see me, Kay? Someone who asks nice? Knows

her place?' Kathleen's eyebrows were raised, a sign that sharper words were stabbing in her brain.

'That's not what I meant. You want to be the next prime minister. You need to stand on a world stage, in front of billions of people. And the first photo they will ever see of you is naked and bleeding.'

'Who the hell ...' Insley advanced on Kay. Kay shrank into Aaron, who recognised Insley's posturing and just sipped his tea.

'Insley,' – Kathleen's voice had none of its usual warmth – 'you don't need to speak for me. Jesus, can the pair of you just let me speak? Please?'

Insley knew when to back down. She perched herself on the arm of the sofa, next to Aaron.

'What is wrong with that, Kay? With the population seeing their future prime minister stripped down, exposed?' Kathleen's voice was composed. Insley was proud of her.

'It is unstatesmanlike,' Kay replied, just a little petulantly. Insley failed to stop herself from sniggering.

'Worse than, say, incarcerating children? Than burning rainforests? Or being accused of raping multiple women? These statesmen, they stand up there with no shame. If the worst I've done is stand naked, then I'm not going to feel inferior to men like that. I'm not going to be ashamed.'

Insley took a sideways look at Kay. She looked rebuked. Insley grinned to herself, but Aaron spotted it and shook his head at her. Kay turned down the dial – she was losing her audience.

'Look, I don't disagree. But it isn't me you've got to convince. It's the voting public. It's Joe down the pub with his mates. It's Nora at church, dishing up the tea and scones. It's those people. You can't do the work if you don't get the job. Our priority is just to ensure you remain electable. And that may mean some sacrifices.'

Insley felt all the eyes in the room on her. It was fairly bloody obvious what Kay meant. She was about as subtle as the garish pink dresses she wore.

'I will not pretend I'm someone else, Kay,' Kathleen responded, cutting Insley off before she could speak again. Insley tasted the blood in her mouth as she bit her tongue just a little too hard. If she waited, Kay could dig her own grave and save Insley the hassle.

'I'm not suggesting you do, Kathy.' Insley hated hearing Kathleen's name, abbreviated. What she disliked more was Kathleen not correcting people. She watched Kathleen bite her top lip the way she did when she self-edited her thoughts. Could she taste blood now, too?

'But Aaron here has said there's a story coming out that you are in a relationship with Insley. The woman who almost caused a riot at a peaceful protest today. The granddaughter of Bodie Hughes, feminist activist, the person behind this new Women's Party that is springing up out of nowhere. It looks suspicious, doesn't it, Aaron?'

'You can't possibly agree with this, Az ...' Insley looked at her best friend. She hated it when he was so weak.

'No, Insley.' Aaron's head was spinning from Insley to Kay. 'Kay, that's not exactly what I ...'

'You said Queentide could end up being a liability to Kathleen ...' Kay said, wide-eyed. Insley wanted to rip her false eyelashes off.

'No.' Aaron was speaking to Kay, but he was looking at Insley and then Bodie. Bodie just raised an eyebrow. 'I said that it might start looking like Kathleen *is* hiding something ...'

'Jesus Az ...' Insley wrestled with an urge to pull his beard or kick him in the shins like she used to when they were small.

'What I was getting at was ...' Aaron said, almost over the top of Insley. 'What I think is ... we should just be open about it. Let's say that Queentide is backing Kathleen. Let's grab the narrative. Queentide is doing remarkable things for women from all different backgrounds in this country. It is nothing to be ashamed of.'

Insley noticed that Kay had shuffled further away from Aaron. No surprises there. She wasn't getting what she wanted. Aaron looked hurt, though. And that made Insley angry. Kay's time was fast approaching. Even if she was Aaron's girlfriend. But the time wasn't right. Insley had to wait and let her speak.

'But there are things to be ashamed of, aren't there? Things I didn't know you guys were involved in when I endorsed Kathleen going along with this election plan of yours, Bodie.'

'Like what, Ms Conway?' Bodie was using her professor's voice. Kay was in trouble.

'Like using intimidation against members of MASC,' Kay replied.

There were some tiny shifts in the room that Kay probably didn't notice, but Insley did. Bodie's eyes sharpened, meaning she was worried. Aaron's head dropped a degree, meaning he felt guilty about something. He didn't need to – Aaron hadn't told Kay anything new. She'd heard it all from her secret meetings with Ben Hamilton. And his information was coming from MASC. But it wasn't time to say that.

Insley muted that track in her brain and concentrated on what Kay was saying so she could craft her response. Insley noticed Kathleen staring at her, but she couldn't decipher the look. There would be time later. She focused on the muscles in Kay's face. The tone in her grandmother's voice.

'I have no idea what you are referring to, Ms Conway,' Bodie said flippantly.

'I am saying a future prime minister cannot be associated with a vigilante,' Kay replied.

'Hey, Kay?' Insley bounced off the arm of the sofa, enough to jolt Aaron and Kay. 'Why don't you say that to my face? It's obvious it's me you are referring to.'

'I'm sorry to interrupt.' Lilith's quiet voice drifted into the silence, diffusing the tension like a waft of lavender in the air. Insley wondered how long she'd been waiting, finding the right time to speak. Lilith Green had turned out to be as smart as Insley thought she was. It was going to be a little more difficult to persuade her than Insley had planned for.

'Oh, Lilith, I didn't see you there.' Kay gave a saccharin grin to Lilith. Aaron had told Insley months ago that Kay didn't trust Lilith. So it had piqued Insley's interest to see Kay be so nice to her. It gave Insley her strongest lead, in fact.

'I came to get Bodie. There's a journalist on the line, from *The Guardian*, Bodie. He said he has an interview lined up with you?' Insley looked at Aaron, he shrugged. He clearly knew nothing about it either.

'Thank you, Lilith.' Bodie struggled to get herself to her feet. Kathleen got up to give her a hand. They said something to each other, but Insley was too focused on Kay to make out what it was.

'So what are you saying, Kay? That Kathleen can't be associated with Queentide because of me? Aaron, it might be time to become an alpha male and pull your bloody girlfriend into line.'

'Maybe I should do that too.' Kathleen's voice hit Insley worse than the punches had. 'Bodie, I'll follow along in a minute. I need to talk to Insley. Alone.'

All of Insley's nerves stood on end. The way they did just before she swung a punch in a brawl. The anticipation of pain. Hers. Theirs. The blow always hurt them both.

'Kathleen, I don't know anything about this interview ...' Kay was standing now, between Insley and Kathleen. Aaron stood too. He gave Insley a sympathetic look. He knew he'd be needed later to contain her explosion.

'We can talk later, Kay,' Kathleen said, terminating the conversation.

Kathleen didn't sit. Insley was unsure what to do. So she sat on the sofa. Allowing Kathleen to stand tall over her.

'I'm sorry about hitting that guy.' An apology seemed like a good place to start.

'Why did you do it?' Kathleen's voice was even.

'Why?' Insley decided to tread carefully, looking for traps. She couldn't see any, so she pushed on. 'Because he hurt you.'

'You stole my anger,' Kathleen said.

'What?' Insley wasn't sure she'd heard right.

'You stole my anger.' Insley looked at her girlfriend. She could now see the bandaid on the side of Kathleen's face. Insley felt ashamed when she realised she'd almost forgotten Kathleen had actually been injured. 'I don't need you to protect me, Insley.'

'I am always going to protect you, Kathleen.' Insley was feeling dizzy again.

'Even when I ask you not to?' Kathleen was keeping her arms at her side but clenching her fists.

'Jesus, Kathleen. I was helping you.'

'No, Insley. You weren't.' Kathleen released her fists and came towards Insley. 'You were angry, and you acted on it. You didn't think about how it would affect me. If it was what I would want.'

Insley scratched her nails over the threads on the chair's arm where the velvet should have been. She couldn't look at Kathleen. Kathleen started walking towards the door. Insley released her breath, not realising she'd been holding it, sure Kathleen was going to land the big punch. End it. But then Kathleen turned back around. Insley inhaled again.

'You don't believe I can do this on my own, do you?' Kathleen asked calmly.

'What are you talking about?' Insley replied, playing for time.

'You don't believe I can win this election without you,' Kathleen said. Insley started to reply and then stopped. None of the answers in her head was what Kathleen wanted to hear. She was too tired to come up with anything intelligent. 'I don't want to win if it means being no better than the system I want to dismantle.' Kathleen shook her head and left the room.

Insley's head was throbbing. She'd sort things out with Kathleen later. She was just upset. It was all Kay's fault for bringing shit up like that. Insley winced as she pulled her phone out of her back pocket and found the number she needed. Time to step things up. Kathleen had to win. It would be iconic. Insley had to make it happen. She was the only one who could make it happen.

'Hey, it's me. I need a favour …'

Kathleen would forgive her when she realised that she did need Insley's help.

Chapter 23

Bodie had known the seawalls would be built. The waves were getting too big, too close, for them to ignore. She was sure, in fact, that she could hear the boulders dropping into place, even over the chants of support for Queentide. And now it wasn't just Bodie's coalition of the pissed-off who were joining in.

Bodie's manifesto was being bought, shared, copied and read by young girls, looking for the signposts and older women trying to get back on their path. They all wanted to know how to get out of the forest, and they all started finding their way. Their own way.

Bodie had spilt an idea into the country, and now it was running off into unexpected valleys, pooling in unforced reservoirs. Queentide wasn't in control of it anymore.

A day hadn't gone by for weeks without something, somewhere, springing up. Things that surprised even Bodie. Things that not even Insley could have thought up. There were the naked protests, of course, lasting just a few minutes. By the time the police got there, the women had already redressed, and they had already made their point. At the local shopping centre in Fremantle. At the post office in Bathurst. On the Melbourne trams - of every single one of them, that one was Bodie's favourite.

Then there were the women who did nothing. They just stopped. All at the same time, across the country. Every Thursday at 3.24 pm. The time, because of the pay gap, that most women started working for free. The teachers, the nurses, the childcare workers, the supermarket staff. They stopped doing, stopped caring, for two minutes. That, Bodie guessed, was about as close to breaking point as they dared take their hearts. Children waited to have grazed knees cleaned and hurt feelings soothed. Elderly people sat in their chairs and lay in their beds, waiting to be fed and asked about their life before their care-home days. Customers queued, waiting for their change and a chance to complain about the cost of milk. Patients waited to be saved – for some, two minutes was too late. The country stopped and waited, like a little kid standing outside the bathroom door, waiting for his mum to open the packet of chips in his hands.

After a few Thursdays, it happened. The movement changed into a revolution. There was no planned event, no fanfare. No individual, not even a Kathleen, making a rousing speech. Bodie had learned, through so many constructive failures that had led her to this point of almost-success, that change didn't happen on a stage. It happened in private. In the conversations people had in their living rooms with their dad and brothers. And in talks they had in the dark, with themselves.

Bodie was relieved as she saw the memes and hashtags fly and the boycotts planned on social media platforms she hadn't even heard of. She slept easier as women stepped forward to be candidates, and Insley vetted them to make sure they'd fit the bill. She breathed more steadily as she watched, from a distance, as activist groups that thought they had nothing in common, formed alliances and got behind Kathleen.

But something ticked in the background that stopped her from letting go completely. Bodie had worked to diffuse enough bombs to know there was always a second wire. Just when you thought you had them beat, when you thought you'd neutralised them, you'd hear the ticking continue, see the seconds fall off the clock. You'd not even have time to prepare yourself for the bang. What worried Bodie was that she couldn't hear a tick, didn't see a counter. She didn't know when the explosion was going to come. But Bodie was sure it was coming.

When it eventually did, it came with a whimper. Bodie heard it in the crime statistics that Helen would analyse. Crimes against women were climbing. Convictions in domestic abuse cases were falling. Women were being made unemployed at a rate that made no sense. Female presenters were being dropped from networks. War on women hadn't been declared. It had been whispered.

It didn't take long, though, for the shouting to start. Online at first. Candidates found themselves on deepfake porn sites. They were trolled on social media. Private messages with violent threats. Public threats by violent mobs. The police told them there was little they could do. No one had been physically hurt.

When they did start getting physically hurt, the police told them there was not much they could do. Then the bomb went off, and the police finally did something. The police told the candidate whose car had exploded in Ben Hamilton's electorate that she might want to reconsider running. She did.

They were meeting today to work out what to do. For the first time, in fact, since just before the first protest. There had been decisions to make, of course, mostly about the donations that were now flowing into Queentide. She left that to Lilith, mostly. Bodie chuckled as she remembered the look on Lilith's face when Bodie told her to work it out. But then she did. She worked out how to fund the candidates' election campaigns and what to do with the rest. And what Lilith did was weave a safety net out of all of that money, with the help of the other activist groups, and cast it wide. Scholarships, legal services, health services, things that would stop women, all women, from slipping through the cracks. Lilith Green, who knew? Bodie did. Even that first time they spoke.

It had always been the plan, at least Bodie's, to give the movement room to grow. To plant the seed, find good people to water it and then let it run wild. She'd started to look forward to just sitting back and watching it bloom. She didn't expect to have to do so much weeding so soon.

Bodie was sitting in the large room, leaning back on a plastic chair, trying to see out of the too-high window, only able to glimpse the blue sky. She rubbed her left arm. It started to ache just thinking about the arguments that she would have to referee. The egos to manage. The tongues to bite. In her younger years, she would have looked forward to the mental challenge. Now, she just wanted to tell them all to grow the hell up and get on with it. Grumpy old witch, she thought to herself.

She was just so damn tired. The night before had been too warm – she'd barely slept. Spring was coming too soon. She wasn't ready to let go of winter just yet.

Just as Bodie spotted a cloud that looked like a rabbit, Lilith walked in, carefully avoiding the curled Persian rug at the door, splashing some water on it from the jug she was carrying. She thought about telling Lilith about the rabbit-cloud and the spilt water but decided against it. They had things to discuss before the others arrived. Bodie was running out of time.

'Lilith, please sit for a moment.' Bodie pulled out a mismatching chair next to her and motioned for Lilith to sit. Lilith obliged, but not before handing Bodie a glass of water.

'I wanted to be the one to share this with you.' Bodie swept her hand over the table, pushing a large envelope towards Lilith. 'Before you open it, I want you to know I will respect whatever decision you make afterwards.'

Lilith's face was motionless, apart from a muscle twitching near the edge of her mouth. She lifted the flap on the large manila envelope.

'What is this?' Lilith's voice was shaking in time with her hands as she flicked through the photos and words.

'This is MASC's file on you,' Bodie responded. 'They have one on each of the candidates and the inner circle of Queentide.'

'I am neither of those.' Lilith continued to look through the papers.

'You have become more involved this past month—' Bodie said.

'But with logistics. I haven't stood in a protest. I have said nothing in the press about Ben,' Lilith replied, putting the papers down, then taking the glass of water Bodie had offered her. She drank the whole thing.

'You are a threat. As long as you could do damage to MASC's cause, tarnish their poster boy, they are going to come after you.'

'But they already have been. I've been getting threats ever since I left Ben. You know that.'

Bodie nodded.

'I thought if I just stayed quiet, kept a low profile, they would leave me alone.' Lilith looked out of the window. Bodie wondered if the rabbit was still there.

'Insley believes they intend to go to Channel 9, sell you as a vengeful, man-hating woman who is using Queentide to get back at your poor ex-husband. It's a hatchet job, but the media won't care about that. There's footage of you at meetings here, edited, so it looks like you are running the show. Which, operationally, I might add, you are,' Bodie continued, watching Lilith build up a wall so Bodie couldn't see her emotions.

'They have footage of Katy and Hannah running around the parade ground with some anti-MASC placards in their hands. If I recall, they were using them as dragon-wings, but obviously, that is not apparent in the video. Then there's you at the medic station at the Opera House, surveying the whole thing. Directing it, they will say, I presume. And there is you, with Sibel's daughter. Looking friendly.' Bodie sighed and rubbed her eyes – she really was so tired. 'Too friendly.'

Lilith laughed. 'Akara? Really? They are saying I'm in a relationship with Akara? She's only fifteen!'

'Well, you do hate men, so there can be only one explanation. Besides, her age makes it a much more interesting explanation.' Bodie smiled ironically.

'What's the point of this?' Bodie knew Lilith hid her emotions, but now she wondered if she had any left. Some days she just seemed numb. Which wasn't uncommon for the women there.

'Honestly?' Bodie ripped off the bandaid. 'Insley believes they are going to drag you through the mud, allowing Ben to go to court and get custody of your children.'

Lilith nodded and picked up the papers, straightening them so they could slide back into the envelope. She put it with the rest of her papers. She poured more water for Bodie and herself.

'And so what decision is it you will respect me for?' Lilith asked calmly.

'The decision to run against Ben, or not,' Bodie said. 'We need someone to replace the candidate who has dropped out. I think if you stand—'

'If I stand, it will help Queentide.' Lilith finished her sentence almost.

'And it will help you, ultimately,' Bodie said, believing it to be true.

'Will it stop me from being dragged through the mud?' Lilith's eyes were clouded, but she was gritting her teeth. The tears were being denied an exit. 'Will it stop me losing my children?'

'No, but this organisation will do everything we can to help you. Even if you don't run. We will help you.' Bodie put her hand on Lilith's. 'Lilith, they have already lit the flames. You can either stay still to prove your innocence and let them burn you anyway. Or you can turn the stake into a flaming broomstick and rain hell on the bastards.'

'I want to be able to do this, Bodie, but—' Before Lilith could finish, Aaron and Kay walked in. Lilith stood up, discreetly picked up the envelope with the other papers. Kay ostentatiously hugged Lilith, not even giving Lilith time to hug her back, and left a red lip-shaped brand on each cheek.

Aaron quietly set up the remaining glasses. He was a good man. There were always good men, Bodie thought.

Then Janet and Helen arrived with a box of doughnuts. Lilith left, saying she would get some plates. She returned after a while, too long to have only been getting plates with Insley. They had been talking, Bodie could tell. Crumbs of words were still hanging on the corners of their mouths. But they sat apart.

Insley next to Bodie, her usual spot next to Aaron occupied by Kay. Leaving Lilith nowhere to sit but at the head of the table. She distractedly took the seat, not noticing the position of power she was in.

Bodie noticed Aaron raise his hand up from the table towards his best friend, nervously looking sideways at Kay as he did it. Bodie couldn't see her granddaughter's face but could feel her eyes rolling skywards. Bodie felt her own do the same.

Then the meeting got underway. Bodie wondered who would point to the elephant first. It was Janet. And she spray-painted the damn thing neon pink.

'So, who's going to put their hand up to run against Ben Hamilton and risk getting a bomb planted in their car?'

'You make it sound like he planted the bomb,' Kay interjected.

'And you make it sound like he had nothing to do with it.' Janet had her court voice on. 'Let's drop the pretence, Ms Conway.'

'All I'm saying is that maybe we shouldn't fixate on Ben Hamilton. It could distract us. He's not the only candidate we need to beat. There are plenty of other seats Labor hasn't got a hope of getting. You need to focus on getting your candidates into those seats. If that's still what this organisation, or movement or whatever the hell you are calling it now, is still here to do.'

Janet was about to respond but was beaten to it by Insley.

'He's the only one with direct links to a group that has been threatening and hurting our candidates.' Insley was calm, which made Bodie concerned. 'I'd say that makes him exactly the candidate we need to beat.'

'Are we still on this MASC thing?' Kay turned to Aaron, who was trying to reach the box of doughnuts. Bodie inched it towards him.

'Why do you keep defending Ben Hamilton, Kay?' Insley replied. 'He's a massive threat to Kathleen too. Don't you want to get her elected? Isn't that what you are still here to do?'

'If you are so sure, Insley, then go to the police.' Kay pulled the box of doughnuts towards her, away from Aaron, and reached in.

'As you know, Kay, we have no evidence to link him to the attacks. We will look like conspiracy theorists.' Insley pulled the doughnuts back across the table but didn't take one. She passed them around. 'It will look bad for Kathleen.'

'Since you two have broken up, I'd say the damage you can cause to her reputation is now at least contained. She's running her own race, Insley. She doesn't need you. I'm not really sure what this group is even still here to do.' Kay paused to take another doughnut from the box, which had made its way back to her.

'This group is here to get a female-led government estab-lished and to make sure scum like Ben Hamilton get thrown out of parliament.' Insley's voice didn't have its usual spark. Her break-up with Kathleen seemed to have taken some of the fire out of her. Or she was burning so hot now that the flames wer-en't even visible anymore. She'd been like that once before. A long time ago. It was a dangerous time.

'It's only one seat, and let's be honest, he is probably going to win anyway. He's got an approval rating of 67 per cent. We could put our energy into better things.' Kay bit into her doughnut.

'Unless Bodie has found us someone to run against him, who might be able to cut through?' Janet looked at Lilith a little too long as she spoke. Lilith moved her gaze between Janet and Bodie. 'Isn't that the expression, Kay?' Janet said, giving a sly smile to Insley before taking a careful nibble off the edge of a doughnut.

'Well—' Bodie didn't finish her sentence. Lilith did it for her.

'I'm standing against Ben.' Lilith's voice was clean and pol-ished. Like steel.

Bodie looked around the table – two reactions surprised her. Kay's anger and Insley's lack of surprise.

'Seriously, you Lilith?' Kay laughed. 'You do not have to do this, Lilith.' Kay's syrupy voice had a bitter tone to it. 'Don't let Insley talk you into this. I mean, think about the girls. You were so worried about how all of this would affect them. Going after their father. Won't that be bad for them?'

Bodie was about to interject. Then she felt Insley's firm hand on her bare arm. Bodie remained a spectator. This was not her battle. Lilith spoke up.

'Growing up in a country where we all pretend men like their father are good people, just to keep the peace, will be bad for them, Kay. I've played nice, I've followed all the rules and where has it got me? Or them? They are growing up to expect men to

behave like this. They will become adults and work out themselves that I have lied to them. That it was all just a fairytale
and that not all frogs are princes. Sometimes they are poisonous
toads. And if I don't show them how to tell the difference now,
they may end up making the same mistakes I have. It's time for
me to tell my story. The real one. I think it's time we stopped
playing pretend. Don't you, Kay?'

Insley stroked Bodie's arm as Bodie glanced out the window.
The rabbit had gone, and Bodie's bones didn't ache anymore.
At least, not the way they had before. They ached with relief.
A letting go. The way it felt when she surrendered to the ocean
and let a wave take her weight.

As Kay wrestled her pout under control, Aaron spoke. 'I'll
help you prepare something, Lilith. If you want?' He kept his
eyes on Lilith, carefully looking past Kay. It was wise. He would
have been cut to shreds by the daggers flying out of Kay's eyes.
'You know, to announce that you are running.'

'Thank you, Aaron,' Lilith replied, her voice sounding in-
creasingly confident.

'You can't do this.' Kay sounded annoyed. 'You're British,
aren't you?'

'Really, Kay?' Insley spoke for the room. It sounded desperate. Bodie suspected Insley had been right about Kay. It was just
as well Bodie had kept her close. It must have made it easier for
Insley to keep tabs on her. Bodie hoped her granddaughter was
as devious as she suspected.

'Ben made me renounce my citizenship when we got married,' Lilith replied. 'He thought it would be bad for his career
to have an English wife.'

Aaron chuckled and shook his head.

'You think this is funny, Aaron?' Kay spat the words out.

'No, as a matter of fact, I think it's awful.' Aaron put his
half-eaten doughnut down and looked sincerely at Lilith at the

end of the table. 'I think what you went through, Lilith, was awful, and I think you are brave for doing this. We should address the citizenship thing first when we make the announcement. We should also explain why you denounced it. I'm not letting the fucker get away with anything.'

'I've had an idea,' Lilith said cautiously. 'We ask our candidates, and the Labor candidates and Queentide supporters, to share the threats they've received ... And their hospital photos.'

'Jesus' – Kay jumped up – 'you don't really think people want to see that shit, do you?'

'They might not want to see it, but they should see it,' Insley said. 'I think it's a great idea, Lilith. I'm sure Aaron does too. He just can't tell you that in case his girlfriend tells him off.'

Aaron pretended to throw a doughnut at Insley but then took a bite instead. Bodie warmed on the nostalgia of them play-fighting.

'I do think it's a good idea, actually,' Aaron said, keeping his head down. 'It might be good to start with the candidate from Ballarat. You know the one who had the baby formula cans thrown at her from the moving car?'

Bodie winced. The candidate, Sally, had been heckled about being childless. She'd had five miscarriages and decided to not keep trying. She'd decided not to talk about it publicly because she was worried people would think she was making it up to get sympathy. One of the formula cans had split her head open – she'd been in hospital for days.

'I'll share my story first,' Lilith said, 'if you want. I'm happy to publish the threats made against me from MASC. And from Ben.'

'Sure ...' Aaron began to answer.

'You can ask the hospital for the photos too. From the night Ben assaulted me.'

'What?' Kay looked incredulous. 'You've always said he

wasn't violent.'

'He was. Once. It's what made me decide to leave. I knew if he did it again, one of us would end up dead because I wouldn't let him do that again without fighting back. So I planned, and I left.'

Bodie noticed Kay's jaw clench. She was angry, it seemed, at Lilith, but that made no sense.

'You can't do that, Lilith.' The syrup was growing stale in Kay's voice. 'People won't believe you. It's been so long since you left Ben and the girls ...'

'I didn't leave the girls, Kay. They came with me,' Lilith said flatly.

'Whatever. My point is that no one is going to believe you. The voters will think you've manufactured this so-called abuse to win an election.'

Bodie looked up to the ceiling, hoping to find some patience there. But all she found was peeling paint and a broken chandelier.

'Ms Conway,' Bodie boomed, the exertion making her heart skip just a little, 'the truth of Lilith's story is not to be questioned. Not in this room. Not by you.'

'I'm sorry,' the younger woman retreated. 'It's just that it's such a personal thing. Does she really want to be bringing that up in public?'

'I think that's the point, Kay,' Insley said sarcastically.

'So you'll be volunteering your very personal story, will you, Insley?'

'What are you talking about?' Insley's voice was relaxed, but Bodie could feel her granddaughter's foot tapping under the table, the way it did when it was the only safe place to store her anger.

'Well, my *boyfriend* tells me that you've got quite an interesting story to tell.' The malice in Kay's voice made the air feel thin.

Bodie looked over at Aaron, chewing his doughnut very slow-ly and avoiding looking across the table. He wouldn't have told Kay, would he? His head was hanging the way it did when he was a kid, and he'd been caught stealing marshmallows from the kitchen to give to the bullies at school. Bodie wanted to hug him but slap him in the face at the same time.

'Well, I think your *boyfriend* is maybe saying things to try to impress you. Or get into your pants. Maybe he should have just offered to get you a job. I hear that's all that's usually needed.'

'Nice, Insley. So much for feminism.'

'I can still be a feminist and think you are a manipulative bitch who doesn't deserve the job she's got.' Insley was on her feet now.

Kay soon followed.

'I'm not scared of you, Insley. This tough-girl routine does nothing for me. And your opinion of me really makes no differ-ence. You are a liability, Insley. Do you know that? If Kathleen fails, if Bodie fails, it will be because of you.' Kay pulled her jacket from the back of the chair. 'I'm done here. While she is part of this, Bodie, I want nothing to do with Queentide, and neither will Kathleen.' Kay strode towards the door and paused. 'Come on, Aaron.'

'I'm staying here, Kay.' Aaron held his chin up high. 'I want to help Lilith.'

'Suit yourself,' Kay said dismissively. 'When you decide to start thinking for yourself again, you know where to find me.'

The room was silent. No one seemed to want to talk or leave until it was certain that Kay had gone. After a few moments, Helen and Janet made their apologies and left. Lilith offered to make coffee. Bodie suspected that Lilith felt the same thing – Aaron and Insley needed some time. Bodie excused herself, but Insley wouldn't take her hand off her arm, so she stayed.

'Hey Insley,' – Aaron's voice broke the silence – 'do you think you can you give me a ride home? Or give me more advice on how to talk to women?'

'How about you shut the fuck up, Az.' Insley had her arms crossed. 'It sounds like you've been talking to women a little too much recently.'

'I didn't tell her everything, Insley.' Aaron made a sign with his middle two fingers. Bodie recognised it from when they were kids. She never found out what it meant. What else had Bodie missed along the way? What had she not done to help her granddaughter while she was off saving everyone else?

Chapter 24

Insley had been young when her dad had killed her mum. So young, in fact, that people sometimes assumed she wouldn't remember or know the details. But Insley did. She knew them all intimately. Bodie had kept all the press cuttings, had not ignored questions, had not shushed away cries, had not dismissed Insley's night terrors as just bad dreams. Bodie was not going to pretend her daughter had never lived and that a part of Insley hadn't died.

The ten-year-old Insley, who saw it happen, didn't die, though. And she never really grew up. Little Insley stuck around like some distorted Peter Pan, motherless. There was always a sound, a smell, or even a word that would take Insley to Neverland. To the place where she could never forget.

Bodie tried hard to do everything right for Insley. She was being tortured by her own cruel pixie, reminding her *she had not known.* On the nights at the community when Insley couldn't sleep in case she dreamed, she'd sit on the stairs, the step that didn't creak, and listen to the women's circle. Bodie would join in. The great Bodie Hughes, mother of modern feminism, could not even stop her own daughter from ending up dead. Battered by her husband. What a cliché. Where had Bodie been while her daughter cried out for her? (And she did – Insley was there, she heard her call out to her mother. She thought it might help Bodie to know that her daughter had wanted her. It didn't.) She was off helping other women in Nevada with their own bruises and tears.

Insley didn't tell Bodie that she'd been sitting on the non-creaking step and heard Bodie's pain escaping. Insley thought, somehow, that would make it all the worse for Bodie, that she'd feel she'd done something wrong. So Insley couldn't tell Bodie that it wouldn't have helped if Bodie had been in Sydney and not in Nevada. Insley couldn't tell her that loads of people had told her mum to get out, and she'd even tried. Once. But she was like a rabbit that had heard a gunshot. Frozen, not sure if it was safer to stay or run. So she stayed. Insley swallowed that all down and instead loved her grandmother fiercely, as brightly as she could. Hoping it would burn out any guilt that remained.

Bodie had been determined that Insley would not hate men. Her father had not been a man, she would say. He had been a murderer. An alcoholic. A narcissist. Bodie would say over and over that he was a reflection of his past. He had been abused himself. He'd grown up not knowing how to love someone. Insley would listen, sometimes nod, but it was his hand around her mother's throat. His bones and muscles that had tightened and tightened, crushing her windpipe. Extinguishing her.

Bodie seemed happy that the only friend Insley had was a boy. But, to Insley, he was just Aaron. He was different from everyone else.

Insley hated school – it was just a waiting room for her. Somewhere she had to hang around until her real-life began. The kids at school would annoy her, fluttering from one thing to another, TV show, popstars, which boys were looking at which girls. They never landed on anything important. And there was so much in the world that was important. So she tried to show them that some things were important. She protested to ban meat in the school cafeteria, which involved lots of tomato sauce and specimens from the lab. She wore her skirt to school but stitched it down the middle to make it into trousers, which girls weren't allowed to wear. She painted a mural on the side of the school, with Aaron holding a torch, of the massacre of Aboriginal people that had happened right there, under the concrete of their netball courts. She tried to make them take notice. And they did, but usually to laugh at her and call her a freak. Except for one person. A girl who never said a word, but she smiled. Kindly. And that smile, or maybe it was the kindness, made it worth it.

One day she spoke. She invited Insley to a party when they were sixteen. The girl was popular but different. There was a frequency in her that matched Insley's. Transmission understood.

A quiet room was found, and, in the darkness, worlds and lips met. Too tuned in to each other to remember there was a world around them. Too tuned in to each other to hear a door open, and two men, called boys in the trial to get some sympathy, walk in. Insley noticed them in the darkness, watching. The girls tried to leave. The men wanted a show. The girls did not want to put one on. That wasn't an option. The girls struggled. The girls were overpowered. Insley was held by her hair and made to watch one man pour himself over and inside the girl with the kind smile, then throw her in a heap on the floor to make room for Insley.

Insley claimed, in the trial, that she didn't know what happened next. The men did not tell because, if they did, they'd have to admit what they did – they would be found guilty. But Insley did remember. There was no red mist, no loss of senses. The thing her father had claimed in his own trial. There was absolute clarity. There was a choice. She knew that she could sacrifice some hair, let it be ripped out of her scalp, and she would be free. She could get to the locked door and get help. But she knew that wouldn't be enough. So she decided instead to attack. In the trial, they said it was unprovoked because she could have got out at that point instead of smashing a beer bottle over the poor boy's head. And picking up a broken piece of glass and running it down his fresh young cheek. Leaving him scarred, branded for life. The boys ran out of the room to get help. Leaving Insley to explain the crying girl and the blood to the other kids, who already thought she was weird. They told her to get out. They'd take care of the girl. She'd obviously done something wrong.

When the police came to speak to Insley, she thought the girl must need her help. She told the police everything, then it became clear they had no idea what she was talking about. She was being arrested for assault; she wasn't being interviewed about someone else's rape.

The girl wouldn't support Insley's story, their story. She called Insley to say sorry. The day before Insley's trial. She couldn't be a witness. She couldn't say what they had done to her. She couldn't explain why she had been alone in a dark room with Insley in the first place. It was too much shame. Her parents. Her friends.

On the morning of the trial, she was found hanging in the very room where she had been attacked. A shaven-headed Insley pleaded guilty at the hearing – the only words she spoke – and withdrew her statements, saying she had lied. Insley walked out with a good behaviour bond – conviction recorded – a court order to see a psychiatrist and a distrust of the legal system.

The psychiatrist talked about PTSD, suggested therapy and pills. Insley played along. She didn't want Bodie to worry. But Bodie had already decided that a different sort of kiss would make it all better.

When her father's parole came up, the police asked if Insley wanted to make a victim impact statement. It might keep him in longer.

'I'm done with being a victim' was all she said. Bodie didn't release the question, even though Insley could see it squirming inside her – why, for the love of God, would she let that man walk the streets, free after only eight painfully short but cavernously long years? She didn't say this. She didn't ask. She trusted her granddaughter.

It isn't hard to get away with something when people think you are too weak to do anything. They don't suspect. They can't even consider the possibility that they are wrong about you. Even with her criminal record, what was the danger in her seeing her father? What was the threat in their meeting alone, without a parole officer? She had learned her lesson; she wouldn't cause any trouble. She was seeing a psychiatrist and doing well. The reports said so. Saying all the right things. Putting on the track they wanted to hear. And he was repentant. He wouldn't risk going back in. He wouldn't hurt her. He was putting on the right track too. Like father, like daughter.

Bodie was less sure. She didn't want Insley to go, at least not alone. She did not trust him. She offered to go too. But Insley said she was scared Bodie would hurt him. She was honest. Insley *was* scared that Bodie would hurt him. Before she got a chance to herself.

So, on the day of his parole, Insley picked him up from the prison gate. She had got her licence just weeks earlier. They drove to a farm that Insley was working at. A place that had a problem with foxes. They'd hired Insley when she showed them what a good shot she was. Strange for a girl to enjoy shooting foxes. But she was good at it.

Nothing to fear, a farm. Plenty of people around, witnesses who saw nothing unusual. Insley had told them she was picking up her dad. She arrived. It was a few hours later when they heard the gun go off and saw Insley run out of her room, screaming for help.

'What has he done?' they asked.

'He got my gun. He wouldn't let me leave.' Insley put on the track she had prepared earlier.

They ran in and saw him, still holding the gun, impossible to tell where his head and the pool of blood separated. Insley was held back, told not to go back in. She even confessed that it was her fault. It was her fault he was dead.

No, they said. He did this himself. They didn't believe her.

Insley stopped confessing. But the second track in her head played over. Of course he didn't do it. It was always someone else's fault. Never his.

Chapter 25

Kay tried to hold her hand steady as the car took a corner. She slid on the plastic-vomit-coloured seats, her stocking catching as she slid over a ripped piece of vinyl. He could have at least sent a car for her instead of making her slum it in an Uber.

'Jesus. Can't you drive a little better?' Kay found a tissue in her bag and corrected the line around her top lip. His house was only a few minutes away. She checked her eyeliner in the small compact she'd got free from a magazine. It wasn't quite perfect, but it would have to do. She hadn't been able to buy a new eye-pencil this week. Her credit card was maxed out. Payday was still a long way off. Last month's payment hadn't been deposited yet, which was odd. She had given them what they'd asked for.

Still, the dress was perfect. He would like it – it would have the desired effect. After tonight, Kay would be able to afford all the things she deserved and pay off the damn credit card.

Kay had hoped Aaron would have taken the bait on the money stuff. But he never did. He'd run her baths and pour her wine and tell her she was smart. All the things men thought women wanted. Maybe some did. But not her. She wanted someone to buy her things. And what was wrong with that?

They were in his driveway. The lights were only on in the bottom part of the house. He'd opened the first gate for her, so she went up the path to the front door. The girls' gumboots were lined up neatly on the porch. Identical, with little cat faces on the front. They had different ones in the community. She'd seen them wearing them when she'd filmed them running around with those placards. Ones with rainbows. When she was a kid, she hadn't even had one pair. She had a pair of trainers that she had to blast with a hairdryer if they got wet.

She could hear Ben on the phone. She rang the buzzer. He flung open the door, clearly annoyed. 'Just a second mate, someone's at the door.' Then, spitting at Kay, 'Couldn't you hear I was on the phone? Come on, before someone sees you.'

'Nice to see you too, Ben,' Kay said to herself. Ben had already gone into the lounge room to continue his call. Kay took off her heels and followed him. She'd learned not to wear them on the carpet.

She looked around as he talked. She'd been here so many times before but very rarely got to see this room. There were portraits of the girls, printed on giant canvases, but no other signs that children lived there. No messy drawings anywhere, a lounge so pale it would scare even the most careful adult. No picture books on the shelves, no toys decorating the wool carpet. Ben was finishing his call. Kay arranged herself perfectly on an armchair, hoping to match the décor. She glanced in the full-length gilded mirror fashionably leaning against the far wall. Yes, Kay looked like she belonged here. She'd fit right in. She was sure of it.

Ben finished his call, then without even speaking to her, headed over to the drinks trolley. He pulled the stopper out of the decanter, the crystal clinking as he tossed it on the silver tray. He took a drink of the bourbon he poured himself, then walked to where Kay was sitting, swirling the liquid as he walked towards her. She knew it was Michter's. She knew quite a lot about Ben Hamilton. More than he realised.

'Where's mine?' Kay tried to sound unbothered.

'You aren't staying long enough to have one,' Ben replied. 'I've got somewhere to be Kay. What are you doing here? You said it was urgent.'

'Lilith is going to run against you,' Kay said bluntly.

'My Lilith?' Ben said.

'Your ex-wife,' Kay corrected him. 'Yes.'

'We aren't divorced yet.' He drained the rest of the glass. 'She's still my wife.'

'Well then, Ben,' – Kay smoothed her hair – 'your wife is going to run against you.'

'I thought you had this under control?' Ben was back at the drinks trolley, refilling his glass a little more generously than before.

'Who the hell would have expected her to grow a spine in the space of a few months?' Kay got up and joined him at the trolley. She poured herself a drink. 'I thought you were handling that side of things anyway. Or don't you have that under control?'

'Watch it, Kay.' He snatched the glass out of her hand and slammed it on the silver, a few dollars worth of bourbon spilling over the sides. 'So what are you going to do about it?'

'Do about what?' Kay tried to take the quiver out of her voice. This was not going how she had planned.

'What are you going to do about Lilith? Can't you get that boyfriend of yours to intervene?' He was drinking quickly, almost nothing left in the glass.

'I don't think you understand, Ben. I'm done. I can't keep doing this. I've done my bit here,' Kay said. 'I've told you everything they've been doing. Every protest, every article Aaron has planned. I've given you contact details. Jesus, I've even sabotaged Kathleen's campaign for you. I've made myself look fucking useless – giving her the wrong time for radio interviews, letting your fucking neo-Nazis in through back doors ...'

'They aren't neo-Nazis, Kay. They are men's rights activists.'

'Well, they are fucking racist ones. Honestly, you should consider getting some new friends.' Kay checked her reflection in the mirror. 'Some of the shit they yelled at her—'

Ben's face arrived in the reflection in a matter of seconds. He grabbed her chin and pulled her face towards his.

'Don't you ever, ever, fucking tell me who to be friends with,' he yelled.

Kay got her arm underneath his and flicked it away, his fingers reluctant to let go of her face, pulling her skin like a leech. Having grown up in a rough neighbourhood had its advantages. It had given her a chance to practice some self-defence that she'd had to use over the years.

'Don't you ever, ever, fucking put your hands on me again. I'm not your pathetic ex-wife.' Kay rubbed her cheek where his fingers had been. 'Sorry, wife.'

He slapped her hard. Before she had time to feel the sting, she scraped her nails down his face, pausing only long enough to decide it was worth wrecking her manicure.

'You bitch.' He had dropped his glass to hold his face. Crystal and bourbon sprinkled all over the carpet, refracting coloured lights all over the bare walls. 'You've been hanging around those fucking witches too long, Kay. Caught yourself a bit of feminism.'

'Please,' Kay spat back, 'I don't need to be a feminist to know you are an arsehole.' A part of Kay wished Insley had got to hear her say that. 'Just give me my money, and you'll never have to see me again.'

Ben laughed. 'You think I'm going to give you money? For what exactly? Our deal was you kept them under control, and I'd pay you.'

'And I did.' Kay felt the anger rise. She could accept the rejection. Even the violence. But she hadn't thought he wouldn't pay her. 'You can't break a deal.'

'Actually, I think you'll find I can.' He stepped over the broken crystal, went to the tray and found a new glass. He tossed it up in the air and caught it. 'You see Kay, I was brought up to value things. Look around you. I don't buy cheap things.' He looked her up and down. 'And no matter what packaging you try to wrap yourself up in, you, my dear, will always be bargain-basement goods. And I'm not buying.' He smiled and took a swig of his expensive bourbon. Then he reached into his pocket and pulled out his wallet. 'I'll tell you what,' – he pulled some fifties loose from the stack, counting them – 'I'll pay you for the sex, how about that? We've done it, what, five times? There you go, three hundred for your trouble.'

He stuffed the money into her cleavage. She was too shocked to respond. She stepped back and stood on some crystal. It dug into her foot, but she ignored it and held her head high. She walked out silently and slowly, picking up her fake Louis Vuitton shoes and the equally phoney matching bag on her way out.

Once she was out of the gate and had hobbled a little way down the path, she let the tears out. She looked down. There was blood on the path. She sat on some rich person's sandstone wall and examined her foot. The sun twinkled on the glass in her foot like a bloodied diamond. She used her chipped nails to dig it out, then flung it into the garden bed behind her. She didn't want a little kid to stand on it.

She squeezed her bloodied foot into her shoe. Then checked her face in her mirror. At least the cheap mascara hadn't run. She pulled the crumpled money from her dress and straightened it, counting as she went. At least she could get a decent cab now. She called Silver Service, giving the street name and the number on the letterbox next to her.

Then she took a breath and called Aaron. She still had something someone would buy.

'It's me … yeah, I know I said don't call me, but I'm calling you. Look, if someone had information on Ben, solid stuff linking him to the threats to the candidates and to MASC, do you think Queentide would buy it?'

Chapter 26

Kathleen was on Safe Street for the third time. Since Kay had left, Kathleen had managed her campaign precisely the way she wanted. Kathleen refused all the offers of new chiefs-of-staff. A few of her colleagues were worried – they thought she was too naïve, too inexperienced, to do it herself. But, after a couple of weeks, even her most vocal critic had finally shut the hell up and let her get on with it.

The Prime Minister still hadn't been down to see Safe Street, and he was getting a lot of backlash for it. Of course, everyone forgot that he couldn't see it, anyway. It was a woman-only zone.

They had barricaded two ends of Pitt Street. In the heart of Sydney on an ordinary Wednesday afternoon. They'd used flat-packed planter boxes that they assembled right there. A line of women in combat pants patrolled either end. The police came down and politely asked what they thought they were doing. They provided their pretty simple demand. Give us one street where women can feel safe. The Lord Mayor sent down some chrysanthemums for the planter boxes. They weren't blocking any shops. They weren't blocking any traffic. This was Safe Street. No one was put in danger. Tents appeared, put up in an orderly line down one side of what had been a bustling street. Food was distributed from a kitchen. The sounds of a guitar and poetry being read were always in the air. Kathleen thought she'd heard Insley reading one day when she was there but, then again, Kathleen thought she heard Insley everywhere she went. She didn't want to, but she missed her.

The rules of Safe Street were displayed at the entrance. All female-identifying people welcome. Free childcare provided. No men. No violence, physical or emotional. Legal aid and healthcare were free for all. Everyone was expected to contribute and support Safe Street. For a week or so, it felt like a festival. Social media buzzed, wondering if more streets would appear in other cities.

Before they could, MASC came. They tried to storm both entrances, throwing flaming rags into Safe Street. A tent caught fire, but no one was hurt. Everyone expected that to be the end, but instead, a woman called Wendy, who had been appointed the President of Safe Street, challenged the country on live breakfast television to show that it could let women feel safe on just 500 metres of concrete.

Within an hour, busloads of men had arrived to guard the entrances. But that was not what they wanted. And that's why Kathleen was there.

'It makes us feel like a bloody harem, a bunch of men fencing us in like this.' Wendy said.

'They are trying to keep you safe,' Kathleen said diplomatically. 'Their intentions are good.'

'We asked them to show us they could respect our safety, and this is how they have to do it? By forming a human barricade?'

'Look, I get it. But you've got to play the long game here. You've got a bunch of men publicly saying that they want women to feel safe,' Kathleen said. 'They are literally getting between you and MASC.'

'I know, but it's so fucking demeaning, you know?' The woman's shoulders dropped. Her head shook defeatedly.

Kathleen nodded. She'd spent her whole life seeing the effects of people doing what they thought was right, without asking.

'What do you want, Wendy?' Kathleen asked.

'I want women to stop having to carry their keys in between their fingers when they walk down the street. I want there to be no such thing as a rape victim anymore. I want women to be able to have kids and have a job. Or not have kids and not feel guilty about it. I want trans women to not have to worry about going to the hospital. I want the fucking world to treat us the way it treats straight white men.' Wendy was almost shaking as she spoke. 'That's what I want. And they can't even fucking manage to do that in this tiny little space. How the hell is this country ever going to get any better?'

'By electing a gay Aboriginal woman?' Kathleen smiled. Wendy laughed but was also crying a bit.

'I think that would be a bloody good start.' Wendy hugged Kathleen. 'And I guess, to do that, you kinda need the blokes on side, right?'

Kathleen shrugged. 'They make up half of the electorate. I need some of them to vote for me. The men who dropped everything to come down here are probably my best bet.'

Wendy nodded. 'Okay, I get it. I'll have to speak to the woman who's been heading up security, though. I can't guarantee she's going to think as strategically as I am. She's a bit more radical than most of the women here.' Wendy looked a little embarrassed. 'I think you know her, actually.'

'Insley Hughes?' Kathleen asked, knowing the answer. She'd been out of the papers for a while, but not long enough for people to forget it was her ex-girlfriend. 'I'll talk to her.'

'Sure, if you think that will help.'

'I've no idea,' Kathleen smiled. 'but I'll give it a go.'

'You'll find her at the southern end. It's where we get the most trouble,' Wendy said. Of course, it is, thought Kathleen.

She weaved through the groups of people. Stopping to shake hands and have selfies taken. The time it took to get to Insley from the time she saw her seemed forever. It was probably no more than a minute. Insley stared at her the whole time, while Kathleen smiled at her supporters and waved to little kids. Insley was trying to look calm, but her bouncing foot gave her away.

Kathleen finally reached her. Up close, Insley looked terrible.

'When did you last sleep?' she asked, stopping herself from stroking Insley's grey face.

'I don't need to sleep anymore – Starbucks is giving us free coffee.' Insley smiled. 'Has Wendy sent you down here to pacify me?'

'More like reason with you.' Kathleen wondered if Insley could tell she missed her.

'No need. If I wanted the GI Joes gone, they'd be gone. I figured it was good publicity having some testosterone out front.'

'What, you're okay with this?' Kathleen wondered if Insley really was sleep deprived.

'I'm more than okay with it. I organised it.' Insley took a sip out of an oversized paper cup. 'Jesus, this tastes worse than Bodie's.'

'What do you mean you organised it?' Kathleen was getting a familiar feeling of not wanting to have her fears about Insley confirmed.

'I got the men down here.' Insley half-smiled. 'I even put the buses on for them.'

'You are staging this?' Kathleen demanded.

'Jesus, Kathleen. I'm not a complete psychopath. They want to be here. They aren't actors or anything. They're dads, brothers. Just people I've got to know. They all owe me a favour. One way or another. I've helped them take care of their women. Now they're helping me take care of mine.'

'Fuck, Insley.' Kathleen looked around. No one appeared to be listening. 'What have you done?'

'I've helped, Kathleen,' Insley replied. 'You need men to vote for you, right?'

Kathleen didn't answer; she let Insley continue. 'If men see other men backing women, backing a female prime minister, they won't worry about being called soft for doing it too.'

'I told you I don't need your help.' Kathleen turned to leave.

'It's not just about you, though, is it Kathleen?' Insley shouted.

Kathleen reluctantly went back to Insley. She couldn't have a scene.

'I'm not just helping you.' Insley thankfully lowered her voice. 'If you get elected, women, all women, are going to be better off. They are going to feel safer.'

'You are a complete psychopath.' Kathleen shook her head.

'I get it. You are angry. I've done the one thing you told me not to do. But this has to work, Kathleen. This is everything Bodie has worked for. I'll do everything I have to do to make this happen for her. And you.' Insley added, sadly, 'I'll even lose you.'

'You've already done that, Insley,' Kathleen said.

'Then I guess there's no need to stop, is there?' Insley took another gulp of coffee. 'You can tell Wendy that I'll behave. Aaron's waiting for you to give him an interview – he's at the north end. You can tell him how fucking awesome you are. You've brought peace to Safe Street. You are so happy to see men and women working together.'

Kathleen shook her head.

'I wanted to love you, Insley.'

'You did love me, Kathleen.'

'That wasn't enough for you?' Kathleen's voice was going croaky.

'It was too much, actually.' Insley's lips twitched. 'I didn't deserve it.'

Kathleen tried to breathe, but the air caught in her throat. She heard someone calling her name. She practised a smile, telling her eyes not to blink in case a tear fell, then she turned around and shook more hands. Accepted more selfies. She wondered if anyone would see her broken heart in the photos.

When she got to Aaron, she couldn't see his usual smile underneath his beard. In fact, he looked worried. Before she could even ask, he was telling her why.

'It's Lilith. She's just called,' Aaron said. Kathleen was glad they were spending time together. They'd both been flogging themselves over Kay's betrayal. Kathleen was just happy she was gone. And that she'd never trusted her. It did not surprise her that she had been Ben's spy and had been trying to derail the election. 'Ben hasn't brought the girls back.'

'Maybe he's just running late. I mean, he's an arsehole, but he's not an idiot. The custody case is tomorrow, isn't it? He'd lose them straight away.'

'I don't think Ben is worried about that. He's told Lilith she's not getting them back unless she pulls out of the election.'

'Well, I hope she's told him to get fucked,' Kathleen replied. Lilith could do that now, Kathleen was sure.

'She's worried,' Aaron said. 'She thinks Kay maybe gave him some other ammunition that he could spring on her tomorrow.'

'Like what?' Kathleen asked.

'Let's talk somewhere else?' Aaron guided Kathleen into a doorway. Kathleen flapped her hand at her bodyguard when she saw him lift his walkie-talkie. She was getting used to him being around. She didn't like to admit it, but sometimes she was scared.

'What's going on, Aaron?' Kathleen asked.

'Lilith paid Kay,' – he stumbled over his words – 'well, Queentide did. For some information on Ben. I'm not sure I should tell you any of this. It's putting you in an awkward position.'

'Like I wasn't before?' Kathleen smiled. 'Okay, so Kay got some money out of Queentide, and Lilith authorised it. Not that big a deal.'

'She's a candidate in an upcoming election, using donated funds to pay your former chief of staff for information on her opponent.' Aaron sounded more nervous than usual.

'What information?' Kathleen demanded.

'Kay had emails. They were from a random email account, but they were traceable back to Ben. She had phone records, even bank account details – do not ask me how she got those.' Aaron shook his head. 'Anyway, they all link him to MASC, organising and paying them to threaten the candidates. Attack them. Even you.'

'Aaron, take it to the police,' Kathleen angrily whispered. 'This is serious. You and Lilith can't be playing Tintin and Nancy Drew with this shit.'

'I can't, Kathleen. If we do that, they will want to know how we got the information and ...' Aaron trailed off.

'... and it looks like we've paid Kay to spy on Ben,' Kathleen said exasperatedly, 'the opposite in fact of what has actually been going on.'

'And Lilith loses her girls,' Aaron said.

'So, what can we do?'

'We do nothing. You need to stay out of this. Act like you know nothing. And I play a bit of James Bond,' Aaron joked. 'I've always seen myself as a bit more of a James Bond than a Tintin ... and I get Insley to help me not fuck things up,' he added nervously.

'You do not need her,' Kathleen said, a little too sharply.

'I do, Kathleen,'–Aaron nodded, 'as much as she needs me.'

'I didn't think she needed anyone.'

'Everyone needs someone. Especially the ones who tell themselves they don't.' Aaron smiled and walked away from Safe Street.

Kathleen motioned to her bodyguard to bring the car around. It was time for her to leave too.

Chapter 27

Insley had made it all sound easy. Lilith was to call Ben and tell him that she was pulling out. Aaron had written an article that she could send to Ben if he pushed for proof. Aaron had even filed it with a couple of news outlets, just in case Ben decided to check. Aaron would just pull it once Ben brought the girls back.

When Ben arrived, and the girls were safe, she would show him the other article Aaron had filed, using the information in Kay's file. He didn't need to pull out of the election. Ben didn't even need to stop harassing Lilith, but he had to roll over like a good boy at the custody hearing. If he didn't, the article would be published before he'd even roared away in his car.

Insley was betting on Ben's arrogance. After she announced her candidacy and her story came out, people quickly moved into two camps, those who believed her and those who didn't. The split wasn't even. Ben was still expected to win by a significant amount. The people who supported him didn't seem to think there was anything wrong with giving your wife a black eye. The pressure of the job and all that. Lilith had no chance of securing their vote.

On the face of it, what Lilith was offering him was a chance to win the election and defeat her. And the price was simply to give up something he didn't want anyway, custody of his children. He got to play weekend, dad, and Lilith got to concentrate on her campaign. Insley had plans for that too.

She sat nervously on the stairs, on the step that didn't creak, waiting for him to arrive. Insley's shaven head emerged from the door on the right, which led to Bodie's office and crossed over to the lounge area. The rest of the community was settling into their rooms; it was bedtime for the children. Lilith hoped she'd get to tuck her own kids in soon, too.

She got a text from Aaron, wishing her luck. He'd wanted to be there, but a man in the community at night was not allowed. That's why she was going to have to talk to Ben outside. Insley would be already in place, in the dark. Just in case. Bodie would stay with the girls and wrap them up in stories and hot chocolate until it was over.

The child-charmer emerged from the office, then paused, putting her weight against the doorframe. She let her head fall back, her eyes closed, wincing. She seemed slower recently. The fire in her was still there, but more like glowing embers than the licking flames that Lilith had first seen only a few months earlier. Lilith was running Queentide now, Bodie gradually shrugging off decisions to her, maybe because it had stopped being a movement and was now a business, selling its range of reliable female candidates who could meet even the pickiest voter's needs. And, just like any product, there was quality control to consider, return on investment, marketing, sales. Queentide wasn't just demanding that society change. It was giving the country the means to change it.

Insley had become more distant, knowing her dirty hands weren't on-brand for an organisation trying to be taken seriously as a possible governing body. No one wants to see blood or hear chants in government. They want to see babies kissed and policy documents published. Nevertheless, the blood and chants had to continue if they were going to succeed. Insley was happy to oblige with protests and strikes and whatever the hell else she did. Lilith had stopped asking.

'Lilith, my dear' – Bodie jumped as she looked up the stair-well – 'is that you? That takes me back, seeing you there. Many a night, I'd have to uproot Insley and convince her that small humans needed more than four hours' sleep.' Lilith could just make out her smile in the dark.

'I didn't mean to scare you, Bodie,' Lilith replied.

'A woman sitting alone, at least in this house, doesn't scare me.' She ambled towards the stairs, lowering herself until she made contact with the third step. She stretched her legs out, tapping her feet together, the same way Insley did. The white rubber from her converse boots glowed in the dullness. 'So ... are you ready?'

'Yes,' Lilith said, but her tone said something else.

Bodie nodded. 'Trust her. Insley, I mean.'

'I do. She's thought this all through. I don't see how this can go wrong.'

'If you can't see how it can go wrong, then you aren't pre-pared.' Bodie tilted her head to the side. 'Optimism is great, but pessimism is useful.'

'That makes me feel so much better, Bodie!' Lilith gently laughed. The older woman was, thankfully, not offended.

'Don't panic, Lilith, if something does not go to plan. We have to give a little of ourselves to destiny and trust it will do its job.'

'And what is destiny's job?'

'She's a tour guide. She takes us to the place we are meant to be.' She used the wall to steady herself as she got up. 'But like all good tour guides, she will take you down the most unfamiliar, interesting paths to get there. Whenever you think you're going the wrong way, destiny is just showing you something inter-esting.' Bodie was on two feet now. 'I'm going to get the milk warmed up for the girls. I expect he will be here momentarily.'

Lilith watched her hobble towards the lounge room. She stopped at the threshold as though she had forgotten something.

'Trust her, Lilith.' Bodie looked up at Lilith. Lilith nodded just before Bodie disappeared into the illuminated room. Even though she knew Bodie wouldn't be able to see her in the dark. Even though she didn't know if Bodie meant Insley or destiny. Lilith wondered if they were a difference anymore.

It wasn't long until the car announced itself on the gravel. A chill went through Lilith as though the corridor was filling with ghosts. It was time for the exorcism. Lilith took a breath and descended the stairs, avoiding the creaking ones. She opened the door, the headlights making her squint her eyes. Before the shadows had cleared from her sight, the girls had clouded around her, hugging her and telling her about all the things they'd done since they last saw her. Ben hung back near the car.

'Go on in, girls,' he shouted. 'Your mother and I need to talk.'

Hannah clung to Lilith's long grey cardigan, hiding herself in its folds.

'Yes, go on in, girls.' Lilith beamed at them. 'I think Bodie might have hot chocolate ready for you.'

Hannah was unwrapped by her squealing sister, and they ran inside, dumping their backpacks near the door.

'Get in the car,' Ben snapped at her.

'What?' Lilith responded, confused.

'You heard me.' Ben waved his hand at the open car door. 'Get in the car. I'm not talking out in the open like this.'

Lilith walked towards the car, then reminded herself that the time of her obeying Ben was over.

'No. I won't. What we need to discuss won't take long.' Lilith breathed, trying to drain the blood that had rushed to her brain. 'You know what security is like up here. If you are worried about reporters in the bushes, then you don't need to.'

'What about that one you are shagging now?' Ben spat out the words. 'Jesus, Lilith. I mean, even you could do better than that.'

'Excuse me?' Lilith laughed. 'Do you mean Aaron?'

'Yeah, that piss-poor one that keeps telling us how we need to be nicer to women,' Ben said, 'like he's not just doing it to get laid.'

Lilith felt fractures forming, years of held-back words ready to break through the dam walls. A rabbit passed between Ben and Lilith, hopping through the streams of light that separated them. It was unconcerned by them. It had somewhere to be and carried on. She did the same.

'I won't be pulling out of the election,' Lilith said clearly.

'Really?' He let out a deflated laugh. 'Well, I guess you'd better get used to not being called Mum then.'

'You won't be fighting for custody tomorrow,' Lilith said. 'You won't be taking anything to the police.'

'I don't remember ever saying that you got to tell me what to do.' Ben's brow furrowed as though he didn't know who the woman in front of him was.

'Look at this.' She handed him the folder; he snatched it out of her hands. He held it near the headlight so he could read it.

'He can't publish this.' The car headlights uplit Ben's face, making it look even more crumpled.

'Why?' Lilith tilted her head to the side, savouring seeing him on the back foot.

'It's slander.' Ben's voice sounded panicked. 'I'll deny it.'

'Aaron is a good journalist.' Lilith smiled uncontrollably. 'He has corroborated evidence.'

'That bitch ...' Ben shouted.

'Yes. Kay was, wasn't she? I mean, fooling Aaron and me, that's one thing. It's easy to make lonely people trust you, isn't it? You just have to show them a tiny bit of love.' Lilith let the fractures widen. She was done bearing the pressure for him. 'But tricking you, Ben Hamilton, the expert at manipulation and cheating, you could have done better.'

'If you don't shut the fuck up right now ...' Ben's fist was crushing the folder. Lilith felt her own fists clench too.

'You'll what?' She laughed. 'Hit me? The element of surprise is gone there, Ben.'

'Don't push me, Lilith.' The folder was now lying on the ground, the wind picking up the edges.

'At least you are giving out warnings these days.' Lilith heard some gravel crunch behind Ben. It was Insley. She held her finger to her mouth. She didn't even move when Ben advanced on Lilith.

'You really are a nasty little bitch – do you know that?' Ben sneered.

'Fuck off, Ben!' Lilith screamed. Both of them jumped, surprised at her venom and volume.

'What did you say?' He had recovered and was now right in front of her, blocking Lilith's view of Insley.

'You need me to repeat it?' Lilith yelled in his face, 'Fuck. Off.'

'Don't ever speak to me like that.' His hand was over her mouth. 'Do you hear me?' He pressed down harder. Lilith tried to prise his fingers off her. She kept trying to talk. He pressed harder. 'I am sick of hearing your voice. On the phone to the girls. Your fucking fake motherly cooing. On the radio, pretending like you are someone. You are no-one Lilith Henderson, do you understand me?'

He was shaking her now, making her panic bubble to the surface. Lilith kept fighting to get the words out. From the corner of her eye, she saw some rabbits emerging from the shadows, watching the spectacle. Then they scattered. Lilith was pulled forward and saw two skinny arms wrap around Ben's head like tattooed snakes. Insley's leather cuff grazing Lilith's cheek as she tried to pry Ben off Lilith. He released his grip on Lilith's face, and she stumbled backwards.

Insley had now jumped off Ben's back, and before he could refind his centre of gravity, she'd kicked his feet out from under him. He was sprawled on the ground, and Insley was standing over him.

'Hey there, Benny.' Insley was out of breath. 'I don't think we've been formally introduced.'

He scrambled to his feet and lunged at Insley. She sidestepped him elegantly, as though they were in a dance, as though the whole thing had been choreographed.

'Bit too much bourbon tonight, Ben?' She kicked his feet out from under him again. 'Looking a bit unsteady on your feet there. Now, I'm going to make this very easy for you. You are going to get in that flash car of yours and drive away. You'll turn up in court tomorrow, the picture of cooperative parenting, and we'll all forget that you just tried to kill my friend Lilith over there. Am I understood?'

He nodded slowly. Insley turned briefly towards Lilith. 'You okay?' Lilith tried to answer, but all she could manage was a nod. 'You'll be fine. Now straighten that fucking crown, princess, and go see your girls.'

Insley smiled as Lilith put her hands to her head and made the sign that Lilith had seen Kathleen and Insley exchange at that first meeting.

Insley was still smiling when Ben came up behind her and hit her with the rock. She unravelled onto the ground.

Lilith was still screaming Insley's name when Ben grabbed her and dragged her into the darkness.

She felt twigs and branches catch in her hair and pull at her cardigan as he dragged her along the walkway, like a child

clamouring to stop their mother from leaving them. She recognised this part of the forest, even in the dark. It was the trail the
girls enjoyed. The one Lilith never let them finish on their own
because it came out at the unfenced headland. The realisation
hit her in the stomach, and she stumbled on a rock, Ben's tight
grasp around her waist preventing her from falling, ironically.

Lilith screamed out, not words, just desperate sounds. Ben
wasn't trying to stop her – it was as though he didn't even hear
her. He wasn't saying anything, just powering on and hefting
her along the path, as though she was just an awkward, heavy
piece of furniture he was trying to move.

The smell of eucalyptus was getting fainter – they were approaching the rocky outcrop near the edge of the cliff. Lilith
tried to make herself a deadweight, but then Ben swept her off
her feet, carrying her in his arms, the grip more aggressive than
on their wedding night.

She briefly stopped screaming, and in the silence, she heard
something moving, gaining ground. She thought of all the
foxes she'd seen from her bedroom window. She looked over
Ben's shoulder, hoping to catch a glimpse of one last animal.
The beam swept over them from the lighthouse on the opposite
headland, then continued on its way. In the clearing, only a few
metres from the edge, all noises were drowned out by the waves
crashing against the rocks. No more animals. No more hope.
But then came Insley's voice.

'Put her down,' Insley yelled in between sea blasts.

Ben spun around, still holding Lilith. He was struggling with
the weight, his feet shuffling.

'That's exactly what I plan to do,' Ben said flippantly.

Lilith's veins were pulsing. She squirmed, trying to break
free. His grip tightened.

'Do you think I'd let you get past me if you did that? You'd be
finished, Ben.' Insley was edging closer. Ben's breathing slowed,

his grip becoming a little looser. The reality was catching up to him. The lighthouse beam swept over them again.

'Let her go like I told you and get in your car.' Insley was so close, Lilith could see the blood glistening on her temple where the rock had hit her. Where Ben had hit her. Lilith wanted to reach out and make it better. Insley winked at her and pushed the imaginary crown on her head.

'So what's it going to be, Ben? You going to put her down?'

Ben flung his arms out in a flourish, sending Lilith crashing to the rock slab at his feet. She scrambled to get away from the edge.

'Well done, Ben.' Insley clapped. 'Finally making some good life choices.'

Ben didn't move away from the edge. Insley kept her eyes on him as she helped Lilith get back on her feet.

'Go back to the house, Lilith,' Insley said. 'The girls are waiting for you.'

'No, I'm not going without you.' Lilith stared at Ben, not wanting to take her eyes off him.

'Benny and I are just going to hang for a bit.' Insley gently pushed Lilith towards the path. 'Go.'

Lilith walked sideways. Trying to keep them in view as she made her way to the path. The light made another sweep, and she could see the two figures at checkmate on the rock. Then a little further along, at the entrance to the alternative trail, there was a third figure. The grey spikes reflected like peaked waves in the light.

It all went dark again, and then she heard Ben shout. As the lighthouse beam made its rounds, the three figures flickered and moved like a flipbook. Ben had hold of Insley. Bodie was still a little distance away. Ben had dragged Insley to the edge. Bodie's figure was now merged with Ben and Insley. Insley had broken free. Ben had hit Bodie. Bodie had fallen.

Lilith waited for the light, waiting for Bodie to get back up. But when the light came, only two figures remained. Lilith ran back to the edge.

'Bodie!' Insley's voice filled the entire sky. Ben stood frozen, looking at the rocks below.

'What did you do?' Lilith yelled as she reached him. She shook his arms, which were limp at his side.

'I didn't mean ...' Ben stuttered.

Insley was curled in a ball, close to the edge, looking over. Lilith wondered if she was trying to find a path down. As the light came around, Insley screamed again. Lilith went to Insley, wanting to make it better. Even though she knew she could never.

'It was an accident ...' Ben's voice was further away. He was heading towards the track.

'You bastard.' Insley was scrambling after him.

'Insley, leave him! We have to get help.' Lilith knew, even as she said it, that it was too late for help. And that Insley would pursue Ben Hamilton for the rest of his life.

For days afterwards, time became jumbled. The world had been shaken like a snow globe, and events swirled and twisted, refusing to settle.

Lilith could only remember what had happened, not when it had happened or what came first. She remembered the relief at finding the children in their beds and the initial panic when she saw their backpacks missing from the corridor. There was a police officer who took honey in the tea that one of the community women had made him while trying not to cry. She remembered Janet De Marco's silence when she had called her to tell her that her best friend was dead. Insley refused to have her face cleaned by anyone and left a bloodstain on her grandmother's blanket, which Lilith had wrapped around her on the sofa where she slept.

Lilith could still hear the helicopter groaning through the air as it made its pass over the headland and remembered bawling when she heard it land on the large oval behind the community. The place where they brought all the bodies of the people who destiny had abandoned on the unfenced headland.

A memory of Ben's car not being there when she returned to the community to call the police. There was the custody hearing that Ben didn't show for, but Janet did and made Lilith show her face, too, somehow. She remembered the news bulletin telling people to not approach Ben but to report his whereabouts.

Lilith remembered trying to explain death to two little girls who still believed in magic, who would always believe in Bodie. She remembered Insley leaving, taking the tarot card out of the frame on Bodie's desk, and refusing to tell anyone, even Aaron, where she was going.

There were media and opinions everywhere, and truth shredded and scattered among it all: Ben had killed Bodie; Lilith knew more than she was saying; this would only help Queentide. Lilith remembered being shocked at how many ways people's hearts could break: with remembered moments, with anger, with remorse, with guilt. She remembered the Bodie-shaped hole that appeared immediately in the world and the realisation that materialised, just as quickly, that it could never be filled and instead would keep expanding until it swallowed everything.

Lilith remembered, most of all, hoping that Insley had gone to hunt Ben down and kill him.

Chapter 28

He had been found dead in the garage, his car's engine still running, just before Bodie's memorial service. The husband of the missing woman. At the back of the tiny theatre, with its wooden chairs and lavish organ at the front, Aaron looked over his notes from the media conference. Not one journalist had asked about the search for the wife or about the husband's connections to MASC. He was starting to think Insley's idea of a quota for women journalists at media conferences wasn't such a bad idea after all. He was getting kind of tired of being the voice for women at these things and the grief he got from the other journos for it.

The old door creaked as a few mourners entered. One was Janet De Marco, or at least a version of her. It was the first time Aaron had ever seen her without makeup, her hair tied back. He waved at her. She dabbed her eyes with a lace-edged handkerchief and gave a half-wave to him. The woman Janet came in with, someone Aaron recognised from Queentide meetings, guided Janet to a chair, and slipped her a hipflask. Aaron hoped there would be someone to do that for him when he had to say goodbye to his best friend. Aaron always had a feeling that day was closer than he wanted it to be.

Janet raised the hipflask towards the massive photo of Bodie on the stage, next to a lectern. More mourners came in, and the seats near the front filled up. There must have been about three hundred chairs lined up in there. He felt a little nervous. He'd have to get up to speak soon. With Insley still missing in action, the job had been left to him to deliver a eulogy. He'd half-jokingly asked Lilith if he could hand out copies instead of speaking. She hadn't even smiled. Insley would have done. Then punched him in the arm and told him to stop being pathetic. He missed his friend.

He'd spent the first few days trying to find her. He'd left messages, gone to her safe houses, went into the chatrooms he knew she hung out in. He'd had no luck. But then he got a call from a magazine editor, asking him if he wanted to write an article about the spread of attacks on men who'd been found guilty of rape. She wanted a female empowerment angle on it – she knew it was his sort of thing. When he'd stopped rolling his eyes, he listened and pretended to know what she was talking about. Since Bodie had died and Insley had disappeared, Queentide was drifting, and it wasn't monitoring developments like this. The editor explained that the attacks were all along the east coast, on men who'd just been released from prison. None of the men could, or would, give an accurate description of their attacker. But there was one similarity – they'd all been held down and branded on their left cheek, a big R burned into the side of their face.

Aaron started mapping the attacks. He got his police contacts up and down the coast to tip him off if they got a report of one. The last one was in Ballarat, just outside Melbourne. Near to where the husband had been found dead. One of Insley's associates there – she had no friends anywhere – had seen her a day before. Aaron pushed the two facts far away from each other, not allowing them to connect.

A blue-haired woman took her place at the organ and began to play. There was an incongruity stopping Aaron from identifying the tune. He laughed when he finally realised she was playing 'Plump' by Hole. A few people turned and stared at him, reproachfully. Aaron sank a little into his seat. Shuffling backwards to let someone pass, he awkwardly moved his legs to the side. He glanced down as their feet shuffled past him. Who would wear Doc Martens to a memorial? He looked up and realised that she was the person he loved more than anyone else in the world.

'She'd be glad someone laughed – she'd picked out her funeral tunes ages ago. She'd probably be surprised they got played on an organ.'

'Insley!' Aaron burst into tears. She sat down, keeping her grey hood on. The leather jacket she wore over the top creaked a little as she found a pack of tissues in her pocket and handed it to him.

'Here, I came prepared,' Insley said.

'I didn't think you'd come,' he said as he blew his nose, the tissue shredding a little on his beard. Insley smiled, called him a dork, and brushed it away.

'I didn't think I would either,' she whispered. 'Aren't you going to ask where I've been?'

'No.' Aaron looked at Bodie's photo. 'I think you'd tell me if you wanted me to know.'

'I know you've been tracking me, Az.'

'Oh, I didn't mean ...' Aaron said apologetically.

'It's alright, it was kind of nice to know there was still someone left to care about me.' Aaron didn't respond – there was no need.

'I came to pack up her stuff, too, at the community. I was wondering if you'd be able to arrange storage for it.'

'Sure.' Aaron ventured a question: 'Why can't you do it?'

'I'm going to be on the road for a while after this. I'm not sure when I'll be back,' Insley said distractedly. Aaron looked in the same direction as Insley to see what had broken her concentration. Kathleen was being flanked by bodyguards as she made her way to the front.

'Did you know she'd be here?' he asked.

'No,' Insley confessed. 'I assumed her security would have said no.'

'They did.' Aaron stroked his beard, displacing some stray tissue, and smiled. 'Kathleen said yes.'

This seemed to make Insley happy. Aaron hoped she was happy.

'Look, there's some other stuff that needs sorting too. Can we get the committee together after the memorial? I want to have a meeting about what happens with Queentide while I'm gone.'

'What happens?' Aaron was confused. 'Are you saying you are running the movement now?'

Insley turned in her chair to face him.

'Who else would be?' Insley's foot was bouncing.

'Well, I assumed Lilith …' Aaron said matter-of-factly.

'Lilith?' Insley's eyes were wide. 'Why would she be running it?'

'Oh, I don't know, maybe because she has been since Bodie died. Before that even.' Aaron felt a bubble of anger inflating in his chest. 'Bodie had handed most of her responsibilities to Lilith while you were off playing little armies.'

'And while you were off shagging Ivana Humpalot.' Insley spun back around and crossed her arms.

'Oh, drop it, would you, Insley? I already feel like a fucking idiot for thinking she actually loved me. I don't need you rubbing it in.' It was Aaron's turn to cross his arms.

'So you're shagging Lilith now, is that it?' Insley asked in a childish voice.

'Grow up.' He paused. 'If you must know, we've been hanging out. She feels as stupid as I do about trusting Kay. I don't think a woman like that would ever be interested in me anyway.'

Insley kicked his foot.

He kicked hers back.

'You know, if Bodie could see us right now, she'd be telling us off,' Insley said, smiling.

'Yeah, and then making us a hot chocolate with a marshmallow angel floating on top.'

'Don't put yourself down like that, Az. Any woman – Kay, Lilith, whoever. They'd all be lucky to have you.' She looked at him intensely. 'I'm lucky to have you.'

He looked over, distracted by a fragment of a memory. A phone call from Insley just before her father was paroled.

'I miss her, Az.' Insley's eyes looked like a river about to burst its banks. Aaron wondered how much it hurt to hold it all in.

'I know.' He pulled a tissue out of the pack and handed it to Insley.

'I can't let him get away with this.' She roughly rubbed it over her eyes.

'I know that too,' Aaron said. When he knew that she could see him, he held up his hand and made a sign with his middle two fingers.

The music had changed. It was now a profoundly syncopated rendition of an old Aerosmith tune. The one about a girl and a gun.

The friends looked towards the stage, where Janet De Marco got up to say goodbye to her oldest friend. Aaron said no more. He just turned the key and put yet another secret in his Insley vault.

Chapter 29

The children had come to the memorial service. Lilith wanted them to say goodbye to Bodie. She and the girls had enjoyed all of the stories Janet De Marco had shared and had been speculating since they left the memorial what secret it was that Janet had said she was keeping as her own bit of Bodie that was no one else's. The girls were sure the secret was that Bodie was magic and had just turned into a bird and flown away. Lilith swallowed the lump in her throat and told them to go play.

She had seen Insley at the back of the theatre, sitting next to Aaron. They hadn't noticed her come in. They were too deep in conversation. She had tried to catch Aaron's eye during the eulogy, but he didn't look her way. He didn't look anywhere except at his notes. They trembled as much as his voice. Then she had tried to catch them on the way out, but Insley was avoiding her, and manoeuvred Aaron deftly through the crowd. And there were all the people who kept stopping Lilith, wishing her luck in the election. It seemed like a foregone conclusion now. With Ben gone, she was standing unopposed.

She'd been glad when her phone pinged, and saw Aaron's name, then concerned when she read his message. Insley wanted to talk to the committee, what was left of it. Lilith had come into Bodie's office to get some files, then paused as she looked around the room. Nothing had moved since she'd died, apart from the tarot card missing from the frame on the sideboard. It stood, displaying its emptiness.

Papers were exactly where she had left them, neatly stacked and ordered. Her laptop was closed and plugged in. Ready for her to start the next day's work, Lilith ran her hands over it, wondering what she had planned to do, what things were left suspended. Where the cursor was left blinking.

Impulsively, she opened the laptop and was greeted with the login box, imposed over a photo of the lighthouse on South Head, the one that had illuminated them that night. Lilith tried a few passwords they'd used on confidential files. None worked. Then she noticed a photo of the girls on the pinboard, along with photos of the other children who had lived or still lived in the community. Lilith smiled as she remembered the stories she would pour over the children and the ones they would make up about Bodie the Dragonslayer. No, that wasn't right. Dragontamer. Lilith tried it. The computer whirred, and in front of her, a window into Bodie's mind opened.

She hesitated, then decided to climb through it. A document was still open, Lilith's heart fluttered a little, then she jumped into it before she could change her mind. She scanned the introduction. It looked like a memoir. Of course it was. Bodie was always explaining how women's stories had been wiped from history. She would not let that happen with Queentide. Scrolling through the pages, Lilith saw there were sections about all of them. Kathleen, Helen, Janet, Aaron, the architects of the movement, the people who had made it possible. As Lilith wondered when Bodie thought it would have been safe to publicise Kathleen's involvement, she saw her own name. She scrolled to her section, her stomach sinking the way it did when she'd hand her school report card to her mother. She was shocked to see Bodie thought of her as the person who would lead the movement in its second phase as a political party. She kept reading, hoping to see how it would end, but there was nothing there –

they hadn't reached the future yet. And if Lilith wanted to get there, she was going to have to start writing her own story.

Instead, what she found was Bodie's prediction for post-election Australia. Some of the policies were familiar. They were part of the Women's Party election campaign. A new office, established under Kathleen's prime ministership – an equity office, ensuring all government policies did not discriminate on gender, age, income, skin colour or sexuality. Plans for reducing domestic violence through early intervention in schools. New Family Law, to stop children being split in half like assets. New ways of teaching to eradicate unconscious bias. Gender targets for the judicial system. She had described a matriarchy. Feminist views saturating throughout the government. A female gaze over life, adjusting things to take care of everyone, to mother the country.

It seemed possible, this country Bodie described. Ben's disappearance and connection with Bodie's death seemed to have tipped the election in their favour. The Women's Party candidates were all polling well, as were female candidates in the main political parties. If people voted the way they said they would, Australia would have a majority female government. The party associated with the patriarchal system would be decimated. The one led by a woman would form a government with the Women's Party. And Lilith would be part of it.

There was one last section that Bodie hadn't finished. It started by explaining that Australia was a Petri dish, ready to start a new life that would be transplanted and replicated all over the world. Bodie wasn't going to stop at one country, just like she was never going to stop at a commune. She wanted the entire world to be a safe space for women. There was a note that said: 'Speak to Insley.' Those were the last words in the document. Lilith wondered if she'd got the chance to before she died. If Insley even knew about her grandmother's plans.

Lilith started looking to see if there were other files with more information in them, directions to this new world Bodie had described. She found nothing. If Lilith wanted to get there, if she wanted her children to see it, she was going to have to finish the map herself.

Lilith closed the laptop and took it with her across the parade ground to the meeting room. When she got there, everyone had taken the usual spots, leaving an aching space where Bodie should have sat, like a picture removed from a wall, leaving behind a shadow.

Helen and Kathleen were talking, Insley and Aaron sat together, looking like they were having a conversation without words. Janet sat at the far end, staring out of the only window. She didn't even seem to notice that Lilith had walked in. She put the laptop on the table and opened her mouth to speak to Insley, but Insley didn't give her a chance.

'Right, now that everyone's here, let's get started. So, um, thanks for today. For giving Bodie a good send-off. Janet? She would have loved what you said.' Insley bit her lip as Janet started to cry again. Then she looked at Lilith. 'Lilith, thanks for organising everything. I'm sorry I left it all up to you.' She held Lilith's gaze, and Lilith willed herself not to look away. She won. Insley turned to Kathleen.

'My grandmother started this organisation to bring about equality through radical action. For her, this wasn't just about empowering women. It was about changing the system that was designed to repress them. The same one that repressed people of colour. People with a disability. People who aren't straight. Bringing down a system designed and protected by a minority to further their own needs and wants.' She paused. 'If the polls are right, we are on track to achieve that next week.' She paused again. 'I know a few of you want to put out some sort of statement, distancing Queentide and the Women's Party from these so-called attacks that have been happening—'

'They aren't so-called attacks Insley, they are violent assaults,' Helen interrupted.

'On men who have raped and hurt women.' Insley spoke slowly, not stopping to allow Helen to speak again. But Helen was not going to be intimidated.

'Violent attacks that have been perpetrated in the name of feminism. You'd know better than most of us the chatter that's happening online. Teenage girls are getting radicalised. They are organising gangs to attack men. They think this is how they show they are feminists. They think this is how they honour Bodie.'

'They are targeting men who deserve it,' Insley said even more deliberately.

'And who gets to decide who deserves it, Insley?' Kathleen interjected, knocking Insley slightly off her rhythm.

'They do their research. They only go after people they know have done something.' Insley's voice was now gaining speed. Lilith could feel the reverberation along the old floorboard as Insley's foot thumped on the floor.

'And what if they make a mistake?' Kathleen asked.

'Then I guess one innocent person gets hurt, Kathleen and the not-so-innocent ones get a warning ... and maybe fewer women get hurt and killed.'

'What are you saying, Insley, that it's okay for a guy to get hurt, if it maybe, might, perhaps, will stop another man hurting a woman?' Aaron looked genuinely confused.

'You learn quickly, Az.' Insley turned to him. 'Good boy.'

'I can't support this, Insley,' Aaron responded.

'You've supported a lot worse,' Insley shot back. Aaron shook his head.

'Insley, the Women's Party needs legitimacy to govern. It has to be taken seriously. If you don't condemn this violence, it won't be. And I won't be forming a government with it.'

Insley spun in her chair. 'You don't get to make that decision, Kathleen.'

'Neither do you, Insley,' Kathleen responded.

'This is my grandmother's organisation,' Insley shouted.

'And this isn't what she would have wanted it to descend to.' Janet stood up, shakily.

'Those men have all deserved it. Every last one of them. I will not distance us from that. This is exactly what Queentide was about. Levelling the playing field.'

'Bodie would not have wanted to level the ground by scorching it.'

'Insley, Janet is right,' Aaron said gently. 'There are many men, me included, who support the Women's Party.'

'I know that, Aaron. I'm not saying this because I think that there aren't *any* good men. I'm saying it because there aren't enough of you. The ones who can't behave need to be shown how to.'

'Insley, for God's sake ...' Aaron shook his head. Lilith wanted to help him and Insley.

'Insley, I know you are hurting ...' Lilith tried to make it better like she did for the girls when they cried and asked where Bodie was or why they hadn't seen their dad for ages.

'I was wondering when you'd pipe up.' Insley glared at Lilith. 'Hurting? You have no idea.' Insley was on her feet, moving around the table towards Lilith. Lilith shrank back in her chair, memories of Ben pushing their way into her mind. 'It's not hurt, Lilith. That's not possible because there would have to be a part of me left to feel it. I've been obliterated.' Lilith didn't turn away. The least she could do was hold space for her.

'I am not saying this out of revenge. I am not saying this be-cause I hate men. Jesus, Aaron, I love you. You are the most important person to me.' Insley's eyes were red and crumpled, but no tears were coming out. Maybe she had none left, Lilith thought. 'I am saying this because I am sick of women being killed. I am sick of women trying to play by the rules, to slowly change the system, to think for a second that they will play fair. Trust me, they won't. We can't play fair either.'

Lilith took a breath and then jumped into the silence, hoping there would be something to break her fall.

'But Insley, this isn't the world Bodie wanted. I found this today. She wrote it just before she ...' Lilith stumbled. There was nowhere to land. Saying Bodie had died felt incomplete. Saying she had been killed was just too much. 'If you'd just look ...' Lilith opened the laptop. Insley slammed it closed again, making Lilith jump back.

'Don't you fucking dare tell me what my grandmother thought, Lilith. Bodie is dead because you were too bloody spineless to deal with that bastard husband of yours.'

The words hit Lilith hard. She couldn't defend herself – her hands were full of the blame she was already carrying.

'Insley, there is no point turning on each other. I miss her too. Desperately.' Janet's voice cracked. 'I made Bodie a promise years ago that I would always protect you. But I also made her a promise that I would protect this movement. You do not lead Queentide, Insley. You were off doing god knows what ...' Janet trailed off.

'I was off doing the dirty work that no one else wanted to do,' Insley said.

'Meanwhile, Lilith was here with your grandmother, doing the work that gave this movement legitimacy,' Janet replied. 'We have a chance here, Insley. A really good chance to form a government. To make Bodie's vision a reality. Please don't make this a choice between that and you.'

'It sounds like you've already made the choice, Janet,' Insley said.

'Yes, I have. I'd like to put forward a vote that Lilith Green is declared leader of the Women's Party, to be put to all members this evening via digital ballot. She will stand, unopposed. She's got a good support base; she knows this party inside out. It's a formality.'

'I'll second that.' Helen spoke for the first time.

Lilith looked around, waiting for someone to ask her what she wanted. She was relieved when they didn't because she didn't really know.

'And you, Kathleen. Is there any point even asking you what you think?' Insley asked quietly.

'I don't get a vote, Insley. You know that.' Kathleen replied bitterly. 'I'm not a member of the party. I guess someone else gets to make a decision for me.'

'Jesus, are you serious? You are going to let the fucking secretary run the movement? My grandmother trusted you, Lilith. So did I. What a fucking mistake that was.' Insley whirled around the room, making Lilith feel nauseous as she tried to maintain eye contact.

Lilith's default setting kicked in, the apology making its way to her lips. But then she put her hands on the laptop, remembered the world Bodie had described. They'd never get there if they followed Insley. Lilith knew that.

'And your grandmother trusted you too.' Lilith held the table so Insley wouldn't see her hands shaking.

'And what is that supposed to mean?' Insley growled.

'It means she would be ashamed of you right now.' Lilith shot the words out like an arrow. 'She would never have condoned what you are doing, what you've done.'

'You have no idea what I've done.' Insley was eerily calm.

'Don't I?' Lilith felt a heat rising in her – she was sick of being underestimated. 'I know enough to bury you if I need to. I might have been just your grandmother's secretary, but that gave me access to a lot of information.'

The women stared at each other. Lilith was determined not to be the one to back down.

'Well, well, well,' – Insley smiled – 'it's a shame you couldn't have found your teeth in time to save Bodie, isn't it?'

She calmly walked out of the room, followed quickly by Aaron. He paused just long enough to squeeze Lilith's shoulders. When she had gone, Lilith breathed. She waited for the familiar thump to start in her chest, but it never came. The rabbit was finally safe in her burrow.

'What the hell was that all about Insley?' Aaron asked, slightly panting, as he caught up with Insley in the middle of the parade ground. 'I mean, the man-bashing I can just about stomach, but attacking Lilith like that ...'

Insley looked at Aaron's red, sweating face. She pushed the joke aside that was trying to get out. She had hurt his feelings enough for one day. Insley found she had reached a boundary she didn't know she had.

'You really don't think she deserves just a bit of blame for what happened to Bodie?' Insley was sure to sound upset but not dramatic. Aaron would spot it and know she was up to something.

'Do you, really?' Aaron sounded unsure.

'Yes,' Insley lied. She needed to push Lilith to see how much the movement really meant to her. To see if she'd fight for it. Bodie would have been glad to see Lilith put Insley in her place like that. And if Lilith felt a bit of guilt, well, that would probably come in handy. Later, at the right time. She tried not to smile.

'Well, I don't,' Aaron said. 'The blame all belongs to Ben Hamilton.'

'And I told you,' Insley said, 'I won't let him get away with it.'

'It won't bring Bodie back,' Aaron was almost pleading.

'You are right.' Insley couldn't stop the smile this time. 'But it will mean she is never forgotten.'

'And that guy?' Aaron asked. 'The one they found dead in his car? Did killing him stop everyone forgetting his wife? Because, you know what, I haven't seen her mentioned. Not once.'

'You think I killed him?' Insley asked. She hadn't expected this. She ran through a few scenarios until she found one that worked.

'Are you telling me you didn't?' Aaron shook his head. 'They don't even know where she is now, Insley. There's zero chance of her being found. How has that helped?'

'There's one less man on the planet,' Insley said. 'I think that helps.'

Aaron put his hands in his messy hair and then let his arms drop. 'I'm done here, Insley.'

Insley wanted to hug him. Aaron had given her exactly what she'd needed. It was time to stop punching holes in his wall. She turned away from her angry friend and walked quickly before Aaron remembered how to forgive her.

Chapter 30

From the newly installed chair, Kathleen swivelled around to survey the office once again. It was starting to feel like a space that belonged to her. The drab paintings had been replaced with art that inspired her, a few books had been added to the shelf that informed her. The first few days had felt claustrophobic, too full of history that did not include her. To escape, she had looked out the window towards the steps of Parliament House when taking calls from other prime ministers and presidents congratulating her. The women leaders, especially, had been enthusiastic to see their small international club growing.

Recalling their words, she smiled softly, cracking the ochre on her skin. She had thought about washing it off and spraying on some perfume to disguise the smell of smoked emu bush leaves, but she wanted to carry the ceremony with her as she addressed parliament for the first time as prime minister.

It would not be the speech she had written just after the Governor-General confirmed the coalition government between Labor and the Women's Party. When she wrote that speech, Kathleen thought the election was the watershed. That everything aft er the election was the future. And in that future, the one Kathleen had talked of in her speech, there wouldn't be a woman left dead in front of Parliament House. Visible to all the new female MPs as they looked out across the forecourt. But that had happened this morning. So Kathleen needed to rewrite the future.

They had asked Kathleen to cancel or at least move the smoking ceremony. They hadn't been able to get it clean. The blood had seeped and stained the Aboriginal mosaic that spread across the forecourt. Kathleen spoke to the Elders, and they agreed that they would not remove the stain or change the ceremony's timing. The smoking was needed.

A video had emerged on the net, of the woman being killed, of a man claiming to be from MASC taking responsibility. He had threatened more attacks if the coalition government wasn't disbanded and a new election held. When she'd told the two male bureaucrats from ASIO that she wanted MASC declared a terrorist organisation, they had patronisingly told her it was just one angry man. She'd calmly took down the file from her bookcase with all the thousands of photos from the election campaign. She resisted the urge to hit them over the head with it and instead showered the desk with images of swollen and bruised faces.

She'd asked if they thought it was the same angry man who had left them that way too. She'd have to get Lilith to accelerate the bureaucracy reviews. There was no point being in power if the people who worked for them were on the wrong frequency to hear their message. There needed to be some retuning.

Lilith's office was a couple of doors away from Kathleen's. The rooms in between had been converted to a playroom for the MPs' children. Lilith had moved out of the community last month after the first threat was made against the children. She'd moved into one of the secure apartment buildings in Canberra. Kathleen had arranged security for her and the girls and the other female MPs who had got death threats, which was all of them.

Kathleen had got used to hearing children running around

the corridors and playing next door. In a way, they'd built a new community right there in Parliament House. Bodie would have been happy to see that. She wondered if Bodie would have been happy to also see her second book being published, the one Lilith found on her laptop.

Kathleen had asked Lilith to stop by, so they could discuss the speeches they would each give. As a coalition, they needed to speak in harmony. A few weeks ago, Kathleen wouldn't have thought this was a problem, but recently Lilith was singing in a different key.

Kathleen couldn't shrug off the feeling that Insley was somewhere tapping out a rhythm to distract Lilith. In fact, it felt like Insley was always there. Since she left two months ago, after the memorial, Aaron, Lilith, everyone, in fact, had avoided the topic of Insley. So much that they had created her outline. Letting their thoughts hit up against her, but never saying her name. They had coloured in a whole page and left one space conspicuously blank, the focus now on what they were ignoring. Kathleen couldn't ignore it; she was there in bright relief against the darkness around her.

She had thought about getting ASIO to find her. Now she was Prime Minister Rae, she realised how easy that would be. It would just need someone to look at all the information that was passively collected on everyone, just in case.

But Kathleen was worried about summoning her, about bringing her back to life. It was unlikely to bring any peace of mind. In fact, it would probably be like inviting a poltergeist into the house. There were enough ghosts for the new government to deal with already.

There was a knock at the door, and Lilith Green – her Deputy Leader and Minister for Equity – came into the room. She had appeared to grow in the past few months. Every interview, media conference and speech seemed to nourish her, helping her thrive. She stood taller, her chin always held high. She wasn't afraid to show her true colours anymore, and this scared Kathleen. Because they were proving to be a very different, darker shade than the ones she'd worn in Queentide or on the campaign trail. They were shades that clashed severely with what Kathleen wore. Kathleen wondered who was casting the shadows over Lilith Green and changing her palette.

'Did you watch the video?' Lilith asked her.

'Yeah, sick bastard.' Kathleen shook her head. 'I've given ASIO a kick along. We're declaring MASC a terrorist organisation. Today. Here, it's in my speech.' Kathleen handed the pages to Lilith. 'We will also issue an Interpol notice for Ben. The police have finally decided there's enough evidence to charge him with Bodie's death, even without Insley's evidence.' Kathleen noticed Lilith lose her composure for a second, like a rain-cloud passing overhead but being blown out to sea. 'Since his disappearance, there's also been some substantial evidence emerge that links him to MASC, puts him at the head of it. Orchestrating the attacks on your candidates, planting the car bombs ...' Kathleen trailed off. Lilith was intently reading the speech. 'Are you okay? I mean, I know this is probably a little upsetting.'

'It's not upsetting.' Lilith still didn't raise her head.

'It's just that, well, I mean, he's still the girls' father ...'

'He stopped being that the day he killed Bodie.' Lilith finally looked up. 'As far as I am concerned, he is already dead.'

'Already?'

'I mean, I assume he's dead.' Lilith began rereading the speech. 'No-one has seen him for months.'

'True, but then look at that woman from Melbourne ... What was her name?'

'Monica.' Lilith's lip twitched into a small smile. 'Monica Gaumond. I met her actually the other day. We were both on *Good Morning Australia*.'

'I didn't see it, but I heard about it. Poor woman, they shouldn't have had her on. She's clearly still suffering.' Kathleen tutted.

'She seemed to be okay to me,' Lilith said flatly.

'How can she be?' Kathleen asked. 'She's still saying she killed him. He was found weeks ago, and the place they found her locked up was hours away. What are we saying here? That she escaped, drove hours without anyone seeing her. Killed him and made it look like suicide, then drove back and chained herself back up?'

'All I know is she's confessed, and the police won't arrest her. They won't believe she could do it. I guess that's what they get for underestimating a woman. They let her get away with murder.'

'You don't seriously think she did it, do you?'

'I think she wanted him dead.' Lilith had a strange look on her face. 'Sometimes that's as good as murder, isn't it?'

Something made Kathleen shiver. This wasn't the first conversation she'd had with Lilith that made the hairs on the back of her neck and arms stand up. Something felt wrong but familiar, like she was seeing Lilith but hearing someone else, as though she was possessed.

Lilith finally handed the speech back to Kathleen. 'The name is wrong, the dead woman this morning. It was Gemma Stott, not Scott.'

'Jesus, thanks for that.' Kathleen corrected it, feeling a little off-kilter that Lilith had made no other comment about her speech. She had been proud of it, feeling that she'd struck a good balance between strength and compassion, what she hoped would become the hallmark of their government. She scolded herself for still seeking approval. Wasn't it enough that she had become the Prime Minister? 'So, can I read yours now?'

'Of course.' Lilith looked through the small blue folder in

front of her. Some papers spilt out while she rummaged, and a large tarot card slid across the table, washing up on Kathleen's side of the desk.

'Looks like the girls have been helping again,' Kathleen joked as she picked it up to hand it to Lilith. She glanced at it, realising why it looked familiar when she saw Lilith's frozen face.

'This was Bodie's, wasn't it?' Kathleen asked rhetorically. 'It's the one Insley took out of the frame.' Kathleen almost expected the table to begin shaking as she said the name she'd tried so hard to avoid.

'Yes, it is.' Lilith reached her hand over the table. 'Could I have it back, please?'

Kathleen obliged, happy to be rid of it. Even holding something belonging to Insley felt like it brought her closer. Kathleen did not want her there. She decided not to ask. In exchange, Lilith gave her the speech to read.

Kathleen focused her attention on the words in front of her. They started off the same way the first draft had done, the one Lilith had shared with her a couple of weeks ago. A dedication to Bodie, a restatement of the Queentide values and an acknowledgement of the ripple effect of female empowerment. There was a pledge to protect all women, regardless of heritage, sexuality or how they had found womanhood. All familiar landmarks on the journey she had travelled with Bodie and the one she hoped to continue with the new coalition government. But then, a few minutes in, there was a sharp U-turn, so sudden it gave Kathleen whiplash.

'What's this, Lilith?' Kathleen looked at Lilith, pointing to the paragraph about new gendered employment laws. Lilith didn't answer, so Kathleen kept reading, unable to turn away, even though she knew it would be like seeing roadkill. She could already smell the blood.

'You can't give this speech, Lilith. You will alienate half of the population.'

'I think that's a little dramatic, Kathleen,' Lilith replied.

'You are relegating men to a lower position in society. You are taxing them more, removing them from jobs if companies haven't reached their female quota. And what's this about custody? You are saying it should automatically go to the mother?'

'It's from Bodie's second book.' Lilith nodded.

'Bodie wrote that?'

'The details weren't all there,' Lilith said quietly, 'so I've started to fill in the blanks. The book must get published, Kathleen.'

'This isn't what Bodie wanted. She never wanted to treat men like the enemy.'

'Well, maybe that's where she went wrong.' The steel in Lilith's voice struck Kathleen like a crowbar. 'Maybe that's the reason a woman ended up dead in the forecourt this morning. Or why I've been getting vile emails telling me how they are going to kill my children.'

'That is happening because MASC is a bunch of sick fucks.'

'Which has got more violent and increased in numbers since we started this campaign,' Lilith implored. 'It's going to get worse, Kathleen. That woman this morning was just the start. You declaring them a terrorist organisation only confirms what we already knew. You know, as well as I do, for centuries, when women have got some control, a backlash isn't far behind. Every time we try to tip the scale just a little, so we get somewhere close to a balance, they pile on hard and send us flying back up into the air. Well, this time, I'm not going to sit back and watch them build the bonfires. We have to take the wood off them so they don't even get the chance. We've tried every other way. We've tried being compliant. We've tried being collaborative. It's time we started being combative.'

'So we go after the ones who are attacking women. We will bring down MASC ...'

'And then something else will pop up in its place.' Lilith's eyes looked different to Kathleen. The wariness that had clouded them for the past year had solidified into anger. 'We have to put some more weight on our side of the scale, and if that means taking away some privileges—'

'Rights, Lilith. You are talking about taking away some of their human rights.'

'And what's wrong with that? They've taken ours away from us for centuries.'

'You don't need to lecture me about suppression, Lilith.' Kathleen bristled.

'This isn't about race.'

'Isn't it?' Kathleen reminded herself to stay calm. 'These men you are going to strip of their privileges, as you call them. Some have probably already been stripped of a few already under the old Government. How is what you are suggesting going to make life better for First Nations men? Or any man who's on the poverty line. Gay men. Disabled men. Male refugees.' Kathleen handed the speech back to Lilith. 'I can't allow you to make this speech, Lilith.'

Lilith picked up the sheets of paper and carefully placed them into the folder.

'You can't stop me, Kathleen,' Lilith said, with no malice, as she left the office.

When she had left, Kathleen noticed that the tarot card, Bodie's wheel of fortune, was still on the desk. She didn't know if Lilith had meant to leave it or if she had done it without realising. Either way, it was now something Kathleen couldn't ignore.

She closed her eyes and took a deep breath to smell the cleansing smoke that was still in her hair. She hoped there was still enough there to ward off the bad spirits that Kathleen could hear knocking at the door.

Chapter 31

She didn't scream when she saw it. Finding dead rabbits on the parade ground at the community had become part of life there. And finding elaborate death threats had become part of living away from it. Lilith gently stoked the motionless animal, its fur still soft over its rigid body, as shouts bounced around the corridors, like a dystopian Christmas morning, as though she were trying to prevent it from being spooked by the noise. Rest in peace.

There was a sound of standard-issue boots and smart leather-soled shoes running down the corridor. Security had stepped up even further after the blood had been cleaned up from the forecourt following the ceremony. They were there to cover up the nerves that were pulsating at the surface. A cheap band-aid that had no hope of healing the wound.

Right now, guards and plain-clothed officers would be talking in gentle and rational voices to all the MPs who had found the final shove towards the edge in a box on their desk in the most secure building in Australia. They would be trying to pull them up to safety, but they wouldn't be able to. Because the women would have decided that it wasn't safe up there anymore. They might as well cut the rope and take their chances on the fall.

Lilith had already made that decision, just after the election, when two pigs' heads had been left on the girls' car seats, in the few minutes she had left the car to collect them from gymnastics. The trio took a cab home and a plane to Canberra the next day.

Lilith felt naïve now when she thought of how she had told Insley that all they needed to do was win. They just had to get enough men to vote for them.

She had wanted to call Insley, to brag to Insley, when the election results came in. She felt proud and finally able to say to Insley that it had all been worth it. She could finally think of Bodie and not feel guilty.

The Women's Party had taken out 25 per cent of seats. All Labor's female candidates had won their seats, a handful of Greens and some independents, even some Liberals. Kathleen had taken her 30 per cent and formed a coalition with the Women's Party. Altogether, the Australian Parliament, the one that was about to sit for the first time, was now over 70 percent female. The women had taken over the boys' oak-panelled treehouse. Or at least sent them an eviction notice.

It felt like dawn had finally arrived after a restless night. There were parties and hope-filled social media posts and readings from *Queentide* given on street corners. Female singers topped the charts, women commentators and journalists were given the post-election narrative. The female voice, for a little while, wasn't silenced or told to be less. But they didn't get to enjoy the colours of the sunrise for very long. Their wind had changed direction, but it had brought the thunder clouds closer, not pushed them further out to sea. It sent the women running for cover, each finding shelter for themselves in any way they could.

In among the swirling grey, Insley appeared, unexpectedly. Like an umbrella held over your head by a stranger in a storm. Lilith had been glad to hear from her and didn't question, at

first, why she had decided after almost a month to make contact. She had forgotten that umbrellas bring the electricity right
to your hand. They don't protect you.

It was a landline number with a prefix that Lilith didn't recognise. A place somewhere in the world that she had never vis-
ited. She expected it to be Insley. The small circle of people who
had Lilith's mobile number only had one break in it.

Insley told her she was in New Zealand, in a town with a
name that hadn't been anglicised and one that Lilith hadn't
heard since her last year at university in Oxford. It was where
Ben had got a summer job running a hostel, the place he'd fled
to when Lilith turned him down, the place where he'd won her
back or wore her down, depending on how you looked at it.

Lilith expected an I-told-you-so, but Insley had told her she
had done an excellent job and that Bodie would be proud, which
was worse. There was a silence, the two women separated by
the wall of guilt that Bodie's death and Lilith's apparent betrayal had built between them. She had to find something to use as
a ladder.

So Lilith told Insley about the manuscript she had found on
Bodie's laptop, which Insley had refused to look at when Lilith
had first tried, and her hopes to publish it posthumously as a
tribute to the woman who had made a female-led parliament
possible. Insley had listened this time as Lilith told her eagerly
because she'd had no one else to confide in, that Kathleen and
Aaron were opposed to the plan. They thought it was a bad idea.

Insley had reassured her that it was what Bodie would have
wanted and offered to help fill in the blanks. She was, after all,
the closest person to Bodie, so she would know what to say.
They could work on it remotely – she still had some things to
take care of in New Zealand.

Insley had ended the conversation before Lilith had a chance
to share the strange coincidence about the town being where

Ben had run off to. She reminded herself to tell her the next time she called. She didn't remember. Instead, they talked about the attacks and how a change to policing just wouldn't be enough. They needed to be proactive, to destabilise MASC's base, which was all men really. They talked about how Bodie always had thought positive discrimination had a place. And what better place was there than in an Australia where women just couldn't get a job? They worked up policies to tackle domestic violence that involved local civilian teams of women who would make some high-profile swoops on perpetrators to deter others. They wouldn't use the word 'vigilante'. It had the wrong connotations.

It was a scorched-earth policy, but sometimes that was the only way to make something new grow. And grow back stronger. Besides, none of this would be forever; it was just temporary, a way to make women feel powerful and in control. Once they had that strong foundation, they could slowly allow the power balance to become more equitable when things had finally changed.

Lilith didn't react during one of these conversations when Insley told her that she had found Ben. Lilith had already known, in that part deep down where the truth gets hidden for being too ugly. The coincidence was just too big – destiny wasn't a reliable enough guide to lead her to that sort of justice. But Insley was.

Ben was using a different name and was working as a labourer on a local farm. Insley had been watching him for a week and doing some digging to make sure it was him. He had arrived in New Zealand the day after he killed Bodie (those words had not lost their impact in the months that had passed), coming into town a few days later. Insley had proof he was still controlling MASC and was behind the attacks and threats. He was still a threat. Lilith asked what she planned to do next. Insley asked her the same question.

As the weeks went by and the storm clouds got heavier and closer, Lilith's plans changed. It had seemed so simple at first – find shelter. Go to the police and tell them where he was. Stop Insley from doing something that could not be undone. But as the lightning hit and her children were threatened, and Lilith's life was turned upside down, more women got hurt. The rain just didn't stop. She wondered why she was trying to stay dry anymore.

When Insley showed Lilith the emails that proved Ben was behind the threat against the girls, his own children, she was ready to burn the last drop of moisture out of the air. The rage that Lilith had always politely built firebreaks around was now burning a hole in her chest, where her guilt and compassion used to live. Insley asked Lilith what she wanted to do, and Lilith replied that she wished destiny would take Ben Hamilton to the place he was meant to be.

The tarot card had arrived in the post that morning, in between the dead woman and the dead rabbit. Lilith turned it over in her fingers, the way she had seen Bodie do so many times, and then slid it into the pocket of the blue velvet she was wearing. She would take it, as an amulet, into the chamber to give her maiden speech.

Hearing Hannah and Katy's excited voices approach, Lilith quickly put the lid on the box.

'What's in there, Mummy? Did someone send you a present to wish you luck?' Hannah's little hands were advancing on the box. Lilith tickled her to distract her.

'It's not a present, sweetheart. It's just a box of things we don't need anymore, things that we can forget about now.' Lilith gently ushered the girls towards the door. 'Come on, it's time for Mummy to do some work.'

The girls were feeling the sleeves of Lilith's jacket, and she couldn't blame them – it was the sort of fabric you just had to touch.

'This looks like the ocean at home, Mamma.' Hannah still called the community home, so did Lilith.

'We, all the women in parliament and some of the men, we are all wearing blue today.' It had been Kathleen's idea. A way to remember Bodie.

'Like a fancy-dress party?' Katy asked.

'Yes, exactly,' Lilith answered. Everyone was pretending to be someone they weren't, at least for now. Until they grew into their new roles.

'Are you ready to be famous?' Katy laughed.

'I'm not going to be famous, sausage.' Lilith began to feel nervous because she realised that's exactly what she was going to be, more than she had been during the election. The speech was going to make sure of that, her diversion from Kathleen's moderate policies. Her veins started pumping. 'Come on, let's get you and Hannah all settled in. You can watch me on the TV.' Lilith tried again to move them out of the office.

'See, you will be famous, you'll be on TV!' Katy was twirling, but at least out of the door. 'Everyone will be watching you!'

Once the girls were settled with the other children, Lilith made her way to the media conference outside. The news crews had asked for all the women MPs to stand together for a photo. Kathleen, at the centre, looked around and said some people were missing. She called for the few men who were part of the coalition government to join the photo. The men, wearing blue too, shuffled as apologetically as they could while some barely audible insults were thrown at them. Lilith wondered if the journalist had heard. Lilith noticed that Aaron was standing with the press pack. She saw him shake his head. He had heard. She looked back towards the camera – she couldn't look him in the eye.

At the far end of the lawn, Lilith saw one of the survivors of the election, Keith Fletcher, talking to another news channel.

'It's a spectacle, a media stunt. It won't stick. We will see that they will fall apart the first time one of them gets annoyed that one of the others is wearing the same outfit as her. You can't have too many women in a room – they'll end up turning on each other. They can't help it.'

Later, in the corridor, Lilith saw him again.

'Good luck, Mrs Hamilton,' he called over to her.

'It's Ms Green now,' Lilith tightly replied.

'No, it's not. You aren't divorced yet, are you? You still belong to him.' His poisonous words polluted the air. 'You know, this equality or equity or whatever the made-up title is that bitch has given you, it means nothing. Men and women are different. We always will be. You lot literally haven't got the balls for this gig. This whole charade you've got going on here is just fucking embarrassing. And it won't last, believe me. You'll get found out when there are tough decisions to make, then we will see where all of this feminine thinking will get us. You'll all be crying about the poor soldiers that might get hurt if we go to war. That's why you need us, why you'll always need us. To make the tough calls. To kill, when necessary. Women won't be able to do that.'

'I guess we will just have to wait and see, won't we?' Lilith smiled at him for just a little too long. His own smile drooped as the discomfort settled on his face. Then the buzzer sounded, and he scuttled into the chamber ahead of Lilith.

Lilith didn't know what the feeling was as she watched him run away, but she liked it. Just a little too much.

Chapter 32

The speeches were being broadcast on the television above the bar. But Insley wasn't watching them. She was watching Ben. He'd drunk more than usual and was sitting on a stool where he could see the screen clearly, instead of the booth where he kept to himself. He still drank bourbon, but it was the really cheap one now. The brand he thought a labourer would drink.

She ordered a round at the far end of the bar. As she paid the bartender, she noticed in the mirror behind how much more like Bodie she looked, with her newly grown spiked hair and the streaks of grey that had sprouted up. She wondered if Ben would recognise her; if he didn't, she'd soon remind him.

She reached him just as Lilith appeared on the screen. He knocked back the dregs of his glass and, before it had hit the counter, she had put the fresh one in front of him. Michter's. He might as well enjoy the drink he was about to choke on.

He turned away from the screen and looked at Insley.

'Do I know you?' His smile dripped with testosterone. Insley dug her new long nails into her palm.

Insley smiled back and raised her glass to his, clinked it and drank. He drank too. He'd been raised to not be rude and had grown up picking up drunk girls in bars. He really was just making this too easy for Insley. She waited until his tastebuds recognised the bourbon. He took another sip.

'She thinks you are dead, you know,' Insley said.

'What?' Ben spluttered.

'Lilith, your ex-wife. Wife. Whatever. The woman on the screen,' Insley said flatly. 'She thinks you are dead, Ben Hamilton.'

'My name isn't Ben Hamilton.' He tried to get up from the stool. Insley pressed down on his thigh muscle, making it impossible and painful.

'Well, it's certainly not the name I've been calling you since you killed my grandmother.' Insley swallowed down the lump in her throat. 'But it is who you are.'

'Insley.' The realisation hit him hard. He turned away from her and slumped slightly over the counter.

'So now we've established who we all are, shall we get down to business?' Insley said brightly. She almost reminded herself of Kay these days.

'What the fuck do you want?' he growled.

'I want lots of things, Ben.' Insley kept her voice low. She couldn't afford a scene in the bar. This needed to go down with no one noticing it. She took another sip, her fingers still digging into his muscle. He was wincing slightly. He didn't want a scene, either. 'I'd like my grandmother back, please. Can you give me that? No? Okay, well, how about, let's start with you watching Lilith's speech like a good boy.'

They sat silently, watching. Insley didn't need to. She'd already heard the speech. Lilith had practised it on her earlier, just like Kathleen used to.

'She's never going to be able to do that.' Ben sneered as she finished the speech. 'She hasn't got what it takes to pull it off.'

'I think you'll find a woman who is capable of killing someone realises she's got what it takes to do anything.'

'Are you telling me Lilith has killed someone?' He laughed. 'You really are as crazy as everyone says.'

'There's more than one way to kill someone, Ben. You've got

a legal degree, haven't you? From Oxford? Impressive. Almost as impressive as the politics degree that Lilith has from there.' Insley let go of his leg and signalled for the bartender to bring another round. 'So, tell me, if a person organises for someone else to carry out a murder, they are still guilty, right? Although, you remember that woman who went missing? She confessed to killing her husband. Actually confessed! And they didn't believe her. Didn't think she was capable of doing it. I guess when you underestimate a woman, you pay the price. Am I right?'

The drinks arrived. Insley swapped the glasses around. Ben looked at her suspiciously and then swapped them back around again.

'Getting a taste for the cheap stuff, Ben? Suit yourself.' Insley knocked back the drink.

'Are you trying to tell me that Lilith has paid someone to kill me?' Ben's face crumpled under the weight of realisation. 'She's paid you to kill me, hasn't she? Like that woman from Melbourne did? I knew it was you when I heard about it. You are a fucking crazy bitch. Kay told me about your father. I know what you did, you know.' Ben's hand shook as he tried to lift the glass. He put it back down again.

Insley sighed. 'That bloke in Melbourne killed himself. At least that's what the police report says. And so did my father. Kay had quite the imagination, didn't she?' Insley paused. 'Besides, they wouldn't need to pay me. I'd kill people like you for free.'

Ben tried to get off the stool quickly, but his foot got stuck in the footrest. He landed on the sticky paisley carpet. A few people started to come over.

'I'm so sorry,' Insley said to the bartender, putting on her sweetest voice. 'It looks like he's had a little too much. I'll take care of him. He just needs a sit-down.' The Good Samaritans sat back down, glad to let someone else deal with the drunk.

She pulled him up and got him to a booth. He stared at her, then held his head in his hands. She could almost hear the thoughts running through it. Because she'd run through them too when she came up with her plan. Who would believe that the pretty young girl who had bought him drinks and helped him up was trying to kill him? He couldn't go to the police because they'd find out who he was. He had no other option but to wait and see if there was another way out. Insley already knew the answer. There wasn't.

'You are already dead, Ben, as far as Lilith is concerned.' Insley was almost whispering. 'And that's enough. For now.'

'What do you mean? Enough?' He looked up at her, his pale green eyes bloodshot from the bourbon.

'Lilith needed to be able to decide to kill the father of her children. If she could do that, then taking a few civil rights away from some anonymous men is going to seem pretty fucking easy, don't you think?'

Ben laughed. 'You think it's that straightforward, do you?' he said. 'Lilith is part of a coalition government. She can't just introduce a policy like that. Your girlfriend, for all of her faults, is a smart politician. She will not go along with this.'

'I'm counting on her not going along with it.' Insley sat back, resting on the overstuffed vinyl lounge. 'I'm not expecting Lilith to succeed, at least not entirely. Kathleen needs to look like a moderate, and she will, compared with your ex-wife. Who, frankly, I have a bit of a girl crush on now.'

Ben got up to leave but abruptly sat back down again.

'Do you really think I'm going to let you get away with this, Insley?' Ben's voice had barbs in it. 'I will not play dead for you.'

'Yes, you will Ben. You see, I've got a bit of inside information. MASC is going to be declared a domestic terror organisation, and I've got evidence that you've been keeping your hand in while you've been over here ...'

'I've had nothing to do with what they've been doing, I would never ...'

'What? Kill someone? You see, I think that's where you and the police would disagree. They have two eyewitnesses who saw you commit murder.' Insley slid the photos and copies of the emails that Lilith had sent her over to him. 'And, of course, there's this. Making a death threat against your own children, Ben? Really, even by your standards ...'

'I did not do this!' He was shouting now.

'You might want to keep your voice down, Ben. I hear the Prime Minister here is pretty hard on domestic violence too. Bloody women, eh?' Insley winked at him.

'I would never threaten my own children or scare them like that,' he replied defensively.

'Just like you would never threaten your own wife. Oh, wait ...' Insley paused. 'It's not looking good for you, Ben, is it? So you see, it might be in your interests to just stay dead. Because if you come back, I can guarantee life will not be worth living for you.'

He shook his head. 'I never meant for this to go this far.' His eyes were completely red. Tears forced their way out. 'I mean with MASC. I never thought they'd threaten children. My children. It wasn't me, Insley. You have to believe me. I mean, who the hell would do that to two little kids? They must have been terrified.' Insley remembered hiding under Aaron's bed in the community on the nights that she had flashbacks. She'd read up on it recently, that younger kids could learn to block out trauma. When Lilith told her that Hannah was having trouble sleeping since she'd found the rabbits' heads in her backpack, Insley switched the tracks in her brain, tried to sound shocked and angry, and told Lilith she'd find her the best psychologist in Canberra to help.

'Someone really desperate, I guess.' Insley left the photos and emails. She wanted Ben to have a reminder of why he needed to stay gone. Besides, she didn't need them. She still had access to Ben's emails. She could go back and find the ones she'd sent any time she needed.

Chapter 33

'I don't know who I'm happier to see, you or that coffee you're holding.' Kathleen took the travel mug from Aaron.

'Jeez, thanks,' Aaron deadpanned. He took a sip and grimaced. 'Don't thank me too soon. That barista downstairs puts way too much honey in.'

'That's the way I like it.' Kathleen smiled. 'It's the way Bodie made it.' Enough time had passed that they could talk about her and remember her life, not just her death. It was a reassuring place to be right now, especially with Aaron there to keep her company.

Aaron had been her chief of staff since the Million Women March. She'd found it easier to choose her own staff since the election and since the disaster with Kay. Ironically, it had been the backroom men in the party who had pushed against Aaron. They were concerned about appearances. The Million Women March had sent a clear message. Women wanted to see the power balance shift. They'd told Kathleen that she needed to show she was as passionate about equality as Lilith. She responded that that was the reason she needed a male chief of staff.

Aaron's appointment wasn't a conflict of interest. Queentide was disbanded when the Women's Party was elected to government. There was no need for it to continue. Most of the members had joined the party as part of the election campaign. The refuges and women's services that Bodie had established were now run by the organisations Bodie had partnered with. Lilith ensured they were funded by the new government. They at least agreed on that. But everything else divided them, and their Cabinet too, split equitably, half from Lilith's party, half from Kathleen's.

'I'm losing them, Aaron.' Kathleen looked Aaron in the eye as she said it. 'There's a growing number of Cabinet members saying they will back Lilith's Private Members' Bill.'

'It's these attacks, Kathleen. They think if we bring in all of these policies, it will send a message to MASC.'

'It will give MASC a great new way to recruit young men who can't get jobs or find themselves locked up for saying the wrong thing to the wrong woman,' Kathleen replied. 'And how's it going to be for a Black man under all of this? Or a gay man? We are promoting discrimination.'

'I do not disagree with you, Kathleen.' Aaron put his cup down as carefully as he chose his words. As though he was worried about spilling both. 'But you are going to have to give them something. I've heard on the grapevine that there's likely going to be a leadership challenge if things don't move forward.'

'After six months? Seriously?' Kathleen rolled her eyes. She focused on the painting behind Aaron of her great-grandmother's country. They had taken her great-grandmother back to the Adelaide Plains to visit, near the foot of the Mount Lofty Ranges, the first time she'd been back since she was four years old and had been stolen from her parents. She had watched as her great-grandmother sank into the place, shipwrecked but finally at peace, out of the storm. 'This is where I belong. I am not going to let them force me out,' Kathleen said calmly. 'I am the right person to lead this government.'

'I know.' Aaron smiled. 'And so do lots of other people. Your polling figures are still solid, across all genders.' Aaron unbuckled his satchel and pulled out some papers, handing them to

Kathleen. 'You are a popular woman, Kathleen. The international press loves you too.' Kathleen felt herself blush. It was nice to get a compliment, even if it was in the context of her political career crumbling. 'It's the thing that is saving us at the moment. It would be a really unpopular move to replace you now.'

'What about Lilith?' Kathleen asked, scanning the page. 'How is she polling?'

'As you'd expect. Great among women. Men, not so much,' Aaron said ironically.

Kathleen didn't need to ask why. Lilith's language had become as extreme as the attacks on women. They had started off as isolated incidents – women stabbed in supermarkets, pushed onto train tracks – but then the mass assaults on the girls' schools and maternity wards started. Women from all over the country marched on Canberra to demand action. They wanted to hear a politician as angry as they were. They wanted a mamma bear to come and protect them. And that's what Lilith had become. The problem was her claws were going to slash some innocent men too. And she didn't seem to care. She was going ahead and publishing that second book. When she did, she'd wake up a whole pack of mamma bears and the mauling would really begin. They had to nip this in the bud.

'You know you can't force her out, right?' Aaron asked cautiously. Kathleen was going to deny thinking about it, but she had. Honesty was sometimes a disadvantage as a politician. Her parents had really hobbled her by raising her so well.

'So what's our option here, Aaron? If it gets out, how divided this government is, we are dead in the water. We might be in control of the government now, but there's still a fairly influential and biased media just waiting for us to fail. And a few big organisations. Jesus, they'd have a field day. I can hear them now: *Look at the women, catfighting after only a few months.*'

Aaron was silent for a while, and then he spoke. 'Go on the front foot,' Aaron said, thoughtfully. 'Let everyone know what's happening. Let's put out a media release or, better yet, give a speech.'

'What?' Kathleen laughed.

'I'm serious. Look, we are handling this like all the governments before us. Trying to hide our disagreements, pretending that there's just one big dick in the room making the calls.' Aaron gave a wry smile when Kathleen scowled at him. 'Sorry, but you know what I mean. Anyway, what I'm saying is that we're forgetting we aren't like any other governments. We don't have to do things the way they did them.'

'So you're suggesting I go out there and say that I can't agree with my coalition partners on the way forward?' Kathleen said.

'Yep, exactly.' Aaron took a triumphant sip of coffee. 'The patriarchy got by for centuries fighting with itself. It still managed to keep control of everything.' He smiled. 'What is going to be different is how you deal with the disagreement. You aren't going to batter each other over the head until one of you submits. You are going to work this out rationally. Equitably. Let's show the voters why what they've got now is better than the old boys' club.'

'Do you think Lilith will agree to this?'

'Yes, I do. Look, we can make concessions on some things. Some of her policies, especially around a reform of the judicial system – they aren't that bad.'

Kathleen nodded, 'Okay, let's go through them. The Cabinet meeting is soon. I want to go in with a clear position. Let's get a media conference organised for straight afterwards. We'll give them a rundown of the new policies that will be introduced and explain where the disagreements still lie. And then I guess we announce the referendum.'

'The referendum?' Aaron looked surprised.

'Yes.' Kathleen looked at the painting behind Aaron again, following the songlines that stretched across the canvas. 'It's time this country started deciding for itself who it wants to be, what direction it wants to go in. It's time to grow up.'

Kathleen paused, her eyes drawn to the tarot card that she now had propped up on her keyboard. 'We just need to make sure it makes the right decision, so it grows up to be fair.'

Aaron raised his cup to Kathleen. 'Here's to a fair society. Finally. Bodie would approve.'

Kathleen parked her honesty and worked out how many more resources than Lilith she had. She was in a better position to spin this. Insley would approve too, Kathleen thought guiltily.

Chapter 34

'Yesterday, my Cabinet met to discuss Lilith Green's Private Members' Bill. Both the Deputy Prime Minister and I have been very open about us not agreeing on everything. And while the old boys' network is trying to use this as an excuse to trot out some views that are as prehistoric as they are, I want to reassure you that this does not weaken our government. It does not show that women are not cut out to run a country.

'In fact, what it shows is that you do want women running a country. Because they will accept that they have differences, and they will sit and rationally work through them. They won't let their egos impede progress.

'You elected us because you wanted a more equitable government, one that represented you. And the truth is, if you want equity, you get differences of opinion. It makes for healthy discussion, and it makes sure you don't get one person, the one with the loudest voice, calling the shots. Those days are gone.'

A murmur moved through the gathered media scrum.

'But one thing we agree on is that the safety of women in this country is our number one priority. If a woman does not feel safe in her home, on the street or in her place of employment, then anything else we do to improve her quality of life is meaningless.

'Our fight against MASC continues and will be ramped up. We are committed to dismantling this terrorist organisation that is not only a threat to women but to our entire society. So, we have agreed that we will be funding, an increase in funding for specialist units across the country, to be staffed by women officers...'

Insley took her earphones out as the attendant checked her luggage.

'You're heading to Sydney today, Ms Hughes?' she asked in her clipped British accent.

'Yeah, I am.' Insley liked the attendant's smile – it was a bit crooked. Not perfect.

'I've got family there, live in Collaroy. Poor things, their house got destroyed by the king tide that came through the other week.' She made a sad face. 'The seawater got into the foundations. They thought it was just a bit of flood damage, but now they think they're going to have to pull it down.'

'You never know. They might end up building something better instead, right?' Insley smiled back at her and ran her hand over her freshly shaved head.

The attendant gave her an appreciative smile and handed her a boarding pass, upgrading her to Business Class. Insley thanked her and put her earphones back in, just in time to hear Kathleen announce the referendum would be held in eight weeks. There was a lot of work to do before then, just as well she was heading back. The movement in the UK could do just fine without her for a bit. The election there was still over a year away. And she'd found a woman who had real potential – she just needed some help.

The speech was over, but she still had some time to kill, so Insley made her way to the lounge. It was busy, but she found a quiet corner to scroll through her phone, flitting from news sites to social media looking for crumbs.

Next to her, a little boy was playing chess on his phone. She watched him for a bit – the computer was winning, and he was getting frustrated.

'Try turning your pawns into queens,' Insley whispered to him. He scowled. Clearly, he didn't recognise a chess master when he saw one. Insley wasn't offended. Very few people knew she played chess. 'It's a good move. Nothing can defeat a queen. And if you've got more than one, then your odds of winning are better. If one is taken, you have back-ups.' She opened her eyes wide. It made kids more comfortable, she'd learned over the years. Kids were good allies if you could just get them to trust you. Insley made sure they always could trust her. She never let them down. 'Serious, give it a go.' She pointed to the screen, making sure the kid saw the chess piece tattooed on the inside of her wrist. The one that was normally hidden under a leather cuff. The one she'd decided not to wear anymore. 'My gran taught me. She called it the Queentide move.'

He made the move, his brow still a little furrowed. Good boy.

'Checkmate!' he yelled and grinned at Insley. 'Thanks. Dad always said girls couldn't play as well as boys.'

'I guess you can tell your dad he's wrong then.' Insley dropped her voice to a whisper. 'Or keep that little move to yourself and just whoop his arse at chess now.'

The boy giggled, and Insley gave him a wink. She turned back to her phone and started scrolling again. There had been a women's strike in Brazil. She made a note of the name of the woman who'd organised it, then started doing some digging and making some calls.

It was time to set the board up again.

THE END

Acknowledgements

Behind every woman who dares to do something is a team of people who tell her they believe in her, even when she doesn't believe in herself. If you haven't got that team, I will be the first member. You **can** do this.

Thank you to my team of family, friends, mentors, writing groups, publishing experts and willing readers who told me to start, keep going and finish this book. Each one of you helped me make it to the end of the street. Especially Kerry and Kelly.

To Alfred, Bina, Diane, Darcy, Kara and James, thanks to each of you for making me brave enough to take the first step and keep on walking.

Donna
26 March 2021

About the Author

Donna Fisher lives in Sydney. She is the founder of a digital platform that increases women's visibility by sharing their untold stories. When she isn't writing about real and fictional women, you will find her drinking tea at the beach and plotting the next feminist revolution.

Follow her on Instagram @shesawwords

Printed in Australia
AUHW022145070422
362029AU00005B/5